RHYTHMS OF LOVE

The theater was hushed in anticipation. Simeon was oblivious of all but the instrument before him as he riffed through the overture.

When he played the first chord of his score, a soulful A minor that would introduce the dancer, the curtain rose. Simeon's eyes glittered. *Brynn!* His fingers ran across the black and ivory keys not missing a beat as he played and Brynn dropped to the floor. As she moved slowly, dragging herself up, she met his eyes. A smile was not in keeping with the drama but he saw the twinkle in her eyes.

Simeon was overwhelmed. If he thought dreams did not come true he was wrong. The woman he loved was dancing for him. And he played for her. With misted eyes, Simeon played

BOOK YOUR PLACE ON OUR WEBSITE
AND MAKE THE
READING CONNECTION!

We've created a customized website just for our very special readers, where you can get the inside scoop on everything that's going on with Zebra, Pinnacle and Kensington books.

When you come online, you'll have the exciting opportunity to:

- View covers of upcoming books
- Read sample chapters
- Learn about our future publishing schedule (listed by publication month *and author*)
- Find out when your favorite authors will be visiting a city near you
- Search for and order backlist books from our online catalog
- Check out author bios and background information
- Send e-mail to your favorite authors
- Meet the Kensington staff online
- Join us in weekly chats with authors, readers and other guests
- Get writing guidelines
- AND MUCH MORE!

Visit our website at
http://www.kensingtonbooks.com

RHYTHMS OF LOVE

Doris Johnson

ARABESQUE

BET BOOKS

BET Publications, LLC
http://www.bet.com
http://www.arabesquebooks.com

ARABESQUE BOOKS are published by

BET Publications, LLC
c/o BET BOOKS
One BET Plaza
1900 W Place NE
Washington, DC 20018-1211

All Kensington Titles, Imprints, and Distributed Lines are available at special quantity discounts for bulk purchases for sales promotions, premiums, fund-raising, and educational or institutional use. Special book excerpts or customized printings can also be created to fit specific needs. For details, write or phone the office of the Kensington special sales manager: Kensington Publishing Corp., 850 Third Avenue, New York, NY 10022, attn: Special Sales Department, Phone: 1-800-221-2647.

First Printing: October 2002
10 9 8 7 6 5 4 3 2 1

Printed in the United States of America

*For my son, Mark Johnson, who insisted there could be no
other title for this story.
And for Linda V. Bain, Lorna Gilbert,
and Brenda J. Woodbury.*

One

Surreal.

Mesmerized, Brynn sat in the audience, her eyes fixed upon the dancer on the stage. The images she saw propelled her into her own out-of-body experience. "My role." Quickly she used her peripheral vision to see if anyone had heard her soft whisper, then, entranced, continued to follow the dance movement by movement.

Moments before the theater had darkened, the ethereal voice had filled the vast cultural center in Barcelona. "Ladies and gentlemen, the roles of Miss Brynn Halsted will be danced by Layle Ambris."

Brynn watched and her palms began to sweat. A twinge forced her to wiggle her injured left foot and her anxiety heightened. Her worst fear was unfolding before her eyes. Another was dancing her role. She had been replaced and she wished to be magically transported to a world far away. If she couldn't dance, it would mean the end of her life!

"Okay, let's see that one more time," Merle Christiansen said brusquely, his sharp gray eyes watching his star dancer. She'd had three weeks off since their return from their successful European tour and he was putting her through her paces. He wanted her back at work. He grimaced and turned away briefly before the pain in his body shot up to his eyes.

"Again?" Brynn wiped her gleaming honey-bronze skin with a towel, then tossed it on the shining wood floor. "But, Merle, I've done this to perfection three times already. It can't be done any better than this," she insisted, her almost-black eyes flashing.

"Oh? I wonder what Layle might say about that." An impish look replaced the shadows. "I thought that would get you going," he said as she batted her long lashes and started to dance.

Watching Brynn Halsted, a principal dancer of the Merle Christiansen Dance Company, move again, dancing the roles she'd made famous for his company made him proud to have been a force in her life. When he'd met her when she was fifteen he knew he'd been looking at a future legend. At twenty-eight her name was already known worldwide. If anything happened to end her career, not only would he be saddened but also the dance world would have a big void to fill. He wouldn't even dwell on what would become of Brynn. That thought made him hold back a question he'd been longing to ask her. *There's still time,* he thought. Her voice pulled him back to the spacious dance studio she'd had constructed in her Harlem brownstone.

"Well?" Brynn said, breathing heavily. Her hands were on her hips. "Where'd you go? You made me go through this and you went daydreaming?" She patted her foot. "I'm not doing this again!" She stared at the tall man with the pale beige skin and the bushy blond hair worn in a ponytail and pulled back with his signature black ribbon. In all the years that she'd known him he'd never lost his accent. Strangers were startled when he spoke. Born in Boston of a Swedish father and a black mother, he spoke with a heavy Bostonian accent, some words carrying the inflection of his father's native tongue.

Merle unraveled his six-foot-long form from the sofa, the one large piece of furniture in the nearly bare room, and walked to her. Chucking her under her chin, he said airily, "You're ready. I expect you at the theater tomorrow. On time. The company's looking forward to having you back." He glanced down at her healed foot. "And for God's sake, be careful. Tripping over a piece of loose concrete I would have expected here in New York City, but in Barcelona?" He tugged at his long hair. "Go figure!"

When he walked down the stairs to the first floor, Brynn was behind him, and her forehead wrinkled when she realized he wasn't taking the stairs two at a time as he usually did. As he slipped on his light-weight jacket that was necessary against the cool mid-September breeze, and opened the front door, she said, "Everything okay, Merle?" In Spain she'd never noticed a loss of weight. But now, she couldn't help but observe his drawn face. Had she been so self-involved? she wondered.

Without turning around to answer, Merle waved his hand in the air and went down the steps. "All's well. See you tomorrow."

Closing the door against the chill, Brynn stood watching him through the glass oval as he hesitated, then turned and walked slowly down the street. Something more than the temperature made her hug her body and she couldn't help but feel that something was wrong. Upstairs, while cooling down, she admonished herself for foolish thoughts. Of course, Merle was okay. What could possibly be wrong?

She flexed her foot and was instantly filled with joy, all disturbing thoughts gone with the wind. In a few days she would be onstage again!

* * *

On Friday evening an exhilarated Brynn waited patiently for her friend and fellow dancer, Claire Jessup. She lounged against a door in the lobby in the huge building in mid-Manhattan that housed the Merle Christiansen Dance Company and also the school where hundreds of students took daily classes. It was after seven and though many of the students and instructors had left, evening classes were still in session. After a full, grueling day of rehearsals, the two women were going to relax over a light meal together, a ritual that had become all too rare for them.

"Hey, girl, let's go," Claire said, marching up to Brynn and linking arms. "I think I want something more than that 'light fare' you mentioned. Gr-r-r, I'm ravenous and could eat a cow. Where're we going?"

Giving her friend a critical once-over, Brynn said, "I think you'd better follow my suggestion, sweetie. That cow you speak of is resting on your hips."

In Grabelli's, two blocks away on West Fifty-first Street and Eighth Avenue, a favorite haunt of the dancers, Claire finished her grilled turkey salad and pushed her plate away after giving Brynn a smug smirk. "No cow here, and I'm quite satisfied." Her dark brown eyes scrutinized the woman sitting across from her as she squeezed lemon into her tea and then sipped the hot beverage. "You look positively euphoric," she said, suddenly becoming very somber.

Surprised at the seriousness of her tone, Brynn tilted her head. "Well, of course I am," she said. "Why wouldn't I be? I'm back." She remembered this morning when she'd entered the building and was greeted with warm welcomes from all whom she'd passed in the hallways. The company had welcomed her and Layle, and other dancers who'd danced her roles had been most gracious and relieved that she was back. All feelings of self-doubt and worry had dissipated with their reception and Brynn had never felt more content. She was home!

Claire sipped her tea. "Nothing is wrong with that, Brynn. I'm glad you've returned and so is everyone else. Especially Merle, who has his star back."

"But?" Brynn was puzzled and felt uncomfortable under the intense scrutiny of her friend.

"But, I'm worried about you. In Barcelona when I looked out on that audience from backstage and saw you sitting there, frozen in place as if mummified, I got a terrible pain in my chest. I was feeling your pain and I was yards away from you."

"That's only normal. We've been joined at the hip since we were seven years old. We feel each other." But her friend was scaring her. "What are you trying to tell me?" she said in the same quiet tone.

"That injury to your foot. It was minor and you're back. What if you're incapacitated for a lengthier time?"

"You mean, never dance again?"

Claire started at the dead look that had come into Brynn's eyes and the wooden sound of her voice. But she said, "Yes. Brynn, there has to come a time for you to face your worst nightmare. I know that all your life you've never wanted anything more than to become a dance diva. You've done that. The world loves you. Then there comes a time when things change. You haven't faced up to that in all the years we've been dancing. Another career has never entered your mind. I'm scared of what will happen to you."

Brynn stared into her teacup as if looking for answers in the nonexistent tea leaves. When she raised her eyes, she said, "Dance is my life. There *is* nothing else for me. You might as well cut off my feet if you expect me to live without dancing."

She stared at the pretty dark brown-skinned woman with the worried brown eyes. Claire's stylish, short hair-cut was tousled and the jet-black bangs fell across her high forehead, while her small hands grasped the mug as if to steady them. Brynn felt a chill crisscross her body, the same that she'd experienced yesterday when Merle was leaving her house. Ignoring the ominous feeling, she said, "You've always known how I've felt." She shrugged. "Why are we having this conversation now? I'm back. Different topic, please."

The astute Claire did not miss the finality in Brynn's voice. Accommodatingly she said, "Has Merle said any-thing to you about, well, about anything that could be wrong?"

"What do you mean?" Brynn heard the fear in Claire's voice.

"You know as well as I do that he's lost weight and his wolf's bark is more like a puppy's."

"I don't think so," Brynn said, smiling at the image. No one could liken Merle's ferocious growl to a small dog's yip.

"Well, I'm worried about him. He should be taking it easy. Even on hiatus, he's working, planning new cho-reography. Everybody should slow down once in a while!"

"Don't cast a spell of gloom over him, Claire. If there were anything wrong we'd be the first he'd tell. Stop worrying." But Brynn felt that shiver again. *Would we?* she wondered.

"You're probably right," Claire said, as they pre-pared to leave. "Look, we haven't done this in a month of Sundays and I miss it. Why don't we do something together one Sunday, since neither of us is performing the matinee? We could use a little change of scenery.

I *live* in Harlem and don't get a chance to enjoy its nightlife. How about coming with me to listen to some cool jazz?"

"Oh, I don't know," Brynn said. "I have a few new ideas I want to try for your piece that I'm putting together for you. I could really use the extra time. Merle is so busy that I can never catch up to him to pick his brain."

Claire glanced sideways at her friend. Brynn didn't realize the immense talent she possessed as a choreographer. If *that* wasn't a second career, Claire swore that she didn't know what was, but she remained silent on *that* topic. Instead, she said, "I know you love your jazz, so don't deny yourself a treat. It's a supper club so we can eat divinely and be entertained royally. You just be ready. And don't put me off for too long because I won't listen to your excuses forever."

When Brynn stepped inside the black wrought-iron gate of her brownstone, a sudden feeling of déjà vu overcame her and she stopped in her tracks. She was twelve years old again! Mired to the ground, she jumped when the taxi horn sounded. Claire was waiting for her to get inside. Brynn waved and hurried up the stairs, and once inside she locked and then fell against the door. She'd had a premonition! Someone was ill and she didn't know who it was.

In the kitchen, Brynn held her breath while gripping the phone. "Ma, how are you?"

Wenona Halsted heard the real question behind the question and her thin brows arched as she laughed lightly. "Don't tell me, Brynn, that you had a premonition. Someone is ill."

"Yes."

"I'm fine," Wenona answered, trying to keep the frown on her face out of her voice. She never believed in premonitions. "So stop worrying. I'm not ill and not going to be. Just the picture of health and you'll see for yourself whenever you get down here to visit me. The citizens of Roensville, North Carolina, still think I'm lying when I tell them that the famous Brynn Halsted is my daughter and used to live here as a child." Wenona kept her voice light as she sat down, stilling her hand from feeling her breast. "And just how are you?" she asked. "Happy to be back on the stage?"

"You know I am and everything is fine, Ma." Brynn listened attentively to any sign that her mother was lying to her. *She* wasn't sick, so it *must* be her mother. Was Merle sick? If not, then who? "So everything else is okay?"

"Stop worrying about me. You're the one who needs to take a break from the hustle and bustle of New York City. I wish you would block out some time and come visit as soon as you get the chance. Maybe after your season there and before you go on tour." She had no fear that her daughter would just drop in on her unexpectedly, so there was no need to be concerned. She knew that she'd be feeling much better by the time Brynn eventually visited. Even the Christmas holiday three months away would not see her daughter in Roensville. That cherished holiday time had long been gone from their lives when Brynn became the star dancer of the famed Merle Christiansen Dance Company. In years past Wenona had spent Christmas in New York with Brynn and had been so proud watching Brynn perform to a full house on Christmas Day.

"I will, Ma." Before hanging up, Brynn said, "You'll let me know if you need anything?"

"Brynn," Wenona said softly, "you haven't had a premonition come true since you were twelve years old."

"That's not true, Ma," Brynn whispered.

Wenona winced. "Okay, sixteen then." Her heart thumped at the memory. "Your father's death was the result of a terrible crime and had nothing at all to do with anything you thought you saw or felt."

There was a moment of silence.

"So stop worrying about me. I'm not sick and not going to be."

Monday morning at nine o'clock, Brynn was dressed appropriately for a brisk walk. The Northeast was having one of the most unseasonably cool Septembers in recent years and this morning the temperature still hovered at fifty-two degrees. She normally would have walked by now, but a call to her mother this morning, and her nagging sense that something was still going to happen had delayed her ritual. By this hour she would have been back home and upstairs in her studio working on her routines.

Brynn pulled her bright red knit cap down over her ears, tucking jet-black, silky, wispy short curls out of sight. She stuffed her key case, an ID card, and some tissues in the small thin case that she wore on a ribbon around her neck and zipped up her black fleece jacket. She always included her identification because she'd hate the idea of having an accident and not a soul would know who she was. A slight smile curved her lips. As if the first person on the scene wouldn't recognize her.

She'd lived in Harlem practically all her life and even if she weren't known as a premiere dancer her long-time neighbors would instantly recognize her. She and her parents had lived in the same brownstone house on West 121st Street for as long as she could remember. That is, until her father had died when she was sixteen and her mother had moved to North Carolina six years ago. Brynn still recognized faces of families she'd known for years. There were many new faces of people who wanted to own a home in the Mount Morris Park Historic District in Harlem. Of course they'd had to pay much more for their property than her parents had had to pay for theirs when she was five years old. The neighborhood like so many others in the city had gone through a period of neglect but now once more displayed the genteel proud town houses of years ago.

Outside the three-story house, Brynn flexed her arms and shook her legs, warming her muscles as she'd done before getting dressed. Her favorite path was usually down her block and to Mount Morris Park West where she walked the perimeter of Marcus Garvey Park. Older residents still referred to the huge recreational public square as Mount Morris Park as it was called over one hundred years ago. But today, she decided to start in the opposite direction toward Malcolm X Boulevard, making the walk around the park her last run before she headed back up her street and home. There was no rush to do anything today since this was her day off and had it not been for her anxious feelings of the last few nights, Brynn would have felt happy and exhilarated.

But as she pushed off, striding briskly and swinging her elbows back and forth in that funny-looking duck-like movement, she frowned. Her mother had always scoffed at the "feelings" Brynn had. But Brynn and her father had not. It was Joseph Halsted who soothed his daughter's fears when she "felt" that way. She always believed that her father was more sensitive than he'd let on to the rest of the world. She remembered his tenderness toward his wife, bringing her flowers, leaving love notes in crazy places where his wife would find them days later, springing up behind her, tickling her sides where she was the most vulnerable. He was a deeply caring man. And when he was murdered, there was standing room only at his funeral. He was also a lover and student of mythology and gemlore and because of this he'd given Brynn an emerald for her sixteenth birthday.

It was the lore of the emerald that had prompted him to buy one for his daughter, who was already a dedicated and talented dancer at sixteen. He'd told Brynn that the stone promoted creativity, and what else could he give his beautiful daughter who was going to be the world's most famous dancer? He'd also said that the stone was prophetic. The legend went that it would hurl itself from its setting to warn of pending danger or illness. He teased her that she'd always know if she was practicing too strenuously and would know to take it slow. There were other properties of the stone. Faith. Hope. A symbol of psychic power and immortality. But that hurling property had never interested her. She was just happy to have a talisman that would help make her dream come true. To be blessed with the talent to become a famous dancer known all over the world.

As Brynn nodded and smiled as she passed familiar faces, the frowns deepened in her smooth, flawless skin, and her black eyes misted with memories. She'd worn her stone proudly and with deep love for her father.

Joseph Halsted had worked as a counselor with the Bureau of Child Welfare. He made a decent living for his family. But like every second or third male in the city, he'd taken a second job. He worked as a security officer in a Thirty-fourth Street department store to help support her dance activities so she wouldn't have to keep a part-time job. At sixteen, Brynn was chosen for her first lead performance at the Albert Prince Dance Company. Two days before opening night, Brynn got one of her intense feelings that something was going to happen. She asked her father to call in sick and begged him to stay in the house all day. Her mother became annoyed but her father soothed her with stories of the fame that would be hers after the city saw her dance. He laughed at her fears that she might become sick and wouldn't be able to perform.

The night before the show opened, her father was shot in the stomach, during an armed robbery. The internal bleeding could not be stopped. Brynn and her mother stayed with him through the night. Her father was conscious and guessed that he was dying. He instructed Brynn to dance for him the following night. To dance as though he were sitting in the second row, center aisle seat, beaming proudly as he usually did at all her performances. He would be with her.

The memory had misted Brynn's eyes so that her vision was blurred. She felt a hard jolt to her shoulder. "Oh, I'm sorry. I wasn't watching where I was going." She sniffled, swiped her eyes, and rubbed her arm as she looked up at the mountain she'd run into. A pair of unsmiling, piercing amber-colored eyes stared down at her.

"No problem. Lot of traffic this morning." Simeon Storey looked down at the woman, though not too far. He assessed her height to be five-six to his six-one. His mouth was about to curve into a smile when recognition leaped into his eyes. Her! He tipped an imaginary hat, mockingly bowed his head, and said, "Excuse me." Sidestepping her, he jogged away.

Brynn turned to look at the loping figure disappear down the street. Momentarily, she had the feeling that she'd met the man before but when the sudden look of dislike had speared her, she was taken aback. She hadn't been mistaken about that raw emotion. Where other passersby had met her with pleasant nods and smiles, that man had actually sent her a look of distaste. *But we've never met,* she thought. She probed her memory. Brynn watched until he became a tall dark blur in his black running suit and black watch cap. She was

certain she'd have recognized such an imposing figure.
And those eyes! It was hardly unlikely that she'd forget
eyes that showed such a powerful animal presence. Yet,
in a glance he'd dismissed her.

Twenty minutes later after walking the four square
city blocks around Marcus Garvey Park a number of
times, Brynn entered the park intending to do the last
ten minutes of her walk inside. Normally, the park
would be empty, but because of the late hour, there
was a crowd of joggers and walkers who, as she did,
finished exercising inside the park and then rested on
the many benches.

She saw him. He was one of several joggers among
many walkers like herself and had passed her at an easy
sprint without a glance in her direction.

Suddenly feeling unnerved by his presence and annoyed that she allowed herself to stress out at a
stranger's obvious dislike of her, she began walking de-
cisively around the circuitous path.

Simeon had seen the tall figure dressed in uninterrupted black save for the bright red hat pulled over
her ears. Twenty minutes ago he'd wondered why he'd
never seen her on his usual jog. On a whim, he'd taken
a different route and had started later than he normally
did and now wondered if fate was in any way responsible for his running into Brynn Halsted. She was the
principal dancer of one of New York's most prestigious
modern dance companies and her face and stature
were instantly recognizable by anyone who lived in the
city. He hadn't been surprised that she hadn't recognized him. Years ago she had barely acknowledged his
presence when they had come face-to-face, so why
would this morning make any difference?

He remembered a day when he had been called in

to play a piano solo that had been written especially for her. A panic call from the artistic director had brought him to the theater where with only two hours to familiarize himself with the music, he'd played for her. He'd barely had time to do a run-through with the star herself. That night he'd played his heart out and she'd danced as if it were the last thing she'd do on earth. She was perfection. After it was all over he'd done his best to get to her through the adoring backstage crowd and the impatient media. Years before, when she'd blasted into the dance world, he'd always had visions of composing a piece just for her and while he'd played for her that night he dreamed that one day she'd dance to his own compositions. Especially to one that he'd already started. When she left her dressing room, followed by her entourage, he awaited her approach, anticipating their meeting. As she neared, blank-faced, no recognition of him in her eyes as the man who'd played for her, he cringed. Impatiently, she rushed by him, flinging an imaginary hand as if waving a peasant aside. And then she was gone. In her wake was a soft exotic scent. That moment had shattered any dream of ever writing a score for her. It shriveled up and died inside him. Such a selfish, uncaring woman could never dance to his soulful compositions.

That had been about four years ago and this was the first time he'd been face-to-face with Brynn Halsted. And she didn't have a clue.

Simeon slowed, hopped in place, and then set off in a warming stride flexing his arm and leg muscles as he walked. He passed by without a glance at the woman who'd been in his thoughts for the last half hour. He felt her stare on his back. After completing a circle he stepped onto the grassy area and did cool-down exercises. Ten minutes later, he was sitting on a backless bench, drinking water. The crowd had thinned and he looked with interest as he saw Brynn Halsted staring at him. He saw her hesitate, then resolutely begin to walk his way. Surprise filled his eyes.

Brynn watched the man watch her as she neared the bench that he was sitting on. Each time they'd passed she could sense the tension though he never looked her way. It was as tangible as slicing a loaf of fresh-baked bread. When she saw him cooling down, she made up her mind. She needed to know what it was about her that rankled him. Of course, she thought, he could be a disgruntled fan but to her amusement she knew that he was hardly going to pull out a weapon and slice her to death or pump bullets into her because he didn't like the way she danced. Then she thought, *Don't be silly; this is New York City, after all.* Just a casual glance could get a person killed. Anything under the sun could and most often did, occur here. But she'd already made up her mind that if the opportunity presented itself she was going to find out what was on the man's mind, dangerous or not. When she caught his look, there was no time for second-guessing and with a great deal of temerity she stared at him.

"Have we met?" Brynn, once again, was taken aback by the man's unusual shade of eye color. His eyes were as bright and alert as a tiger's and looked right through her. But she held his gaze, refusing to give in to the shudder that made her want to hug her body. She convinced herself that it was the fifty-two-degree temperature.

A thick raised brow met her question as Simeon stared. He wasn't certain that he'd remember her voice. The low, well-modulated tones seemed to come from deep inside her. Each word enunciated clearly. He remembered. *As precise as her dance solos,* he thought. He stood.

"We have," he answered, holding her gaze. He could feel the cruel sense of justice rising in him when her black almond-shaped eyes widened at his response.

"We have?" Brynn was at a loss for words. Surely, she'd have remembered *this* man! "I'm sorry, but I really don't remember."

"That's not surprising, Ms. Halsted. I'm sure that happens to you a lot."

Brynn wasn't surprised that he knew who she was. But the way he spoke made her sense that theirs had been anything but a casual meeting. Never in her life had she intentionally snubbed anybody. But this man made her feel as if it were her nature.

"Princessa." Simeon spoke in a low voice as he observed her reaction. "December. Four years ago."

Her solo piece that had become her signature dance. Brynn frowned. *"Princessa?* Four . . . ? But that was the first night that I danced . . ." She peered closely at the man's face, and then gasped. "You played for me."

Simeon tossed the empty water bottle into a trash can. "I did."

Brynn watched as he rubbed his arms. Then with the same mocking bow he'd made to her earlier, he turned and walked briskly away.

Later Brynn's thoughts were on the morning and the abrupt, almost rude departure of the jogger. No, the superb pianist! The encounter nagged her until she decided to learn just what it was about the man that intrigued and disturbed her. The minute she shed her jacket and kicked off her shoes and donned fluffy slippers she put the kettle on for tea. In her bedroom, mug in hand, she picked up the phone.

"Merle Christiansen Dance Company. May I help you?"

"Hello, Brittany," she said to the student receptionist, "this is Brynn. Is Merle in?"

"Hello, Brynn. He just went into his office. Hold on, please."

"So, you can't enjoy a day off like sane folk, honey? What am I going to do with you if you fall out on me from sheer exhaustion?" Merle said in his deep voice. "Can't stay away from us, huh?" He wondered what was wrong.

"Merle, please," Brynn said, laughing lightly. "This is serious. I need to know something."

"Serious? But *life* is serious, honey! All that bowl-of-cherries crap is for dreamers, am I right or not?" He forced the laughter into his distinct voice. He removed his round rimless glasses and set them down on top of a mess of papers, and wearily rubbed his eyes.

"Merle," Brynn pleaded.

"Okay, love, what's got you in a way on this beautiful but blue September Monday?"

"The opening night of *Princessa*. Who was the pianist that you magically got to save my butt that evening?"

A booming laugh filled Merle's office. "Ah," he said, "you finally admit that you were in trouble, huh? Except for the magician as you call him, you, me, and the company would have been stuck in mud for the season." Merle stopped long enough to wonder. "What brought this on after four years? You never once mentioned him. Why now?" Merle was suspicious. "Did you read something in one of those rags?"

"Nothing like that. I saw him today and was iced over," she said. "Could have sliced me up and used me for one side of an igloo." She finished her hot tea and yearned for another cup to chase away the sudden chill when she thought of the man's cold stare.

"Do you wonder?" Merle said, relieved, yet amused. "Simeon was never used to being dissed even by the best of us. You were at your diva best that night after the show."

"What are you talking about? Nothing happened that night after the show. Everyone loved it." Brynn worried the short hair at the nape of her slender neck with long tapered fingers. "Simeon what?" Even the name sounded haughty.

"Storey," said Merle. "No, nothing happened," he recalled. "That's just it. The man was waiting outside your dressing room like all of us. Suppose he wanted to bask in the glory too, since he was a major part of the success that you were that night. But you cruised past him like the regal QE Two, just as untouchable as her namesake is to her adoring subjects." Merle scratched his scalp and pulled the ever-present black ribbon from his ponytail. "I was standing beside the man and your wind cooled *my* heels. Guess his were dusted too. He watched until you were gone. When he saw me staring he just looked at me. He'd said he was coming to the after-party I'd invited him to, but he never showed." As an afterthought, Merle said, "Obviously, judging from today, the man never forgot that night."

"My God," Brynn finally murmured after replacing the receiver in its cradle. She replayed that night in her mind, seeing the hordes of people in the small area outside her dressing room, the shouts of bravo, strangers calling her name, reaching for her. All she had wanted was to go home and lie down and let the fear show through. The fear she'd felt when she first learned that the original pianist had been stricken ill, Merle's frantic calls to replace him, her thinking of not performing her solo—all combined to make her a jumble of nerves, but she played it off to everyone else as if it were nothing. Show business, after all, she'd told the company. They'd thought she was the calm, cool, serene, confident woman, keeping it all together.

Only Claire had known the real deal. She'd stayed in the dressing room with Brynn until Merle appeared beaming that the night was saved. Brynn heard her music being played, and listened intently for a missed beat. She followed her routine in her mind, pausing where she should, picking up or slowing the tempo. When the music stopped, Merle insisted that she run through it just once with the pianist so he could see the choreography. The theater was dimmed and all she saw was a tall slender figure, a man with very little hair and an angular face who stood and acknowledged her with a bow as she took her position onstage. She forgot him and everything else when she heard her music. And then she danced. When she finished the impromptu rehearsal, she'd hurried from the stage, never stopping to thank the man, her only concern being for the show that night. Later, she was immune to the world as she put her heart and soul into her performance.

"He'd been waiting to speak to me! Artist to artist," Brynn said to her reflection in the cheval mirror. Her cheeks flamed. "A diva is right, Merle," she said softly.

Brynn carried with her a constant fear that she would in some way be injured and that she would never dance again. Her mother called it unnatural and said that Brynn was being unrealistic in thinking that she could dance forever. Age happens, bodies tire, the knees go, desire wanes, and it was only the way of things that a life of dance would give way to another career, her mother had said.

But Brynn secretly went through her liberal arts college courses and getting her degree thinking that she would never put it to use. Those were the most boring periods of her life, spending time in a classroom studying the required science and math that had absolutely nothing in the world to do with her dancing. She lived to dance. It was her passion. If that were taken away from her she'd be of no use to herself or anyone else.

Always when she walked she took care that her feet were well padded. She was ever watchful for the zillions of holes and cracks in the city's sidewalks. In the house she never walked around barefoot, habitually stepping into soft slippers the moment she removed her boots or shoes. The slightest cramp or unusual pain sent her to the company podiatrist to rule out any impending problem. Her well-exercised body and legs were pampered weekly with herbal wraps and massages.

Preparing for bed, Brynn realized that her earlier fears were unfounded. Her mother was well. *She* wasn't coming down with anything. Claire was fine. Merle looked tired and she aimed to tell him to take some time off. A smile of relief touched her lips as she gave thanks for a blessed day and that none who were dear to her were stricken with an illness.

Lights out, she closed her eyes with thoughts of tomorrow night's show. She was dancing *Princessa* for the first time this season. Although she had the sixteen-minute solo performance down to perfection, she went over it step by step, and chord by chord, the music as alive as though the pianist were here in her bedroom. *Princessa* was one of the few pieces in the company repertoire that was danced to live music. But she didn't see the face of the man who was a regular member of the orchestra. She saw a pair of amber eyes that stared at her in anger.

Something nagged at Brynn. She realized that the bow the man had given her years ago as he acknowledged her when she took the stage was the same bow that he'd given her today. Before it had been out of respect. Today it had mocked her. Disturbed as she was by her strong reaction to the feelings of a stranger, it was a long time before Brynn was able to fall asleep.

In Roensville, North Carolina, Wenona Halsted lay in bed rubbing her breast, silently cursing her daughter's sharp intuition. Wenona refused to call her daughter's feelings premonitions, and told herself for years that it was nonsense. But when her husband had been shot, murdered, she secretly feared that her daughter had a gift. *How could that be?* she wondered. Then scoffing at the superstition, she closed her eyes. She told herself that the small lump, which hadn't been present at her mammogram a year ago, was just part of her cystic breasts. Whenever she'd gone for the exam her doctor would say, "Oh, the lumps are just shifting around." Always frustrated, she'd never been too diligent about breast self-exams for that very reason.

Next week, she thought, she'd go see about this lump on the side of her breast. Maybe. What she feared more than anything in the world was to fall ill with a terminal disease. The thought of dying—leaving her daughter alone—filled her with the worst kind of dread. But deep down, Wenona was scared. This lump was like no other she'd ever felt. She feared it wasn't just another cyst.

Simeon Storey never went to bed before dawn. But Mondays and Tuesdays, Storeyland, the jazz supper club he owned and operated, was closed and today was his to relax or do mundane things that were a necessary part of living. For most of the day he'd wondered why he'd chosen that route to jog that morning. As before, he attributed it to fate. Or was it that only last weekend he'd gone upstairs to his studio and pulled out some old music that he'd started years ago? Since then she'd been on his mind. Could it be that the new dance season had started and her face and name would be in all the papers? That there would be no escaping that beautiful face, the honey-bronze skin glistening like goldenrods in the sun as she danced? He'd always been enthralled and mesmerized by the movement of Brynn Halsted. For years the music he'd started for her had lain untouched in the seat of his music bench, ever since that night when she'd brushed by him with that vacuous look. There was nothing to note that she recognized him as the pianist who'd played for her not an hour before, saving the night from ruin.

Later, he'd dismissed the notion of writing a beautiful and soulful piece of music for a woman who disdained everyone about her. But try as he would he couldn't get the music he'd started out of his head. Years later it was still unfinished. He used to joke to himself that what musical genius didn't have an unfinished symphony? He mused that one day he would compose it for a dancer who would be worthy of it.

But today after their brief encounter he went to his studio and played the music. Visions of Brynn Halsted danced in his mind as she was before and as she was today. She was even more beautiful than he'd remembered. The cold had flushed her cheeks. Her black eyes stared at him, inquisitive, and her long curly black lashes fluttered with curiosity. There had been nothing in her demeanor to show that she was the snobbish woman of four years ago. He'd seen her walking briskly around the park smiling and nodding at her fellow walkers. People had respected her space and no one had bothered stopping her to chat or ask for an autograph. He'd been surprised at her interaction and had expected the opposite behavior from her. As he walked home he couldn't help wondering if he'd had the wrong impression of her for all these years. Had he been mistaken? Was what he'd seen that night simply the results of a tumultuous evening? A high brought on by the impending disaster and the relief that came after a heartfelt, soul-stirring performance?

Simeon's thick brows drew together in a thoughtful frown. If he'd held her in disdain all these years he'd been wrong and had to set things right within himself. He owed himself that much. And her. Only then he'd be able to finish his composition. In his heart he knew that it would never do another dancer justice. Dared he dream that one day she would dance for him? There was only one way to find out. And this time he would think with his head and not his heart. Going that route once had been enough.

Two

The last day in September was still damp and cool. There had been one week during the month that had been true fall weather, dry and sunny. Brynn had hoped that the dreary weather wouldn't be a factor in keeping patrons away from tonight's program but when she learned that the theater was sold out she became ecstatic. Tonight there would be two premiere performances. Brynn had choreographed one and Merle the other. The preview critiques were highly favorable and there was an air of excitement in the theater. The company dancers had straggled in, happy at the sold-out house and thrilled to be a part of such a renowned dance group.

Brynn was on the stage, going over last-minute glitches with Claire, who was the female lead in the piece that Brynn had named *Élan*. It depicted a woman's flight from fantasy to reality.

"Oh, for heaven's sake. What in God's world is wrong with me today? You'd think I never saw this move until today." Exasperated, Claire stood in her pointe shoes, hands on hips, staring in disgust at her friend. "How can you be so calm about this? After all it's your piece and look at what I'm doing to it!" She groaned and sat down on the floor, flexing her toes back and forth. On the day of a performance she never rehearsed but she'd been exceptionally nervous about this new role.

Brynn joined her, crossing her legs at the knees and rearing back on her outstretched palms. She gave the vexed pretty woman a knowing smile. Claire's butternut-brown face showed anger, but Brynn saw the frustration and fear in her big brown eyes.

"Yes, I'm looking," Brynn said solemnly. "I think you're going to be simply marvelous tonight. That is, if you stop thinking about Raoul's dropping you and your both landing in an undignified heap on the floor." She pursed her lips. "That is not what I planned for my pièce de résistance and major debut in choreography, my dear! Do you dare think that I will take a bow if you guys mess up?" She groaned heavily. *"Mon Dieu.* I would head straight for sanctuary in Roensville and bug the devil out of my mother for the rest of my life!"

Claire laughed. A soft tinkle that sounded as delicate as she looked. "You wish. Go tell that tall tale to someone who'll buy the Brooklyn Bridge from you. No takers here."

A mock sigh escaped from Brynn but she looked warily at her friend. The chatter was working because the tension had gone from Claire's face and her lithe body. She stood up. "Okay, let's try that step before the leap once more. Pretend that I'm the man of your dreams and you're making a leap for life." She caught Claire's hand and pulled her up.

"I'm already trying to do that but I don't think he's ready to be caught." Claire blushed.

"What?" Brynn stared. "Keeping secrets?" Like herself, Claire hadn't been in a serious relationship for years. "So when were you going to tell me? At the altar?" Brynn was pleased about the news.

"There's nothing to tell, yet," Claire answered. "But

I want you to meet him soon. Come on. Let's do this.
I'm ready."

Brynn was high up in the theater, standing in the
darkness of the last row of seats in the middle aisle.
There was not an empty seat in the house. Merle had
just left after the audience had given his composition
a standing ovation and cries of *more!* He'd grinned at
her, and given her a tight hug before leaving. He knew
that she was nervous and wanted to be alone when she
watched her own ballet being brought to life.

The theater was hushed as the audience awaited the
long-anticipated efforts of the company's principal
dancer. A star that the whole world knew would one
day be artistic director of her own dance company. One
that would rival Merle Christiansen's. Brynn wasn't in
the dark about the talk. It was destined that after her
dancing days were over she would naturally assume her
place in the dance world as teacher to the future stars.
But only those closest to her knew how detestable that
idea was.

Years ago when she'd had the chance to become director of the young adult company, along with her principal dance duties, she'd abhorred the idea. To please
her mother, who'd always admonished her to think
about another career in the dance world, she'd tried
it for a month. She'd hated it. While training others,
she'd yearned to be the one dancing, giving her heart
and soul to a performance. She'd given it up and Merle
had only laughed, saying he didn't think she'd last as
long as she had.

Brynn remembered how the rest of the company
had welcomed her back into the limelight, laughingly
teasing her that she'd still be the star when they
brought their own children to Merle's shows.

While Brynn watched Claire and Raoul Salendres lead the company in the finale, she realized that what she'd just seen was a parody of herself. She'd choreographed her life's story! As she watched Claire play out the dreams, the fantasy, the anguish of a young woman on the verge of making life-changing decisions, of facing the truth about herself, she was watching the real fears of Brynn Halsted. No wonder she'd been so passionate about every little move being performed to perfection.

She flushed, her cheeks growing warm. Had Merle and Claire guessed? she wondered. When Merle had praised her on the dance, was he looking at her pityingly, wondering if she was conscious of the ballet's content?

The applause was deafening. Brynn was standing in the shadows as the curtain rose and fell time after time. Her name was being shouted. They'd loved her choreography. The lights came on and Brynn moved aside out of the way of the departing patrons. Still stunned at what she'd seen, the realization of it all, she slid into a vacant seat, staring at the empty stage. She heard her name as some who recognized her sitting so quietly sought to catch her attention. She never acknowledged them and never smiled. It was as though she had been watching herself out of her body—again. Her eyes never left the deserted stage. Even when a voice sounding vaguely familiar called her name, she glanced up numbly, then turned away to stare stoically below.

It was when Merle came looking for her that she was aroused out of her stupor. For months she'd worked with that piece unaware that she was writing herself. But the woman in the dance had made life-altering plans, never to go back to what she once was. No, that couldn't happen to her, Brynn thought. She thought of her recent premonition. I'm *not sick or injured. That can't be all about me.* But she couldn't ignore the slight shiver. She looked over at Merle, who'd slid quietly into the seat beside her.

"You knew, didn't you?" Brynn asked softly.

Merle slipped an arm around Brynn's slim shoulders. He nodded. "It was brilliant."

"You and everyone else must think me a fool," Brynn said.

"No one thinks that. You had a vision and you brought it to life. If it just happened to be similar to your life, then that's what made it real. Your heart and soul was there."

"For the whole world to see," Brynn murmured.

"Honey, what's so bad about that? Isn't everything we do a part of who we are?" Merle removed his arm and took her long slender hands in his powerful ones. "Would you have done anything differently if I had pulled your coat and said hey, that's you up there? Stop, the whole world is going to know the real Brynn Halsted?"

She smiled and rested her head on his shoulder. "No," she whispered.

They sat quietly.

Brynn finally lifted her head. "It *was* fabulous, wasn't it?"

Merle grinned. "It's here to stay, love. Long after Claire stops calling it her own, it'll be here." He stood and pulled her up. "Come on. Let's go meet your public." He stopped at the foot of the stairs and looked down at her. "You know I want you to take over for me one day," he said solemnly. "But if that's not what you want, then I'll be content to watch you dance for as long as you desire. Remember that."

"Take over? And just when might that be?" Brynn chuckled. "I really will be in a state then, barely able to maneuver under my own steam, my nurse having to guide me to the stage. Take over indeed! When it comes to packing it in you're as bad as I am, Merle Christiansen." Arm in arm they went to be lauded by patrons and the company alike. *Why is he talking like that?* she asked herself.

What Merle didn't want Brynn to see was the small grimace he made as they walked. He was glad of the dim light, because he couldn't mask the pain in his telling eyes. He wondered how much time there was before he had to tell her.

Simeon unlocked the door of his brownstone, carried the keys with him up one flight of stairs, and tossed them on a hall table. Preferring the solitude, he was the sole occupant of the three-story building he owned. His main quarters occupied the top two floors. The first floor was reserved for drop-in visitors and rare overnight guests. It was comfortably decorated and had its own kitchen and private bath.

In his second-floor living room, Simeon fixed a vodka martini and flung his long legs onto a huge multicolored upholstered hassock as he rested against the back of a roomy armchair. He'd turned on the electric fireplace on this chilly September night and he watched the flames flicker and lick the air, spreading comforting warmth around the spacious room. His reflection in the glass screen caught the moody look on his long, angular face.

On Sunday night he was usually at his club after spending the day with his family. As he had no wife and children of his own, his parents, his brother, and his sister and her family made up for his lack. Earlier, he'd had dinner with his family. As usual, his mother couldn't resist remarking about his coming alone and firmly stated that before another year passed she expected to see a lovely young thing with a rock on her finger having Sunday night dinner at her table. She wanted more grandchildren.

His scowl deepening, Simeon thought of the wasted night. His rush through dinner to get to the theater. He could have spent more time jawing with his brother Conrad, who was talking about an interesting concept for his new clothing line and his sister, Asha, and her daughter, Amber. Though she was only four years old, Simeon was always amazed that he wasn't talking to an eleven- or twelve-year-old. Kids. They were certainly different from what he remembered when he was growing up.

Because he was a lifelong benefactor of the company he'd had no problem in being seated for the sold-out performance and had specifically requested a certain section. His presence in the theater tonight was important to him. He'd read that besides the famous *Princessa*, danced of course by its creator, Brynn Halsted, the star had done the choreography for a new ballet that would debut that evening. And he wanted to go backstage, this time to act more civilly toward her. His behavior in the park had been rude and childish and he felt he had to make it right. He'd been foolish to have harbored ill thoughts of her for all those years. She was nothing at all like the spoiled, cold diva he'd thought her to be.

The moody look turned to one of instant disgust. How could he have second-guessed himself? Tonight, sitting in a row of the balcony, he'd been stunned to turn to see her standing in the shadows. She'd been oblivious of her surroundings as she stared down at the stage. He could hardly watch the performance for turning to stare at her. But he'd been mesmerized by her choreography. The story itself was heart-wrenching but to see Claire Jessup give it her all had brought the house down. He'd been one with the audience as they stood and shouted and applauded for all they were worth. When it was over he'd watched people file by Brynn Halsted and, upon recognizing her, murmur a greeting. He'd watched with narrowed eyes as she sat like a stone, never tearing her eyes from the empty stage. When he'd passed, he spoke, calling her name. She'd looked at him with that same vacant stare of four years ago, and had turned away, as if he'd never spoken. Not a sign that she'd recognized him as the man she'd approached in the park. Without another word, he'd left the frozen woman.

During the drive uptown to Harlem he'd seethed inwardly, kicking himself for the jackass that he was. Thinking about the music he'd begun writing again, *her* music, he could have laughed out loud. Brynn Halsted was as he thought: cold, uncaring, and so self-important that she couldn't see the rest of the world. And here he was, about to play the fool again over a pretty face! *You never learn, do you, brother?*

Seeking solace, Simeon left the room before long and went up to the third floor where he had his studio. A piano and bench took up an area on one side of the long room. The rest of the space was opulently furnished with a sofa, a chair, a table, and a lamp. The soundproof room was where Simeon composed. On occasion, his band from the club would come by for practice sessions especially when he'd written a new piece that he wanted them to perform.

Simeon played for a long time. Old standby pieces by Chick Correa and some newly familiar by Joe Sample. After an hour, exhausted, he found himself playing the low-tempo, haunting music in A minor that he longed to finish. Brynn's music. A wry smile parted his lips.

"It'll never happen," he murmured.

* * *

Brynn rose early to take her morning walk, though she was tired as all get out. The last three weeks had been so hectic she'd wondered where the days had gone. The success of the new season and the two new performances had had every trade magazine and TV show clamoring for interviews. She'd given some and begged off on others until future dates. Seats had been filled for every performance. She was in the theater constantly, rehearsing her dances as well as ironing out kinks in her own piece. Flaws that only she saw and would have been ignored by the audience. But as long as she knew something was amiss, it had to be corrected. She was blessed to be working with such professionals, for they never complained and were eager to achieve the same perfection of themselves.

After circling the familiar route around the park perimeter at her regular time, she walked briskly inside and spied the tall black-clad figure that she couldn't possibly ignore. Simeon Storey. He'd obviously finished his workout and was about to leave the park when he glanced her way. There was no sign of recognition, not even the mocking bow. Brynn approached him.

"Can we talk?"

Simeon looked at her with a wary expression. "About?" Was he cursed? He'd thought he'd never run into her again.

"Accepting my apology for my bad manners four years ago in not waiting to thank you for saving the night for me."

"Uh-huh," Simeon said. "And three weeks ago?"

"I beg your pardon?" She nearly flinched at his curled lip.

"Why apologize for something that's your nature?" Simeon shrugged. "Everyone believes that rudeness abounds in New York City. Why should you be contrary to that opinion? When fans speak to you there's really nothing to force you into acknowledging that they spoke at all."

Brynn stared. She remembered the voice, the look she gave to a man who'd called her name, the man who was looking at her now as if she were the world's worst shrew. "You were at the premiere."

"I was." Wrinkles creased his forehead as he wondered about the dancer who acted as if she'd just come back down to earth. Was she really a vacuous woman? It suddenly dawned on him that maybe all her performances left her in a stupor. He'd heard of some divas who couldn't function for hours after certain shows, all emotion being drained from them. Could it be that he was standing in front of such a person? "You don't remember?"

Brynn flushed. "Now I do," she said. She removed her glove and extended her hand. "Then I apologize for both times, Mr. Storey."

Taken aback, Simeon stared but then removed his own glove and took her hand. The unexpected warmth from her firm grasp caused him to grip her hand more firmly than he'd intended. Whenever he'd watched her dance he'd always marveled at the power he'd seen as she wove her magic and told her stories with her long arms and slender hands. As well as steel and strength there was warmth and smoothness. When he caught her quizzical look, he released her hand, feeling suddenly bereft.

"It's Simeon. Accepted."

"Brynn." The tingle that started in her fingertips ran up her arm, somehow settling in the pit of her stomach. Her hand had felt quite at home, warm and cozy in the steel grip.

A cold breeze lifted the collar of Brynn's jacket. The

weather was turning nasty as the weather stations had predicted. A slight drizzle had started. She drew on her glove and rubbed her arms.

"This is not the greatest weather for a dancer's legs," she said. "I'll warm up on the walk home." She looked up at him. "Do you jog here often?" she asked.

"Frequently," Simeon answered. "Though I've never run into you before."

"Whenever I can I'm here, weather permitting. On other days I exercise at home. Then you're an all-seasons jogger?"

"Yes. Like you, except for inclement weather. I'm not a duck and really prefer the warmer weather."

Brynn smiled. "Then maybe we'll meet again, sometime, Simeon."

"How far are you going?" *Watch it, brother!*

"One block. Just to the middle of One Twenty-first Street where we met before." She paused. "That day, I started later and changed my route," she said thoughtfully.

"Me too. This is the time I usually get out."

Their admissions brought a silence, each wondering about the follies of fate.

Simeon fell in beside her. "That's on my way, mind if we walk together?"

"I'd like that," Brynn said. She surprised herself. Since when did she welcome the company of a man—a stranger—so readily?

Simeon slowed his walk to keep in step with her, though she walked briskly. He suddenly wished for a warm balmy day on which to stroll. He wanted to know more about the woman that he'd held in contempt for so long. Only a few spoken words had cleared away years of misunderstanding. She wasn't what she seemed. Deep down he wondered if he'd always known that. Otherwise how could he have even begun to write beautiful music with her in mind? Somehow, he had to get to know her better, well enough to ask her to choreograph his score. He'd never heard of her being linked as part of a couple, and just now she'd only removed one glove so he never saw her left hand. He wondered why he needed to know that especially if he only wanted to work with her on a professional level.

"Are you playing in a show now?" Brynn asked.

"Playing?" Simeon frowned. Then he remembered she only knew him as a pianist. "No. Occasionally, I'll get a call to fill in for someone here and there."

"Oh," Brynn said, wondering why a talented musician should be out of work. He had to be in the union and there was always a need for good talent. Was he just lazy?

Simeon observed her closed expression and could guess what she was thinking and was amused. "Mondays and Tuesdays are my own. The rest of the week I'm at the club."

"Club?" Why would such a talent waste his time in a club? Disinterest in her voice, she asked politely, "What club is that?"

"Storeyland."

Brynn stopped. "As in Simeon Storey?" The jazz supper club was a hot spot for New Yorkers and tourists alike. It was a place that Claire talked about and had pleaded with her to go a number of times, but Brynn had always begged off for one reason or another.

"Yes."

"You're the owner?"

"Yes."

"My friend Claire thinks very highly of your establishment."

"Claire Jessup," Simeon said easily. "Yes, she visits whenever her schedule permits."

"You know Claire?"

"Very well."

"Why, she never told me that. . . ." Brynn stopped. Told her what? That the club she visited was owned by this mysterious man? *No wonder she wants me to go to the club with her.* Could the new man she had her eyes on be Simeon Storey? Somehow that thought made Brynn suddenly uncomfortable. Claire and Simeon?

"You've never been?" Simeon asked. As if he didn't know.

"No. I've never found the time. I hear the food is a rare treat for such a place." She blushed. "I didn't mean that the way it sounded."

Simeon shrugged. "No harm done and no offense taken. Your assessment of jazz supper clubs is held by many." He gave her a thoughtful look. "Would you like to come as my guest, one night? My chef will feed you well, and you'll hear some of the best jazz around."

"I love jazz. I listened to Monk incessantly when I choreographed *Élan* for Claire."

"Did you? I shouldn't be surprised. I felt the rhythm."

"Really?" Brynn was pleased. They'd reached her brownstone and she wondered how they'd gotten there so fast. But the rain was coming down steadily and she needn't flirt with a cold.

"Yes," Simeon said. "That's a brilliant piece of work. You should be proud of it."

"I am. It was something I've been wanting to do for a long time," Brynn answered. "I can't tell you the feeling that came over me while watching it. I felt as though . . ." She stopped. How could she tell this man that she'd written about herself? That that was what had put her in a stupor and she'd been unable to see anyone in that moment of self-recognition. Suddenly embarrassed, she held out her hand. "It was nice running into you again. I'd better get inside if I'm going to work tomorrow without sniffles and cramps."

Simeon agreed. "I understand. I'll see you then. At the club?"

Brynn hurried up the stairs, then turned. He was still there, watching her. "Simeon, does your chef do baby back ribs?"

"Yes, on occasion. Whenever he gets the whim."

"Then, let me know when the mood strikes him. I'll come then."

"Let you know?" Simeon asked.

Brynn smiled. "I'm in the book under my mother's maiden name, W. Gilliard." She opened the door and slipped inside.

Simeon started a quick jog. He was several blocks from his home on 137th Street, and glancing up at the gloomy sky he thought that he wouldn't be the only one laid up with a cold if he didn't get out of this mess. But his next thought had nothing to do with the weather. His chef was going to get the urge very soon to do his famous baby backs. And the whim would not be his, but Simeon's.

When Simeon left the hot shower, he was reluctant to quit the warmth of the steamy bathroom. But he'd heard the phone ring and then his machine click on to take the low-voiced message. The voice was male and sounded urgent.

Grimacing, already guessing what he'd hear, he was right when the exasperated voice of his manager, Duke Monroc, rang through.

"Simeon, give me a call. I'm at the club. The inspectors walked in nice as you please like they owned the joint. Left a little surprise."

Unsmiling, Simeon mused at his manager's word to describe Storeyland. He was the first to sound off at anyone who used less than elegant language in talking about the club. Duke was a jazzman from back in the day when New York ate, slept, and played jazz till long after the cows came home and the roosters raucously trumpeted a new day.

"What's the surprise?" Simeon asked when he called back, dressed in sweats and slippers. "And what were they doing coming around the place today? They know we're closed. Who is 'they' anyway?"

Duke grunted and ran a hand over his bald head. "Why wouldn't they come today, knowing you'd be out? You know Inspector Thompson with his wimpy butt self wouldn't want to tangle with you again." He chuckled. "He brought backup with him. Guy who got even a few inches on you. Must be six-four at least. Figured you'd keep your distance, I guess." His voice turned gruff. "Willing to bet Buddy let on that somebody'd be here. Knows my routine."

Simeon grimaced at the name. "Okay, what'd they leave for me?"

"Another summons. Serving minors."

Simeon swore. "Another setup. Just when was that supposed to be?"

"Last Sunday night."

The two young girls that Simeon had personally escorted from the club had reeked of trouble. They'd back-talked him and threatened him with a lawsuit but once they wouldn't produce any ID he'd put them out. He'd seen Buddy Randolph hawking him from the bar, a smirk on his face. Simeon hadn't made anything of it then but now he was certain that his former employee had his fingers all over this one. Just as he suspected that he was behind all the other unpleasant incidents.

Simeon knew that he should have taken matters into hand long before now, confronted his ex-bartender about the rash of unexplained happenings that plagued Storeyland. For over a year the club had been under investigation for alleged charges of illegal activity, of drugs being sold. There were already two citations for attempted rape on the premises, allegedly to have occurred in the downstairs ladies' rest room. A stabbing that had nearly cost a woman her life. Reports of robberies as patrons left the premises. Surprisingly, the incidents did nothing to thwart people from patronizing the club. Business was up a hundredfold and Simeon wondered if it wasn't true that the human element craved danger and fed off the misery of others.

But Simeon found that the stress of answering summonses and appearing in court was not worth the time and effort he put in defending himself. His attorney was kept quite busy these days but offered that further incidents would lead to the revocation of Simeon's license and the club would be closed.

During a light breakfast of Special-K, toast, and coffee, Simeon pondered whether to cancel his plans for the day. It wasn't often that he and his longtime friend and fellow musician, Art Chessman, got together like old times just to shoot the bull. Lately, their only contact had been at Storeyland. They had met as college students in a music class at Yale. It didn't take long before each found in the other a kinship especially when they learned that they were New Yorkers and Harlemites. Simeon recalled that Art had shown none of that fawning that people did once they realized who he was and who his parents were. He'd found a kindred soul. Art went on to NYU for his master's in business, and Simeon did his graduate work in music composition at Julliard. By day, Art worked as an executive at a prestigious insurance company in Manhattan. He indulged his passion for jazz by playing bass at Storeyland.

Duke's news had changed Simeon's feel-good mood and he was set to call Art and tell him to stay home.

"No sense in ruining your day too, man," he muttered and went to the living room to make the call. The peal of the door chime halted his steps. "Damn, too late." He went downstairs to open the door.

"B-r-r," Art said, as he pushed his bulk inside to the warmth of the hallway. "Nasty, nasty, man," he said, shucking out of his long black raincoat and putting the umbrella in the stand by the door. "Where'd we say we were going today?"

"Nowhere," Simeon answered. "C'mon upstairs." On the second floor he led the way into the kitchen. "Coffee?" Without waiting for a response, he filled two mugs and handed one unembellished to his friend.

Art drank the hot brew and stared at Simeon. "Hmm. That must be interesting. I've never been there before. Where is it?"

"What?"

"Nowhere. Where is it? Uptown, downtown, in Connecticut?"

"Very funny."

"Damn right it is, if I'm out in this mess on my long-overdue R and R day just to watch your gloomy mug. What happened now?" Art looked up at the ceiling in mock contemplation. "The club," he said. "Another summons. Now let me see. Another attempted rape? A woman was robbed in the ladies' room? Nah, gotta be serving minors." His eyes lit up when he saw Simeon's expression. "Bingo! Damn, I'm good!"

"Cut the psychoanalysis. You're not licensed."

"You will be needing a psychotherapist if you don't stop this foolishness before it jacks you up." Art's voice was serious. "Look at you. Stiff as a board. You can't even sit there relaxed, enjoying a hot brew in your own kitchen."

"I'm okay." Simeon hugged the mug, letting the heat from the ceramic warm his hand. "Just wasn't expecting another summons. How many more before they shut me down?"

"Won't take too many more. Seems to me the only thing that you haven't had happen in that club is murder. With the way things are going, that can't be too far behind, God forbid." He grimaced. "Shades of old Harlem."

"Let's hope not," Simeon said with heat in his voice. "The place would be shuttered for sure, then."

"Is that so bad?"

"I employ a lot of people from the community. What's going to happen to them? What we don't need is more unemployment. And you and the guys'll be looking for a jam elsewhere." Most of the men in the band were professionals but dedicated jazzmen, happy to keep the art form alive.

"True, but they'll be okay. As long as the economy doesn't go to pot, they'll be able to find other work. As for the band, hell, if you have to shutter the doors, we'll be playing somewhere."

"Why not, if I'm able? I thought that was the idea of giving back from whence you came?"

Art smiled. "As if you and your parents haven't given enough."

"When is 'enough' enough, Art?"

"That was a phrase, Simeon." He reflected on Simeon's background. Dr. Thomas Storey was a gynecologist at Columbia-Presbyterian Hospital. Dr. Jemma Jamison Storey was an esteemed pediatrician. Both were known for their deep concern for and plentiful gifts to the less fortunate in the city. Simeon's mother was born into the wealthy Jamison family, founders of Jamison's Hair and Beauty Products for Black Women. They were millionaires. And Art had never met a more honest and down-to-earth family than the Storeys. When they could have chosen to move out of the city they lived and worked in Manhattan. Simeon had chosen to live and work in Harlem where he grew up.

Simeon glanced curiously at his friend. "What's on your mind?"

"That's my line, isn't it?" Art said with a chuckle. "But seriously, don't you think it's time you gave it up to do what you really want?" He waved a hand to encompass the impressive surroundings. "It's not like you'd starve to death, if you did."

"You know how much I've always wanted a supper club. A great home for jazz. It was a dream that I made happen." He paused. "If I stopped, the kids might suffer too."

"No, they won't," Art said. Simeon had started a music school for the Harlem youth where they could go after school and on Saturdays to study. It was a big hit with the parents and many of the students went on to become music majors. Simeon was like a proud daddy of one boy who'd become a harpist with the Connecticut Symphony. "The kids'll be fine," he said.

"Yeah, I suppose you're right."

"I know I am. In college that's all you talked about. Your school for music. And you did make it happen." He paused. "Maybe it's time for you to move on to another phase of your life. Pick up on another dream that you just buried and forgot."

There was no mystery in what Art was saying. "No. Not forgotten," Simon said.

"Oh?" Art perked up in his chair, his brown eyes inquisitive in his dark brown face. "Did I miss something here?" He lifted his chin toward the stairs leading to the music room. "You've pulled it out of the piano bench? When?"

Simeon's honey-colored eyes held a glimmer of amusement. "About three weeks ago."

"And?"

Simeon lifted a shoulder. "And nothing, yet," he answered. "I play it, but nothing new has been added."

"But you haven't written it off, again."

"No."

Art's gaze was shrewd. "Was it the opening of the season that did it?" He knew that the Merle Christiansen Dance Company had been playing to sold-out houses. And its star dancer had been all over the news media.

"I've met her. We've spoken." He shifted under his friend's intense gaze. "I've invited her to the club."

A low whistle escaped. "Can I believe you?"

Simeon said nothing but gave him a look.

"All right, all right, I believe." Art got up and poured more coffee into his mug. "Now's not the time to emulate the sphinx, friend. Give it up."

Simeon stretched out his long legs and leaned back in the chair. "There's nothing much to say. We barely spoke for ten minutes."

Another whistle. "Must have been some ten minutes."

"I may have been wrong about her."

"So a night at Storeyland will tell you otherwise?"

"Hopefully, it's a start."

Art was thoughtful, his eyes never wavering from Simeon's. When he spoke he was dead serious and soft-spoken. "At long last, I'm going to see the real genius of a man. I'm going to hear a masterpiece, an original score for the piano. Written expressly for the untouchable Brynn Halsted. How many dreams does one man have come true in a lifetime?" His voice turned stern. "What I know is that you have a heavy decision to make. Think about what you're being offered, brother. You've had Storeyland and now it's time to do something with that innate musical genius. You're a *composer*, man. Always have been. By now, you could have followed all the greats into Carnegie Hall, and Ellington would have been right there on that bench patting his foot alongside you." He shook his head. "Guess the rain brought out the preacher in me. But I meant every word, man. You've given back. You've had your fun job. Now it's time to give to you. You owe it to yourself and to the music world."

Simeon had listened to his friend without interruption because he knew he was hearing the truth. It was time to move on, to write his music. Not only on off days or on a whim but to really work at it like he used to. Unsheathing the music for Brynn Halsted had stirred his deepest desire to compose again. But he had an obligation to the many people he employed. He couldn't just lock the door and walk away without a backward glance.

He nodded. "One day," he said. Uncomfortable, Simeon shifted the focus. "I'm wondering how is it that you're able to hold the interest of a lady like Claire Jessup." His amber eyes glinted. "I notice she's frequenting the club more. Should I know something?"

Art crossed ankle over knee and drank more coffee. He knew he'd given his friend food for thought and decided to let it rest. The corners of his mouth lifted. He shrugged, trying to look indifferent but managing only to look guilty.

"In time, man."

"Don't want to jinx anything?"

"Something like that," Art said gruffly.

A sudden reflective look settled on Simeon's face. "Is Claire coming any time soon?"

"I don't know. Why?"

"Ask her if she likes baby back ribs."

Art looked quizzically at his friend.

Three

Simeon tossed aside the entertainment section of the *New York Times* that he'd been reading and pondered his next move. The Merle Christiansen Dance Company would be going on tour soon. That left him little time in which he'd have to keep his promise. Why hadn't he called her by now?

In the past few weeks he'd caught several more of the company's performances. Each time that he saw Brynn dance, whether it was her famed *Princessa* or some of her other roles, he'd been increasingly aware of his growing feelings for her. They had nothing to do with her executing to his music. She was a woman, warm-blooded and beautiful, and the visions of her in ways that no one had seen, at least not on the stage, left him with the emotions of a wanting man. Annoyed by the trend of his thoughts, he promptly ignored them. When he worked with Brynn and he felt deeply that he would somehow convince her to choreograph for him, it would be all about work. He had no intentions of seducing her. On the stage she told beautiful stories with her body. After every role, he envisioned that the next would be her interpretations of his music. So why was he reluctant to call? He didn't need a psychic to answer that question.

There had been a woman, Veronny Walker, who'd blown his nose wide open after they'd met at a gala in

Manhattan. He should have gotten a glimpse of who she was when he learned that she'd come with another brother and had left with him. Even after their six-month torrid affair he still didn't get the message when his sister and mother had given him the raised-eyebrow look as if wondering where his head was. They'd seen right away what he couldn't because he'd been besotted. Veronny was pretty, witty, intelligent, and a talented actress. She was also a charming, conniving, devious woman who'd do anything to achieve her goals and was, as he learned later, using him as a stepping-stone. Art had tried to pull his coat but had given up when they had almost come to blows. The night Simeon had seen the light had been one of the worst in his life.

His eyes darkened at the memory and he stirred. This time when he dealt with a beautiful, career-minded woman it would be all about business. His only goal was to get Brynn Halsted to dance to his music. Nothing else. Without hesitation he dialed a number, spoke briefly to his chef, then hung up. Next, he dialed the number for W. Gilliard.

Brynn was rested and feeling the best she'd ever been. The New York season was going well, everyone in the company was healthy, and she couldn't wait to go on tour in a few weeks. For the next four months, she'd barely have time to catch her breath but she knew that she would love every minute of the grueling schedule. Her debut ballet, *Élan,* had been a success and Merle had changed the program to include it in every city. *Princessa* was also scheduled and the sixteen-minute solo would be more than enough to wear her out. But as always Brynn was looking forward to it.

Even with the whirlwind season, the theater usually the only thing on her mind, to her surprise she had thought many times about her meetings with Simeon Storey. Today was the first real chance that she'd allowed herself to dwell on him. She mused over their last encounter, parting with talk of baby back ribs and jazz and his invitation to the club.

"Guess his chef never got the whim," she said, thinking about Simeon's last words. Wondering if he'd forgotten the phone's listing, she twirled a stray curl at her temple. *Just talk from another fine-looking brother,* she thought. Peeved at his lack of response, Brynn was surprised at her feelings. She wasn't given to romanticizing and swooning over a man. Since her first teenage crush on a fellow dance student, there had never been a man who had had the charisma to take precedence over her passion for her career.

As young women, she and Claire on occasion had dated a few men, but Brynn had always ended the night feeling empty, and she thought that she could have better used her time studying new dance techniques. Eventually she just flatly refused any further invitations and had taken herself out of the market. She'd never met a man who sparked her passion like dance, until lately, when a pair of amber eyes would appear to haunt her at the oddest times, sending an unfamiliar wall of warmth through her. Even the groping hands of those long-ago admirers had failed to evoke the emotion she was feeling from just thinking about the stranger whose beautifully shaped lips had rarely parted in a smile. For one so detached, she thought, he played like a genius. And Brynn wondered if that was the real attraction. The phone interrupted her musings.

"Hello?"

"May I speak to Brynn Halsted, please?" Almost certain it was she, he vaguely wondered if she and her mother shared a home.

"Speaking," Brynn said. Her ear tingled from the

deep resonance of his voice. "Hello, Simeon." Had her thoughts of him been that strong? She nearly laughed.

Taken aback that she'd instantly recognized his voice, and trying not to read anything into it, Simeon breathed in deep before he spoke. Without preamble but gripping the receiver, he said, "Feel like ribs this Sunday?"

"Yes," Brynn said matter-of-factly. Then, "Your chef doesn't get certain whims very often, does he?"

"That's what I was thinking," he said easily. The lightness of her voice lifted the gloom from the day. "It sort of came over him suddenly, though. As a matter of fact, just this morning."

"I see." There was a silence and Brynn finally said, "Then I'll see you on Sunday."

Suddenly, Simeon felt that three days were far too many until he saw her and he wondered why the words "stick to business" kept ringing in his ears. He ignored them.

"Can I interest you in some fabulous oriental before then?" Why was her answer going to be so important?

"Tomorrow night?" Brynn held her breath. She was actually making a date?

"That's fine. Pick you up at five?"

"Five is fine. See you then. My name is on the bottom bell."

Simeon hung up wondering what had gone on just now. He wasn't so obtuse that he had missed the message. She had been waiting for him to call.

Ruby Foo's Dim Sum and Sushi Palace on upper Broadway in Manhattan couldn't have been more of a surprise to Brynn as she finished her sumptuous meal. They were sitting on the second floor of the huge split-level restaurant that could easily have held four hundred people. She turned to Simeon. "It's amazing," she said. "I can't get over the feeling that I'm in a theater. With a little imagination and lots of seats we could be sitting on the stage."

Simeon looked down over the vast space below them. "Actually you're right. I believe this was once a theater. The designer worked his magic." He looked at her empty plate. "How was your fish?"

"Delicious," Brynn said. "I think I made a pig of myself, but it couldn't be helped. How they got a fried bass to stand straight up in the air must be an art. How'd they do it?" She laughed softly.

"I don't know but we can inquire," Simeon said solemnly. He wished that he could think of something funny to say just to hear her laugh again. Her voice was low and deep-throated but when she laughed it was melodious.

"I just might before we leave here, tonight." Brynn's eyes twinkled and she smiled at him. "I'm surprised you never asked before now."

"Are you? Why is that?" Simeon was curious.

"Because you appear to be a man who doesn't leave any stone unturned or nothing to chance. You want to know."

"I'm so easily read?"

"Definitely not." Brynn didn't demur and looked at him directly. "That's my sense of you."

"Then you're not wrong. I've been told that I can be tenacious about some things." He held her look. "As you are, I'm sure."

Brynn nodded. "Not untrue," she said. How could she deny her tenacity when it came to her career?

She studied Simeon. From the time he'd picked her up at five o'clock and driven downtown and parked, he'd been nothing but the perfect gentleman. Even during dinner he hadn't made the slightest off-color remark or put the moves on her. He'd set the tone for the evening and she liked it. He hadn't treated her like an untouchable goddess, watching his every word for fear of offending her. She was as relaxed as she'd never been before in the company of a male stranger.

Her silent scrutiny amused Simeon. "Everything okay?" he asked, an amused glint in his eyes. He straightened his tie and shot his cuffs under the sleeves of his midnight navy suit.

A blush warmed Brynn's cheeks. "I was staring." *At your mouth.*

"Yes, you were." His lips moved in a knowing smile. "It's a family trait," he said. "Most Storey men are afflicted."

"I wouldn't call it *that,*" she said, meeting his stare. His mouth was beautiful. Brynn had never seen an upper lip formed in an almost perfect V. One was almost tempted to trace the delicate outline of it. She found herself thinking that it was downright kissable! And when he smiled it transformed his whole face. It was free of hair, long and angular, and his forehead was high. His jaw was strong and his chiseled chin was dimpled. He didn't have the conventional handsomeness that people looked for. Brynn felt the quiet assuredness of him and without needing to know the man any more than she did, knew that he was not one to be toyed with. Especially his emotions. Those who did were most definitely at his mercy. His fantastically colored eyes had a slight slant and his black bushy brows had expressions of their own. She liked the way his patrician-shaped nose brought his unique look together and wondered from which parent he'd inherited it. The whole effect made him a mysterious-looking man. And she liked it.

"It's Friday," Brynn said, breaking her stare.

Simeon looked amused. "It has been all day."

"I mean, isn't this one of your busy nights? You probably make it your business to stay on top of things."

"You're right," Simeon said. "I'm there when the club is open from Wednesday through Sunday. When I'm not around, my manager makes things move." He looked at his watch. "The first set should be happening about now." His glance was thoughtful. "Would you care to catch the last of it?"

"I'd like that," Brynn said. They were in his car when she said, "It's been a long time for me."

"What's that?"

Brynn caught herself before she said "date."

"I guess you would call it 'hanging out.' Leisurely meals in sumptuous places, listening to good jazz." She looked at him. "It's something I haven't indulged in a lot."

"You mean dating." Simeon held her gaze.

"Yes, I guess that's what you would call it."

"You're not involved?" he asked easily.

"If involved means with a man, the answer is no."

"Involved with your career, definitely."

"Correct. And you?"

"With another woman, no."

"I can hear a 'but' there."

"I'm very much involved in writing music. Mostly for the piano."

Brynn looked surprised. "Have you published?"

"Some. I have a tune on Johnny Brunson's *Here's Johnny!* The lyrics are mine. And my band indulges me when I want to whip something new on them."

"Oh?" Brynn said. "I have that CD. What's the name of your side? The whole collection is beautiful." She smiled. "I probably wouldn't know the name even if you said it. You'll have to sing it for me. I have a good ear."

He laughed. "Now, *that* you'll have to pay for. I don't give free concerts."

"That bad, huh?" Brynn chuckled. "Okay, how much? It's worth the price." She hadn't heard him laugh all evening and the sound was pleasant. Full of down-to-earth honest mirth. She'd pay just to hear that sound again.

Sobered, Simeon said, "Any price?"

"Name it," she said.

"Pasta dinner, tomorrow night?"

Brynn breathed deeply. *Is that all?* She exhaled. "Sold," she said softly. She was glad she was only working the matinee tomorrow.

Simeon found himself gripping the steering wheel again. Then, with an exaggerated sigh, he paid up.

During his rendition of "Butterfly," a tune that Brynn instantly recognized from the album and loved, she couldn't help but cover her ears before he was halfway through. She promised to listen to the CD again if he'd stop but he continued. When he finally finished, Brynn had tears in her eyes.

They were still chuckling when they walked into Storeyland. Brynn hadn't realized that they were holding hands when they stepped inside and he released her to help her off with her coat. The realization brought a faint flush to her cheeks.

Simeon noticed, but wordlessly took her elbow and guided her inside. He fell strangely silent after he spoke to his staffers, instantly picking up on the vibes. The club was packed as he'd expected and there was nothing but soft sounds of amiable conversation under the band's rendition of "Blue Monk."

"I think you'll be comfortable here," Simeon said in a low voice as he seated Brynn at a small circular table out of the way of the crowd in an intimate corner where she had a good view of people and band alike.

"This is fine," Brynn said, with an admiring glance around the spacious room.

"Can I get you something?"

"A spritzer, please."

Simeon signaled a waitperson, gave the order, and turned to Brynn. "It'll be here shortly. Will you excuse me for a moment?"

"Certainly. I'll be fine."

She watched the tall slim figure move in a long easy stride around the room. He nodded to patrons, spoke to staff, and stopped at the bar where he engaged in conversation with an older bald man. Brynn assumed he was the manager from his apparent in-depth explanations as he made gestures around the room.

She had been in many clubs before, at home and abroad, and found Storeyland to be at the top of her list of welcoming havens for entertainment-minded patrons. Especially those who loved their food and music together. There were no greasy-spoon smells coming from a kitchen in a dark far-off dungeon. The big glass-and-walnut-paneled room was smoke-free and there was enough soft lighting that allowed one to see one's companion at the white linen-covered table. There were fresh fragrant flowers in small glass globes, and flickering candles cast a soft glow throughout the room whose décor was sleek modern in colors of beige, black, and brown with splashes of red.

Her drink had arrived and Brynn was sipping and listening to the music when someone touched her shoulder. She looked up. "Claire?"

Claire slid into the chair beside Brynn. "I was downstairs in the ladies' room when I heard that Brynn Halsted had just come in. What are you doing here?" Her large brown eyes flashed in the soft light. "I thought you were going out to dinner."

"I did," Brynn answered. "It was wonderful." She

gestured around the room. "So this is Storeyland. No wonder you've wanted to get me here. It's lovely."

"Yes, I know," Claire said impatiently. "But that still doesn't tell me how you got here tonight!"

"Simeon suggested it."

Claire's jaw dropped. "Your dinner date was with Simeon Storey?"

"Yes."

"So why didn't you tell me?" Claire said accusingly.

Brynn shrugged. "It wasn't anything to talk about. Probably was going to be a one-time thing. I didn't want you to read anything into it."

"It isn't." Claire didn't miss too much.

"What?"

"A one-time thing. You're going out again."

"Dinner, tomorrow night."

Claire was silent wondering whether to be mad or glad for her reclusive friend. Finally a bright smile framed her wide mouth. She caught Brynn's hand and squeezed it. "I'm glad," she said. She didn't dwell on it, unwilling to make her private friend uncomfortable. She released her hand and turned her attention to the band that was apparently finishing up the set.

Brynn followed Claire's veiled glance with interest and was in time to catch a knowing look pass between the bassist and her friend. She observed the man, who was quite good-looking. He towered over his instrument and he wore silver wire-frame glasses and sported a full mustache.

A discreet glance over at Claire, who was engrossed in the music, prompted Brynn to think about the remark Claire had made a few weeks ago that she was interested in someone. Later, a casual mention of Simeon's name had brought no response from Claire, other than that she visited the club and they'd have to go together sometime. That had made Brynn feel easy about her thoughts of Simeon. Now she knew what or rather whose Claire's interest was at the club.

"What's his name?" she whispered.

Claire flushed. "Art Chessman."

"Serious?" Brynn knew of the last man she'd taken seriously years ago.

"I'd like it to be," Claire said in a low voice. She met her friend's cautious look. "It's a different kind of feeling this time."

"Are you sure?"

Claire nodded. "Two people couldn't be more opposite." She glanced at Art, who was looking at her, and smiled. She turned back to Brynn. "Art is not a liar. Lawrence didn't know what the truth was." She patted Brynn's hand. "Don't worry about me. I'm going to be okay."

"I believe you." Brynn heard the conviction in Claire's voice. Five years ago, Claire had fallen for Lawrence Hinson, a sweet-talking dandy who had promised her the moon, the sun, and the stars if they'd marry. And he had the looks to make one want to believe. Claire had told him emphatically that she didn't want to start a family and with marriage that was almost a certainty. Her career was what she'd always wanted. Lawrence had promised that kids were not in his immediate future and she had nothing to worry about. All he wanted was Claire as long as they could marry. Brynn remembered that time as the worst period of Claire's life. When he'd forbidden her—enforced by slaps—to use contraceptives and he refused to use condoms, Claire ran for her life. Merle and the rest of the company had been overjoyed with her escape from the controlling man.

"Hello, Claire."

"Simeon," Claire said with a smile, "how are you? The jazz is great as always."

"Thanks." He smiled. "I wonder if you're just a little bit prejudiced."

Brynn watched the bass player walk toward them. His eyes were on Claire. When he reached the table, he leaned over and gave Claire a peck on the cheek, then straightened and smiled at Brynn.

"Ms. Halsted," he said in a smooth voice. "Art Chessman."

"Brynn. Nice to meet you, Mr. Chessman." He caught her extended hand in a firm grip.

"Now that's hardly fair. Just Art."

Both men joined the women at the table and before long they were engrossed in conversation as if they were old friends. Soon Art excused himself and went to rejoin the band. Simeon left also when his manager summoned him.

Claire's eyes narrowed. Brynn followed her friend's gaze and her lips thinned when she saw a man step away from the bar at Simeon's approach. "What's *he* doing here?"

"He used to be the bartender until Simeon fired his butt months ago," Claire said. "But he insists on hanging around. Guess Simeon can't bar him from the place without courting a discrimination suit," she said in disgust. But there was fear behind her eyes as she watched Gordon "Buddy" Randolph stare down Simeon.

"You knew he was working here?" Brynn looked questioningly at her friend.

Claire nodded. "At first I stayed away. When I heard he was no longer employed here I started coming back. Only recently he's started hanging around again."

"Has he bothered you?"

"Nothing I can't handle," Claire answered. "He knows better than to try something with the men around. You know what a punk he always was." She eyed the man they'd both known as children. Buddy had been a skinny eleven-year-old when eight-year-old Claire's parents brought him into their home as a foster child. She still remembered how he'd charmed his way into their hearts. Behind their backs he was pure evil.

Brynn watched the trio that Simeon had discreetly moved into the shadows of the club, out of earshot of the patrons. She could see the hard set of his jaw and the stiffness in his stance as if he was ready for whatever came his way.

"Jerk," she said in a low voice. Buddy was the one person whom she'd come across in her lifetime that she could actually hate. She detested him. Childhood memories made her wince as she remembered the feel of his hands on the tender buds of her ten-year-old breasts. He'd grabbed her from behind as she was on the way into Claire's bedroom. She'd screamed and turned and kicked him in the stomach. He grabbed her foot and twisted it, taunting her that she would miss dance classes for a week if she told on him. She'd stopped visiting Claire after that except when one of her parents was at home.

"Does Art know about him?" Brynn asked.

"Only that my parents had him as a foster child and that I can't stand him." She couldn't form the words "foster brother." Her eyes darkened. "Buddy keeps his distance from Art."

The women were relieved when they saw the three men disappear from view. Only Duke and Simeon returned.

"He's gone," Claire murmured.

Brynn looked at Simeon as he sat down at their table. "Everything okay?" She could see the muscles in his face relax.

Simeon's eyes narrowed. "It will be." He dismissed the incident and nodded toward the band. "What do you think?"

"I think they're all fabulous," Brynn answered. "Do you play with them?"

Claire chuckled. "On special occasions, we're so honored."

"We've been working on something," Simeon said. He looked pointedly at Brynn. "We figured we'd give it a go on Sunday."

His look told her that she was the "special" occasion on Sunday and the thought made her feel good all over. "I'll be looking forward to hearing it," she said.

On Sunday, Claire and Brynn shared a taxi to Storeyland. At five o'clock it was dark and cold but unlike the past few days it was dry and welcomed. The city had taken on a damp that clung to the bones and seeped into every pore. The women snuggled into the warmth of the car.

"So how was pasta yesterday?" Claire asked.

"Delicious," Brynn murmured.

"Hmm, I bet." She pinched Brynn's arm through the thickness of her coat. "I hope you're putting yourself through your paces, girl. You don't want to hear Merle's mouth if he has to send you to wardrobe." She laughed. "I bet it was delicious in more ways than one."

Brynn pinched Claire back. "Mind your business."

"Like that, huh? He's a fine guy, Brynn. At least from what we all can see."

"What do you mean by that?"

Claire lifted a shoulder. "He's like you. Quiet. Reserved. Picks his friends. I doubt he ever entertains in what I heard was a fabulous brownstone on One Thirty-seventh Street. Art and the rest of the guys go over occasionally to rehearse. He's not quite like what you'd expect a rich boy to be." She rolled her eyes. "Though I've never met many rich boys."

"Is he really?"

"You're kidding me, right?"

Brynn looked blank.

"He's a Storey! You know, the famous doctors?"

"Well, of course, I know about Doctor Thomas and his wife! Who in Harlem doesn't?"

"Then I guess you don't know that she is an heiress to the Jamison fortune. As in beauty-products-for-black-women Jamison?"

"I never knew that," Brynn said.

Claire clucked. "Then you must check out the Black Who's Who? The Storeys have three children. Simeon has a brother and a sister. When they each reached twenty-five, Doctor Jemma Jamison Storey gave her children their inheritance from her fortune. She reasoned, why hold them back from achieving their dreams while they were still young?"

Brynn was thoughtful. "You're right," she finally said. "He's so natural."

Inside Storeyland, the club was packed. Word must have gotten around about the menu because as they were led to their table, Brynn saw plates of ribs on more tables than not.

"I think we arrived in the nick of time," Claire said. "We're not the only ones anticipating what's not good for us."

"Please," Brynn said in a mock whisper. "Don't remind us. Pretty soon we'll be in our hotel rooms in L.A. drinking mineral water and feasting on carrot sticks. Let's enjoy."

Annoyed at having missed Brynn's arrival, Simeon comforted himself that he'd be driving her home while Art escorted Claire. He was in his office double-checking his liquor inventory to give a report to the police. The break-in last night and the theft of most of his top-shelf liquor had left him sorely depleted. Too late to rectify the situation, he gave instructions to his staff to give complimentary first rounds to all and to discount the rest. He was lucky that the thieves had made a racket, sparing him of a complete wipeout. The detectives didn't have to tell him that the alarm wasn't tripped, making it highly suspect that it had been an inside job.

Simeon cursed. If it was the last thing he did, he was going to see that Buddy Randolph got what was coming to him. No one would ever be able to convince him that that loser wasn't responsible for every bad-luck incident that happened in the club. But he needed proof. Not one crime had Buddy's name emblazoned on it. And like Simeon's lawyer said, suspicions don't cut it as evidence.

Buddy Randolph was an inconspicuous figure at the end of the three-deep bar. The place was so crowded that no one noticed him, not even old eagle-eye Duke, who'd invited him out of the place Friday night. But he'd gotten payback. He snickered. Simeon's private stock was swimming around in his belly and he was feeling no pain. He'd spent the better part of the day sampling rich boy's top-shelf scotch. He'd have gotten it all if it hadn't been for one of those clumsy jackasses who'd started sampling as he carried out the stuff.

Buddy hated Simeon. He wondered just like every other brother in the world why the ancient question never got answered. Why was it that the rich only got richer? Buddy knew he had the same savvy to run a club like Storeyland. When he'd asked Simeon to make him assistant manager to Duke, to get the low-down on the workings of the business, the man had almost laughed. Buddy seethed with the memory. Well, he'd gotten even with the stuck-up jerk during the last year. Soon, Simeon would be ready to call it quits even before the police shut him down. Buddy chuckled. Simeon didn't have a clue who was rocking his world.

He shook off the beauty who'd latched on to his arm and whispered sweet promises in his ear. Buddy was used to the attentions of pretty women. If it hadn't been for his looks and talking the talk that he knew they loved to hear, especially the over-the-hill mamas, he'd have been sitting on a rock years ago. He'd learned to make his way ever since the Jessups had thrown him back into the system when he was sixteen years old. And all because their precious daughter wouldn't give it up. For years while he'd been part of their family there were promises of adoption, but it had never happened. He'd thought that he'd finally had a family: a home of his own. But that ended when Mrs. Jessup caught him in Claire's room. Mr. Jessup had beaten him within an inch of his life and thrown him out. He'd sworn to get even with the whole damn Jessup family, especially that tease, Claire.

All these years, he'd never forgotten the way her lips curled and her beautiful dark eyes blazed her disgust for him when he touched her cheek and bent to kiss her mouth. Her voice dripped venom as much as a thirteen-year-old's could when she warned him to stay away from her. He'd been surprised. Ever since he'd turned thirteen he had been having sex with women. His initiation into the world of fornicating was with a twenty-five-year-old social worker who had him in her office each time she summoned him to visit. Afterward he'd had girls and women of any age, anyone he desired. He'd never had to pay rent on any apartment he'd lived in since he was released from the foster care system. Women fell over themselves giving him things. Claire was the only woman that he'd wanted and couldn't have. He was going to prove to her that just like every woman he'd had, she would find him irresistible. She was certainly going to look at him in a different way once he was through with her.

"Art, baby," he muttered, "I'm going to get what you got." A wicked grin parted his lips and the dimples in his cheeks deepened into bottomless bowls.

When Buddy saw Claire walk in with her high-society friend, he scowled. He'd seen them on Friday, preening like peacocks, bowing and smiling at everyone as if they were first ladies of the city. That Brynn Halsted had been pissing him off since she was a skinny little nothing brat, turning her nose up at him even then. But his eyes stayed on Claire Jessup. With every laugh and each smile that she gave Art Chessman, Buddy took another drink and his mood became as dark as the evil in his soul.

Four

As the group prepared for the last set of the evening, Simeon left Brynn and Claire, spoke briefly to the men, and then sat at the piano. When patrons realized that he was going to play, a sudden quiet came over the room. It was a special treat when the owner of Storeyland joined the band, and when he did there wasn't a still foot in the house.

Brynn watched, as she was acutely aware of the admiring glances thrown his way from the ladies in the room. When his eyes locked with hers, as the first notes tickled her ears, she knew that he saw no one but her. She smiled and the mysterious half smile that she'd come to know touched his lips. He turned away as he became one with the other musicians as each worked his magic with his instrument.

The five-piece combo was playing a soft-tempo number that immediately relaxed Brynn. She closed her eyes and allowed herself to drift, swaying to the rhythmic beat. The melody was unfamiliar but beneath the relaxing tune was an undercurrent of excitement that rippled her soul. It caught and held one captive. It was hypnotic. She realized it was a piece for the piano as that instrument went into a solo, and Brynn knew that she was listening to one of Simeon's compositions. She opened her eyes. His met hers in an intimate gaze before he closed them, losing himself in his music.

A sense of peace settled over Brynn. She was more relaxed than she'd been all day. She'd awakened with an unusual feeling, almost a premonition that this day would bring a change in her life. Could it have had to do with Simeon? Last night after their dinner she knew that they were forming a fast bond. After he'd left her she gave careful thought to what was happening between them. Was she ready for a relationship? Was she going to start setting boundaries? Warn him that her career came above all else? But Brynn decided that her feelings for Simeon were not at the center of her discomfort. She felt nothing but a sensual woman whenever she thought about him. That was the way he made her feel and she basked in it.

No. Her feelings bordered on the ominous. Something bad. The first thing that had popped into her head was her legs and feet. There was no pain or cramping and after examining them closely, she'd scoffed at her silliness.

But while showering, she couldn't shake the disturbing feelings she'd had weeks ago, that someone close to her was ill. Deep down she suspected that her beloved mentor and teacher, Merle, was not himself. She'd observed the moments when he'd tried to hide a sudden twinge of pain by wolfing and shouting at the dancers and storming from the room in disgust. But she respected his privacy enough not to intrude, although she worried about him.

All day, Brynn had trod carefully about the house. It was with a sigh of relief that she'd carefully walked down the steps of the brownstone to join Claire in the waiting taxi.

Claire's touch brought Brynn out of her musings. "What is it?" Brynn whispered.

"Lord, this is embarrassing," Claire whispered back. "Gotta go downstairs. Now!"

Brynn sympathized. She knew Claire was in agony waiting until the last possible moment before conspicuously leaving in the middle of the set. "Go on. Hurry back."

Claire, as demurely as she could, left the room, then hurried down the stairs. "Thank you, Simeon," she murmured, "I don't have to wait." Simeon had spared no expense in making his guests as comfortable as possible. The ladies' room was expansive, holding the rare number of five stalls, and double sinks on each mirrored wall. He'd thoughtfully installed a spacious powder area.

Relieved, Claire tossed the paper towel and reached for her purse to touch up her makeup when the door opened and closed quickly. Thinking Brynn had followed her she said from the mirrored enclosure, "You too, huh?" She frowned when she heard the soft click of the lock. She looked into the mirror, and then froze.

Buddy leaned against the wall. "So you give it up for a wanna-be musician and not for me," he said in a low slur. His eyes raked her. "Well, what do you say that I find out just what he's been getting, huh?"

Fear cloaked Claire as she stared in horror. The thing she'd spent her life avoiding was now happening. *How can this be?* she thought wildly. *This can't be real.* Her mouth was dry and she shivered as her body chilled. Crazily she wondered why her body was cold and her hands were sweaty.

"You're drunk!" she seethed, trying to keep her voice steady and showing a braggadocio that she didn't feel. "Get the hell out of my way and let me out of here," she screamed as loudly as she could.

Buddy laughed. "No sense in yelling like that," he said. "With your man strumming his heart out ain't nobody gonna hear a thing down here." He pushed away from the wall. "Besides, I like it rough. C'mere, baby, give me a taste." He stumbled toward Claire, who was too slow in jumping out of his way. He caught her and kissed her mouth, plunging his tongue deep inside. He pulled away and grinned down at her. "C'mon, baby. I like a little foreplay. We got plenty of time." He sneered. "No mama or papa around to stop me this time."

Claire screamed, terrifying images searing her brain. "You scum! Let me go!" Tears of anger and fear burned her cheeks as she swung her arms, one fist catching him in the ear, and her nails raking his cheek. He cursed and she swiftly brought up her knee, slamming him in the groin. Bent over in pain, he let her go. Claire sped to the door, unlocked it, and ran outside, but Buddy stopped her when he caught and spun her around. She fell to the floor.

Buddy was on her before she could scoot away. He slapped her face, and started dragging her back into the rest room. "Shut up, princess. Just enjoy it."

Brynn was on the stairs when she heard Claire scream. When she rounded the corner and saw Buddy with Claire on the floor, she looked in horror and then screamed. "Get off of her. Get off!" She flew toward them, attacking him with flying fists of fury.

Startled by the unexpected and ferocious attack, Buddy dropped Claire and assumed a boxer's stance as if fighting another man, instantly warding off Brynn's blows to his head. He swung out, punching Brynn's jaw and knocking her to the floor. Enraged at the attack he deliberately stomped on her ankle, and viciously ground it into the floor. Brynn screamed in pain. "Damn bitch," he snarled and kicked at Claire, who was trying to grab his foot.

Simeon, who'd gone in search of Brynn and Claire, was on the stairs when he heard a woman scream. Fear of another attempted rape in his club scorched his brain. Disbelieving of what he saw, he was momentarily stunned silly. His blood boiling at the sight of the two women on the floor, crying, and Buddy kicking at them, mindless, he hurled himself at the man who must have gone berserk.

Buddy stiffened and prepared for Simeon's assault, pulling a knife and concealing it behind his back.

Simeon didn't see the weapon but Brynn watched in horror as the click of the blade snapping open pierced her ears. She called out to warn Simeon, but it was too late. Like lightning, Buddy's arm came from behind his back viciously slashing at Simeon. Reflexively, Simeon warded off the strike with his shoulder, instinctively protecting his hands.

Brynn and Claire screamed at the sight of blood on Simeon's jacket. A thunderous commotion on the stairs sent Buddy bolting for the back emergency door. The arriving band members, headed by Art and Duke, instantly grasping the situation, pursued and caught Buddy while he was struggling to open the door.

Bleeding badly, Simeon kneeled down and tried to comfort Brynn, who was writhing in pain. With one look Simeon knew that her ankle was broken. He was sickened by his first thought, that Brynn would never dance again.

Trying to move her foot tore a yell of agony from Brynn's throat, and brought fresh tears of agony to her eyes. When she saw the look of horror spreading over Simeon's face as he glanced at her foot, she turned cold. With fear in her heart she followed his gaze. Gasping at the unnatural angle of her foot, Brynn stared and wondered why the room was spinning around. With a cold, stark reality, she knew her worst fear had come true.

Brynn felt herself falling into a deep black hole. Simeon was calling her name. But she didn't want to go back to him, to the horror she'd seen in his eyes. She liked where she was, floating away in the blackness. She was safe here. She could feel nothing.

Wenona Halsted released her sleeping daughter's hand, and went to sit down in the big chair by the window. The fifth-floor room at North General Hospital in Harlem was pleasantly decorated and aimed to comfort those who came to comfort the sick. The surgery had gone well, the doctor had said. However, dancing was another matter. He firmly refused to commit himself.

Since Wenona had arrived on Monday morning after Claire's frantic call the night before, and had seen Brynn lying strangely quiet, there were ever-present tears behind her eyes waiting to fall. That quiet, almost lifeless form couldn't be her only child. The girl who'd danced around the house like a whirligig, and later as a beautiful young woman, wowing audiences around the globe with her moving modern dancing.

In her wakeful moments, Brynn had stared with glazed unseeing eyes at her and had spoken as if unaware of where she was or why. At first, Wenona feared that Brynn was traumatized to the point where she wouldn't remember. Two days later, Brynn was falling in and out of sleep and Wenona was advised that it was the best medicine. When Brynn realized the extent of her injury it might not bode well for her mental well-being, the doctor had said.

So Wenona sat and waited. Since only family was allowed, there had been no other visitors though there had been many who'd made the attempt. She scowled at the man who came to visit, whose establishment was where the carnage had occurred. What nerve! Wenona had looked at the owner of the place and forbade him entry into Brynn's room. Claire was allowed in once and so was Merle. Wenona had insisted that they both keep their plans to finish the season and follow the tour. Brynn would feel bad enough when she awoke. Ruining the whole tour should not be laid at her feet as well.

"Ma?"

Wenona went to her daughter. "Hi, baby," she said. She took her hand and bent to kiss her cheek. "Do you have a headache?" Brynn had winced when she moved her head.

"No. But what's wrong with my face?" She lifted her hand and touched her cheek. "It's swollen." Her eyes widened. "Ma, what's wrong?"

"Sh-h-h, don't get excited. It's gone down a lot and will heal just fine." Wenona nearly choked, and the ever-present tears threatened to fall. *The only thing that will heal,* she thought, sniffing back a sob.

A moment of confusion had Brynn staring at her mother and wondering why she was almost crying when realization hit. "He punched me!" Her eyes flew to the foot of the bed. The white mound on the left side was telling. "Oh, my God!" she whispered. "My God, no!" She looked at her mother with imploring eyes. "He ground my foot into the floor. He hurt me, Ma." She pulled at the blanket but her mother stopped her. "Ma," she cried, "I have to see." Her lips trembled and her body shook. "I have to know."

"Brynn, you had surgery." Wenona held her hands. "There might be . . . more to come."

"More?" Brynn stared at the mound. "Then that means . . . that I . . ."

"We don't know yet."

Brynn fell back on the pillow, her eyes squeezed shut. Her head moved from side to side as she moaned softly. *"I know,"* she whispered. *"I'll never dance again!"*

A deep sob wrenched her chest. *"N-never dance again."* She gripped her mother's hand. "Ma . . . help . . . me . . ." Her shoulders shook with dry sobs.

Wenona's tears finally fell.

Simeon's shoulder had been badly cut. But for the thickness of his jacket the vicious swipe would have seriously damaged tissue. After almost three weeks, he was not as sore but he was determined to heal without any aftereffects of the fiasco. As soon as the bandage and stitches were removed, he exercised his arm regularly. Today was the first day that he eased a shirt over his head without wincing.

He was in the living room watching the TV news. The media had, to no one's surprise, continued harping on the story of the assault on dancer Brynn Halsted at Storeyland. Reports that her career was ended abounded on every station and in every newspaper. The owner of the club, Simeon Storey, had been stabbed and nearly lost his life. Simeon flipped the channel and caught the New York reporter for Channel Four. Asha Cunningham was the only reporter to give the true facts, stating that Mr. Storey had suffered a cut to the shoulder that was not considered life-threatening.

"You tell 'em, sis," he said, giving his sister a thumbs-up as she made the thousandth report on the incident. He knew that she was only doing her job, as she'd tell him when she called him every evening. But she insisted to her news producer that she wasn't going to follow the other stations' manic style of reporting the incident out of context.

Asha was thirty-four, the youngest and the most headstrong of the Storey children. During a gathering at Simeon's house after he'd been released from the hospital, she was the one who had to be calmed by his parents. His father threatened to sedate her if she didn't stop ranting like a maniac, crying for Buddy Randolph's blood.

Simeon had reassured them all that Buddy wasn't going to walk on this one. His mouth twisted in a harsh smile. No, he thought, Buddy was where he was going to be for a long time. There were so many charges against him that it would be a long time before he would be able to inflict his special brand of evil on others. The attorneys for Claire, Brynn, and Simeon had wasted no time in filing charges on behalf of their clients for attempted rape, assault, and theft. His lawyer failed to secure bail for Buddy after it was revealed to the judge that he'd made threatening remarks against the life of Brynn Halsted.

A picture of Merle Christiansen flashed on the screen. He was being interviewed while on a six-city tour of California. They were in the Santa Barbara Performing Arts Center and the reporters had caught him after the show. Simeon studied the man, who looked drawn and tired. To the world, he was the familiar tall man with the long sandy bushy hair pulled back with the ever-present black ribbon. Simeon saw the tightness of his lips when he breathed and the scrunching up of his eyes, as if in search of the proper response to a question. But he knew better. Something was wrong. Simeon had known Merle since the young dancer had arrived in New York years ago and they had become friends. Years later, it was Merle in a panic who'd called on Simeon to save his show from ruin. It was the night that Simeon had played for Brynn and she'd won the heart of the cruelest dance critic.

Merle was saying that no, he didn't think Ms. Halsted's career was over, that that was an opinion for her doctors. More surgery had not been necessary and yes, she was home and recuperating but not receiving visitors. She sent her love to all who'd expressed their concern.

Simeon turned off the TV. His mouth tightened. He was one of those visitors that had been turned away at Brynn's hospital door the day after being treated for his own injury. He'd barely gotten a glimpse of the woman lying sedated in the bed. Later, Simeon had learned from Merle and Claire that Brynn's mother guarded her daughter's privacy vigilantly. Claire hinted that Wenona Halsted was none too pleased that the owner of the place where her daughter had been attacked wanted to come to apologize.

"Apologize!" Simeon said through thin lips. Slowly, he unclenched his jaw and he remembered that night, the vision of her lying in a heap like a broken doll. Her foot twisted at an impossible angle and the fear he saw in her eyes. As long as he lived he'd remember that look of disbelief when she stared at his face and then the fright when she realized what he was looking at. He knew the moment that she knew. He'd felt her life's energy oozing from her in his arms. He'd seen the light go out of her eyes before she closed them. He'd held her, calling her out of her given name. When he knew she could no longer hear him, he still whispered those sweet things to her, things that only anguished lovers said. His blood dripped on her pretty gold dress and he'd stared at it making crazy, childlike doodles on her. She was so still he thought she'd died in his arms.

That was the last time he'd touched her. The police had arrived and in the confusion the ambulance had sped away without him. Claire had been hysterical and Art had accompanied her to the hospital. Brynn had been taken away alone. There was no familiar friend to hold her hand, to comfort, and to reassure her. Out of all the horrors of that night, that one simple thing remained with him, haunted him, that she had probably felt so alone, almost abandoned.

Restless, Simeon stared at the clock and shook off the bad feeling that was about to erupt in his gut again. The only time that ten o'clock on a Saturday night caught him at home was if he'd been bedded with some horrible foreign bug whose name was always unpronounceable. Instead, he was home, unemployed like the rest of his workers. His liquor license had been suspended and his club was shuttered pending further investigation of criminal activity. His mood darkened when he remembered the looks on the faces of his staff when he informed them the club was closing immediately and indefinitely. Many of his waitresses were single mothers, and some worked two jobs. Some were college students who now had to scour the city for other suitable work. What made it worse for them, Simeon knew, was that they'd find it hard to match their lost salary. He'd never paid his workers the minimum wage. Since he was in a position to do so, he made it a little more rewarding for them to come to work happy and ready to please the boss. He always believed that a happy employee made a successful employer.

Some had no problem finding good places of employment. He'd enticed his chef away from a top-notch downtown restaurant and they'd been only too happy to hire him back. His strongest competitor, Londels, had already snatched up the Storeyland combo.

Simeon reached over to the table by his chair and picked up the small green stone. Brynn's emerald. He'd found it on the floor outside the ladies' room that night before he left the club. When he'd stepped on it and picked it up he knew immediately what it was. It was in his pocket when he visited the hospital but wasn't allowed in to see her. He toyed with it, rolling it back and forth in his hand, wondering if she knew where she'd lost it. He'd never seen her without it nestled at her throat. A good-luck charm? *Some luck,* he thought.

Wenona bit her lip, wincing back the pain. She smoothed the lines from her face before taking her daughter a cup of tea in the living room. It had been nearly three weeks since Brynn had been hurt and it was just that long since Wenona had called her doctor to delay her surgery—again. She'd reassured him that she would be returning to Roensville within the week and she'd call him then. Weeks ago she'd swallowed her fear of the unknown and visited her doctor. She'd gone home in fear, refusing to have the biopsy. Suppose she had cancer? Because she'd ignored the presence of the lump for so long, she was filled with dread that whatever they found had to be inoperable. How much time would she have? Would her death affect Brynn's career? Finally, with fear in her heart, she'd agreed to the biopsy. But that had been before Brynn's accident.

Brynn hadn't moved from her spot in the living room where she sat with her foot propped up on an ottoman. This morning they'd removed the cast and clamped on a heavy white plastic brace.

Wenona watched her daughter silently for a brief moment before making busy sounds as she set the cup and saucer on the table. They'd finished dinner only an hour ago; at least *she* had eaten, but as usual, Brynn had practically touched nothing. Wenona was beginning to worry.

"Are you trying to make yourself sick?" Wenona asked. She indicated the turkey sandwich and tea. "You've got to begin eating something, Brynn, or you'll be right back in the hospital."

"Don't fuss, Ma," Brynn said woodenly. "I'll eat

when I get an appetite." She stared at the TV, and as was her habit since she'd been home, flipped the channel whenever a news spot came on. Inevitably, she would hear her name or the latest in the closing of Storeyland.

Wenona noticed and let out a sigh. "You can't escape it no matter how hard you try. People will be talking about this for months. It's news, baby."

"News." Brynn looked at the screen with disgust. It was the most emotion she'd shown all day. "Feeding vultures! Why can't they just leave it alone?"

"That's the way it is, you know that. When something else catches their attention, you'll be old news." Wenona saw the flicker of pain flash in her daughter's eyes. "You know what I mean," she said.

After a moment, Brynn nodded and said, "No longer the star of the moment."

A lump formed in Wenona's throat. "You'll always be our star, baby. Don't forget that."

"I know," Brynn whispered. Her father's face flashed before her and she could almost hear his voice. Automatically her fingers went to her throat but found it bare. Weeks ago she'd removed the chain from around her neck, no longer able to feel the comfort of her emerald. It was gone. Lost. And she had no idea where it was. In the hospital she'd begged her mother to look high and low for it. She accused the staff of finding it and tossing it in the trash. She'd behaved abominably, like the irascible diva, but at the time she didn't care. All she wanted was her stone. It was only when she got home that she'd removed the chain from around her neck, the mount sadly empty.

"Ma, why don't you go to bed? I'll be okay. You don't have to watch me." Brynn tried wiggling the toes of her left foot. "It's not like I'm going to sneak out to go dancing."

* * *

A week later, Brynn was alone. Her mother called every day and she made Brynn promise to call if she needed anything.

The six o'clock news had just ended and Brynn was wickedly pleased that there was not one mention of her or Storeyland. Instead, the TV newsreaders were hot on reporting the breaking news of yet another rap star artist who was involved in another nightclub shooting. Gleefully, she flipped from channel to channel. When satisfied that she was not going to find a snippet about herself, she idly settled on watching an entertainment gossip program about the stars. Time to hear about somebody else's troubles, she thought.

Brynn frowned at the phone when it rang, glancing at the caller ID. Simeon. She'd refused to take his calls as well as everyone else's. Now why had she done that? she asked herself. But she frowned. She knew. That night had flashed through her mind over and over until she blanked it out. The image of his blood soaking his jacket. Dripping on her as he held her in his arms. The vision was so vivid at times that it made her shudder. It was her fault! He'd rushed in to save her from a maniac and he'd gotten cut. She couldn't think about his never being able to play again because of her. A stiff arm for a pianist meant the end of his career! Fear and shame made her deny her part in ruining his life.

His voice came over the answering machine, the same calm, patient tone, as if he knew that one day she'd pick up.

"Brynn, I don't know what you're thinking, but I would—"

"Hello, Simeon," Brynn interrupted.

For a second, Simeon was taken aback, expecting to

finish his voice message. "Brynn," he said. *Is that all you can say after all this time, fool?*

"Before you ask, no, I won't be dancing again," Brynn said abruptly. "The most I can hope for is to walk like a normal person. No limp. No pain. Is there something else you wanted to know about me?" A brittle laugh escaped. "Consider yourself to be privy to the exclusive. My agent is scheduled to flash the news tomorrow."

There was silence.

Simeon spoke. "Is that your idea of a joke? Because if it is I don't think I'm talking to the same woman I knew before she had the sense knocked out of her as well as getting her ankle crushed." He paused. "If you really want to know why I called, you have my number. Until then, what I have of yours can keep." He hung up.

Brynn's heart beat wildly. She didn't believe she'd done that. That was someone else! She bit her bottom lip. The cruelty she'd just dished out wasn't her. Why did she want to lash out and hurt those who cared? Her mother. Merle. Claire. They'd all offered comfort and solace and she'd spurned them. And now Simeon, who'd only been thinking about her safety when he'd come to her aid. And this was how she repaid everyone's kindness. Tears sprang to her eyes and her shoulders shook. "Why me?" she sobbed. "Why?" The tears flowed.

At last, she'd asked that question. For weeks she'd held back the tears, unwilling to be pitied and comforted. Who could possibly understand her pain? Instead, she'd allowed the bitterness inside to grab hold like giant tentacles and squeeze the goodness from her heart. For whatever reason, fate had dealt the cards and she was the one asking that useless, pitiful question. She'd been chosen and she had to face up to it.

The tears continued to fall and her sobs had quieted to a slow moan as she hugged her waist and rocked back and forth. To dance was all she'd ever wanted since she was a child. That was all. Just to dance. Now what was she to do with the rest of her life?

Brynn must have cried herself to sleep because she awoke with a start when her doorbell rang. She looked at the clock and frowned. After ten? Her housekeeper wasn't expected back until tomorrow. No one ever visited this late. Her phone rang and she glanced at the ID in the illumined window. Claire?

"It's me, Brynn. I'm at the front door. Can I come in? I have my key." She sounded breathless. Brynn hung up the phone after giving permission.

"B-r-r-r, the Windy City doesn't have a thing on little old New York. I'm glad we're outta there!" Claire said as she breezed into the living room bringing in a cold blast of air. She leaned down to hug her friend. "How are you, girl?" Her eyes clouded as she tried not to notice the puffiness and the reddened eyes.

"What are you doing here?" Brynn looked puzzled.

"Merle gave me permission to miss tomorrow's matinee," she said. "Philly's only about a two-hour ride on Amtrak, so I'll get back in plenty of time for the evening show."

The question that Brynn wanted to ask but was afraid to was lost on her lips as she willed her thoughts to other things. "You look good," she managed to say.

Claire heard the unasked question. "God, I miss you, Brynn." Her voice caught.

Brynn smiled. "I miss you too, Claire." She eyed the familiar large red leather bag. "Are you going to stay the night with me?"

"Yeah, if you don't mind. I told you I miss you."

"I'd like that," Brynn admitted. "I—I was having a rough time today. The first time that I—I . . ."

"Cried?" Claire said. Her eyes misted.

"Yes," Brynn said in a low voice. She saw the tears welling up in Claire's eyes. "Now don't you go and st-start." But the emotion she felt was too much and her tears began to fall. "Oh, Claire," she cried, "it's all o-over for me. Everything!"

Claire's tears fell unchecked and she went to Brynn and hugged her tightly. "Brynn," she said. "I'm so sorry."

They cried together.

Claire sipped the hot tea she'd fixed for them both and drew her legs beneath her in the oversize chair. "Is it painful trying to get around? Does that really help?" she asked. The cane lay on the floor beside Brynn's chair.

"Takes some getting used to, but I'm managing. The stairs are a challenge though." Brynn gave her friend a grateful look. "I'm glad you came. Too much self-pity can be a mind-blower. Didn't know whether my body was going to puff up like a blimp and then burst into smithereens." She made a face. "Y'all wouldn't know where to start to pick up the pieces."

"It was time," Claire said. "That was a heavy weight to bear." She hesitated. "Merle told me you called letting him know about tomorrow's announcement," she said softly.

Brynn's eyes clouded. "Would've been cold letting him find out along with a million other people."

"I'm glad you did that." She hesitated.

"What?"

Claire shrugged. "Probably nothing. I was wondering how he sounded to you but I guess you aren't into hearing about anybody else's problems and I can't blame you."

"Is something wrong?"

"No, like I said, probably nothing. Just that Merle

looks so tired lately and he is so quiet all the time."
She eyed Brynn. "I wondered if you noticed anything
when he visited you in the hospital but you were pretty
much out of it back then."

Then I wasn't just seeing things, Brynn thought. "I'd
noticed before that," she said in a quiet voice. *Then
there is something wrong.* "Remember months ago when
we thought that there was something? I—I thought the
premonition was meant for me."

"You never told me," Claire said, equally quiet.
She'd known about Brynn's fear of someone close to
her becoming ill, even dying. This was the first she
heard her speak of it in years.

"I'd thought I was wrong. That I was the intended
victim and it came true." She raised worried eyes to
Claire. "What could it be?" Her voice shook with fear.

"Maybe it's something he's taking care of and will
let us know in due time." Claire tried to sound opti-
mistic. She changed the subject. "A refill?" she said,
getting up and grabbing Brynn's cup. "I need one.
Feels like the cold is still in my bones." She busied
herself with fixing the tea. She gave Brynn hers and
sat down opposite her. "What's the matter?" Her friend
was looking at her strangely.

"About that night," Brynn said. Her long lashes
flickered as she remembered, but she went on. "What
started it?"

Claire met Brynn's gaze head-on, guessing what was
coming. "Buddy?"

"Yes." Brynn looked thoughtful. "It never ended,
did it?" Concern filled her eyes. Buddy had always men-
aced Claire. Even after he was removed from the Jessup
home, whenever he saw Claire in the street he would
taunt her.

Painful, fearful memories pierced Claire's brain.
"No," she whispered. "It never did."

Anger flared in Brynn's eyes. "I never knew why you took that crap from him. If you'd only told your father he would have given him some more of what he gave him when he kicked him out of the house!" Claire's eyes filled.

"My father would have killed Buddy Randolph if he knew." The tears fell and she swiped at them. "I never told you."

"Told me what?" Brynn became alarmed at the sudden look of defeat that softened Claire's body.

"When Buddy was returned to the system, he was a pitiful, angry boy," Claire said. "He blamed my mother for breaking her promise to adopt him. He hated her but always kept it from showing, especially to my father. You know how Daddy loved him in the beginning. At last he'd had the son he could never have. He always overlooked any silly, bad thing Buddy did, sloughing it off as pranks that boys played."

"Was touching you a prank?" Brynn said angrily.

"Mommy started to change toward him but Daddy didn't because he didn't think anything was wrong. She'd changed her mind about the adoption and that infuriated Buddy. But Daddy didn't want to give him up, saying all he needed was a little understanding and love."

"Until that day he was caught in your room trying to rape you!"

"Daddy nearly killed Buddy that day." Her face crumpled with the memory. "Mommy had to beat him with the broom to get him off that boy."

"What happened after he left?" Brynn knew there was more, the part that Claire had kept from her.

"Nothing until six months later." Claire stared into space. Her look was vacant when she turned to Brynn. "I stopped my mother from stabbing Buddy to death."

Stunned, Brynn could only stare. "What?" Her mouth was dry and the word was barely a croak.

"He broke into the house. I was alone. He was on me before I knew it. I was struggling on my bed and I could feel him hard on me." She paused. "God. It was awful. I heard a scream like a banshee and Buddy screamed and rolled off of me and onto the floor. My mother had stabbed him in the shoulder with a butcher knife and was about to plunge it into his back when I grabbed her arm."

"My God." Brynn stared in horror.

"Buddy was howling and scrambling around on the floor, trying to escape. My mother pushed me away and flew after him, determined that he wouldn't get away. She stabbed him in the leg. I don't know how Buddy did it but he half tumbled, half ran down the stairs and was out the door. What saved him was that I was holding on to my mother's arm and grabbing her around the waist. She dragged me and we tumbled halfway down the stairs. The knife cut into her other arm but she never noticed as she tried to run after Buddy. She was like someone gone mad. She finally looked at the knife and me and stared at her bleeding arm, as if she'd just realized what had happened. Very calmly she walked to the kitchen, washed the knife, and put it away. 'Don't tell your father' was all she said to me. We never spoke about it again."

"Buddy never bothered you after that?"

"No. The last time I saw his face it was like watching death. He was scared for his life. Later, I heard he'd moved to Brooklyn. You remember one year, you made a remark that we hadn't seen Buddy Randolph on the streets in a long time? It would be years before I saw him again."

"At Storeyland." Brynn was still shocked. "Lord,

Claire. You and your mother have lived with this all these years? What were you, only thirteen?"

"Daddy never knew," Claire said in a low voice.

Brynn's eyes blazed and her body was warm from the heat that settled over her like a blanket. She tossed aside the throw that covered her legs. "I hope that smug, arrogant punk rots where he is!" Brynn spat as if something vile were on her tongue.

Five

"No, don't walk with me," Claire said, "I'll lock up." She hugged Brynn again. "Thanks for last night. I needed that. I feel like a weight has been lifted from my soul. All those years!" She sighed. "And poor Mommy. What she bore. To think she could have murdered."

"You both carried a burden," Brynn said, squeezing Claire as tightly as her balance would allow. "Thank you for that talk. I needed that too."

Claire stepped back and eyed her with a raised brow. "So are you going to call him this morning?"

Brynn looked worried. "You know it's been a long time for me and relationships. It's like starting all over again. We were getting to know each other. There were feelings. Besides, I'll probably further embarrass myself."

"You won't," Claire said, and squeezed her friend's arm. "I know you'll be hurting for a long time, Brynn. But hiding here, hating yourself and everyone else, isn't healthy. Talking about it and trying to accept what is, is only the first step to healing yourself inside." She kissed Brynn's cheek. "Gotta go. I'll call."

The morning and afternoon had flown by and Brynn still hadn't called Simeon as she'd promised Claire. Soon after Claire left, Ruth, her housekeeper, had arrived, fixed breakfast, and after she fixed lunch and dinner, was gone before one o'clock. Brynn was so sleepy she'd dozed off. At three, the TV newscaster's loud, excited voice woke her up. She listened intently.

"Brynn Halsted, the principal dancer of the Merle Christiansen Dance Company, has retired from dance. The injuries sustained earlier this year have impaired her ability to ever dance professionally again."

Brynn listened as if the news personality were speaking of someone else. Woodenly she stared at the screen, watching her agent fend off the more aggressive of the reporters and smoothly answer questions that were only factual.

She clicked the remote and stared at the blank screen. She breathed in deep, refusing to go there, the funky place that her friend Claire had rescued her from. The deep dark hole that she'd dug for herself. No, she wouldn't go there again and vowed to fight the melancholia that threatened her mood.

Instead, Brynn reached for her phone book, bemused that she'd never memorized Simeon's phone number. After all, he was only going to be a casual acquaintance, wasn't he? There had been no time even to entertain thoughts of a long and serious relationship. She was going to be on tour for nearly four months, so why start something and then leave it in limbo? she'd asked herself way back then.

That last night in Storeyland flashed before her. The looks they'd shared, the ease with which they'd talked, enjoying good conversation with Art and Claire. No, she thought, she was wrong. Something *was* happening between them, only she had been willing to put it on the back burner. "Until when, Brynn?" she asked. The fact that Simeon had called, ever solicitous, told her that he felt something for her. There were feelings and she was ready to ignore them. Maybe he'd still want to talk to her. She held her breath as she dialed the number.

* * *

Simeon swore as he watched the news. When her face flashed on the screen and an excerpt from *Princessa,* Brynn's most famous role, was shown, he nearly gasped for air. Deep down he'd known this was coming but he'd fervently hoped that he was wrong. Now, it was final. Brynn would never dance again! "God, help her," he murmured.

"She knew!" he said. Yesterday, when he'd called, she knew then what the whole world learned today. No wonder she was spitting nails, and he hadn't helped any. "God," he blurted.

"Simeon?" Brynn held her breath wondering why he hadn't answered when he picked up. "Simeon?" she repeated.

"I'm here, Brynn," he said, exhaling. "You caught me by surprise. I didn't expect to hear from you since—"

"You've heard the news," Brynn interrupted. She heard him catch his breath.

"Yes." He didn't try to console her. Commiserating was the last thing she needed, he thought. At least, not at the moment. "You watched?" He began to breathe easier.

"Yes." Then, "How is your arm? Will you be able to . . . to play again?"

"I'm fine." Simeon grimaced. *I can play, but you can't dance.* He heard her let out a breath. Suddenly he asked, "Are you alone?"

"Yes." Brynn was close to falling into a funk. "Yes," she repeated for lack of what to say. She was happy that his arm wasn't injured. Yet, her career was ended. *Don't go there!*

"Would you like some company?" Simeon asked. Before she said no, he said, "I have something of yours."

"I know," Brynn said, swallowing hard. "Yes, I'd like

some company, Simeon." She paused. "Please don't forget my emerald."

Yesterday Wenona had heard the news from Brynn. Now, like thousands of others whose favorite TV programs were interrupted by breaking news, she heard it again. Her baby! The pain Wenona felt was almost unbearable as she listened to Brynn's agent and watched as, inevitably, the film clip of Brynn dancing her most famous role was aired. She wished that she could travel to New York, knowing that Brynn would need her now that her worst fear was revealed to the world. But there was no good reason to tell Brynn more bad news. Not at the time of her saddest hour. Somehow Wenona would do her best to spare her daughter any more hurt, at least for a little while. She'd find a way.

"Coming," Brynn called. She grimaced as she slowly made it to the door on her cane. She unlocked it, then balanced on her good foot when she stepped aside, exclaiming at the giant vase of flowers Simeon held against his chest. "Oh, how beautiful," Brynn murmured. "Please come inside before they die. It's freezing out there."

Simeon cocked his head in a rueful pose. "They?" At that moment when he stared into her eyes, he knew that this was no longer "business" as he'd always thought. His feelings for this woman ran deep.

Brynn blushed. "You too, Simeon." She stared at him and sucked in a breath. His eyes held such a haunted look. *All is not well with him and he's worried about me,* she thought. Taking a little step back, she said, "Just turn the top lock and follow me." She maneuvered herself around. "I'm getting the hang of us-

ing this as long as I don't act like I'm in a footrace."
She walked slowly to the living room.

Walking behind her, Simeon was glad she couldn't
see his face. He knew all the anger and pain he felt
inside was mirrored there. He'd come to be whatever
comfort to her that he could, not to stir up her pain
and agony. It wasn't hard to miss the red, swollen eyes
and the blotched cheeks where she'd rubbed the tears
away. Instantly, he was furious. She stayed here all
alone? No wonder she had so much time on her hands
to think. With her friends away on tour, she had no
one!

"Simeon?"

He realized she'd called him and he hadn't responded. "I'm sorry."

"The kitchen is just straight ahead. Would you remove the cellophane from the vase and bring it back
in the living room, please?" Brynn looked flustered.
"I'm sorry. The coat closet is back by the front door.
I—"

Simeon stopped her. "Brynn," he said firmly.
"Don't. I'm not here to be waited on. I came to see
you and to be of some help if I can. So let me?"

Brynn swallowed the lump in her throat and nodded.

"Good. I'll bring the flowers back to you and my
jacket will be just fine right here on this banister. It's
a little damp anyway. Okay?" When she gave him a
grateful look, he said, "Go on in there and sit down.
I'll find my way."

When he returned, he looked around and found a
spot on the fireplace mantel and stepped back to observe the effect. "Okay?" he said, looking at her for
approval.

"Perfect. What a gorgeous mixture of colors. The
orchids are exquisite. Thank you." As with cheerful rays

of sunshine, there was something about fresh-cut flowers in a room that had no equal.

"My pleasure." Simeon looked around the large room. He liked it, feeling as comfortable and as at home as he was in his own place. Her taste in furniture was similar to his: long, multicolored maroon sofa, a comfortable stuffed back without a zillion pillows that moved when he moved. The two sand-colored side chairs were big and looked inviting with bright-colored throws bringing splashes of color to the large room. Scattered around the room and walls were African art sculptures. A Jacob Lawrence painting held a prominent spot over the mantel.

"Nice," he said, looking at her.

"Thanks." Brynn was sitting in her big chair and suddenly frowned.

"What is it?" Simeon asked.

"I forgot to offer you something," she said, then smiled at the firm look on his face as one bushy brow shot up. "I know, I know, you can manage. Okay, there's plenty of stuff to drink in the refrigerator. Or tea or coffee. Please help yourself."

"Would you like something?"

"No. Not right now."

"Then, I'll wait too." He noticed the faint smile on her lips. "What's the matter?"

"I feel like we're strangers and we're not, are we?" Brynn said softly. "We talked rather easily together and now I feel like we're meeting for the first time. At a loss for words, I think."

"Uncomfortable?" Simeon said quietly.

"Yes."

"It's not so unusual to feel that way." He looked at her pointedly. "Things happened and some things changed as a result." He saw her eyes well up. "Oh,

God," he said. "Brynn, I didn't mean to be so blunt about . . ."

"About my crushed foot?" Brynn tried hard not to let the tears fall. Tried to be adult and bold and sassy about it all. Tried to show Claire and now Simeon how brave she was, that she was handling her misfortune like the stoic sphinx. But she couldn't help the dam that was threatening to burst inside her. She lost the battle when she dropped her head in her hands and the sobs came as fiercely as they'd come yesterday.

Simeon was beside her chair in an instant, sitting on the edge, pulling her to his chest and holding her tightly. "Brynn, sweetheart, I'm sorry. Lord, how I'm sorry," he whispered in her ear. He held and rocked her, caressing her back, smoothing the tears from her cheeks. The more he crooned to her the harder she wept and Simeon could feel the wetness behind his own eyelids. He cried for her too. He held her for a long time, rocking her gently. He kissed the tears from her eyes, then held her until her shoulders were still and the gut-wrenching sobs stopped. He ran his fingers through her damp curls. After a long silence, Brynn lifted her head from his shoulder.

He handed her a tissue from the box on the table and waited until she blew her nose. He took another and dried her eyes.

She looked at him teary-eyed. "This was a repeat performance, I'll have you know." At his inquiring look, she said, "Last night, with Claire. But I think, like Rita Moreno, I won every award in the book for this one."

"As long as it helped, accept it and take your bows." He caressed her cheek and when she caught his hand and held it there, his heart pounded in his chest. She dropped her head on his shoulder with his hand cradled beneath it and closed her eyes. He could feel the soft flutter of her damp eyelids on his palm and the sensation was as if his erogenous zones were being tickled excruciatingly. Almost mesmerized by her softness, the sweetness of her touch, the clean, salty smell of skin and tears, he bent and kissed her mouth. How long he'd been convincing himself that this wasn't what he wanted. When she responded, he deepened the kiss, seeking more. "Sweetheart," he murmured.

At the sound of his voice Brynn wound her arms around his neck. She remembered a dream weeks ago. When he kept calling her. Not Brynn, but sweetheart as he'd done just now. It wasn't a dream after all. She kissed him hungrily. He had hurt for her then and he was still hurting. Delicious feelings swept through her and she was suddenly cloaked in a mantle of warmth. And she'd been a fool even to think about leaving him for four months without a word or thought about their feelings for each other.

In the lengthy quiet they'd moved to the sofa and Simeon was staring at her with a look in his eyes that she couldn't read. Was he sorry for what had just happened? The room was dim and Brynn looked out the window. "It's gotten dark."

Simeon glanced at his watch. "It's five-thirty. I didn't realize it was so close to dinner when I got here. I should have called about bringing something."

"Don't worry about it. Do you like pot roast? My housekeeper starts dinner when she gets here every morning and leaves it for me in the fridge." She brushed a curl from her face. "Are you hungry? Can you stay?"

Can I? Simeon stood, walked over to a tall bronze floor lamp with a Tiffany shade, and turned it on, a soft glow emanating from beneath the colorful stained glass. He walked back to Brynn. "You're looking at a man who loves a good roast no matter what time of year it is." His brow shot up. "There's only one problem."

"What?"

"I never met a housekeeper who could make a mean bed *and* burn. Can she?"

Brynn laughed. "Trust me, love. I found a gem years ago and don't intend to let loose!" *Love?* Immediately, Brynn's cheeks caught on fire. *Where'd that come from?* she wondered. And so easily!

Simeon stared at her oddly. "Don't take it back. I liked the way it sounded," he said, husky-voiced. He handed the cane to her and then helped her up. "C'mon, let's put a hurtin' on a roast."

While the dishes were going through cycles in the dishwasher, Simeon tidied the rest of the kitchen, then looked around scrutinizing his handiwork. He turned to Brynn, seeking approval. "Okay?"

"Fine," Brynn said, smiling. "But don't think I'm letting Ruth go either."

"No, huh? Well, I'm just thinking of how I can put in a request for tomorrow night. How is she with a hen?"

"Wicked," Brynn said, a gleam in her eye. Tomorrow? She flushed. Dinner again so soon with him was not a horrible thing.

Simeon saw what his remark was doing to her and he waited. He wasn't going to be coy about the whole thing. He'd already bitten the bullet. But deep down he wondered if he was going to regret letting his heart take over—once again. He wanted to spend time with her. And if that included tomorrow and the next day and the next he'd be okay with that.

"I'm almost sure there isn't a hen in sight around here," Brynn said softly. "I think she's planning on duck. There's one defrosting in the fridge." She stared at him. "How's Friday night?"

Simeon nodded. "It's a date."

Brynn swallowed. "Don't you like duck?" she asked.

"What time tomorrow?" Simeon asked quietly. Lord help him. He wanted this!

"About now. Six?"

"That's a date too." The gurgle of the coffeemaker interrupted his next thought and he walked to the counter and poured the hot brew in the waiting mugs. He prepared the cups and inquired, "Living room?"

Brynn nodded as she walked slowly beside him. "Thanks, I think it's time to elevate," she said.

Simeon set the mugs on the chair-side table and helped her ease into the big chair. He frowned. "You're not overdoing it, are you? What time is bedtime?" He handed her the coffee and sat down opposite her. He noticed the grimace on her face when she lifted her leg onto the ottoman.

"Whenever I fall asleep," Brynn said, "I . . . I've been having a little trouble with that lately." A cloud settled over her face.

"Then I won't keep you up," Simeon said, worried about her.

"No." Brynn suddenly panicked at the thought of being alone. She was almost sure she'd open the floodgates again. "Please don't go." She flushed. "Well, I didn't mean . . . but if you have something else to do . . ."

"Brynn. I'm here because I want to be. I have nothing to do tonight or tomorrow or the next. At least I didn't until five minutes ago."

She remembered that Storeyland was still closed. "I'm sorry about your club, Simeon," she said. "How is the investigation going? Will you be able to open any time soon?" She waved a hand at the gray TV screen.

"I've been watching. One is certainly kept abreast of current events." She gave him a wry look.

He nodded in agreement, but his light eyes took on an angry dark hue when he remembered that night. "Slow."

From the way he looked Brynn knew there was something else behind his short response. "There's been other trouble?"

"Yes," Simeon said. He held her gaze. "With Buddy Randolph."

The name brought a raw taste to her mouth and her eyes flew to her foot encased in the brace. Swallowing her anger, she said, "Claire told me that you fired him months ago. What happened?"

The dark look on Simeon's face turned to anger. "Buddy was turning Storeyland's decent rep into one of sleaze. People, including some of my staff, were turning me on to some backroom dealings." His laugh was sarcastic. "Backroom is not literal. Since Buddy was my bartender and up front his dealing was going on right under my nose, so to speak."

"He was dealing drugs?" Brynn shot him a look of disgust.

"No." He shook his head. "Soliciting my customers, propositioning the female guests. I knew he considered himself to be a lady-killer and talked his stuff but in his profession he's supposed to make the customers feel at home. If they want to cry on his shoulder he listens. And he did that. The club is where he met all his women. The ones who took him in and made him their boy toy. When he got tired of one or she became too wise and fed up with taking care of him she'd put him out, but there was always another waiting in the wings to have him warm her bed." He shrugged. "Apparently women didn't care about the stories they'd heard about him. They walked into their mess with their eyes wide open. That's how he made his way. Living off women."

"That was why you'd fired him?"

"That was the main reason. When a few women who weren't interested pulled my coat about his aggressiveness, I warned him but that went over with him like a damp Fourth of July rocket. We had a heated discussion but I let him stay on."

"Why?"

"Because he was a good mixologist and he kept the majority of the customers happy," Simeon said. "After our little talk, I think he wanted to put the screws to me and the business." He looked thoughtful. "I think he always envied me and the success of the club. He approached me once about learning the ropes claiming he wanted a similar club one day. I turned him down. Anyway, it wasn't long afterward that the first attempted rape incident occurred."

"He tried to rape someone in the club?"

Simeon shook his head. "Not him. I think he paid someone else. Like all the other incidents that were too suspicious but I had no proof. The underage girls made up to look legal were suddenly a nightly happening. I don't know how many times Duke had to escort them out. I believe Buddy was responsible for their presence and then inviting the police to come and make random checks of IDs."

He didn't miss the look of simmering anger in Brynn's eyes and he decided to ask the question that had bothered him for weeks. "I need to know something." When he had her attention he said, "Why did Buddy treat you so cruelly? That was a vicious act. Understandably he was enraged because you interrupted his attack on Claire and tried to gouge his eyes out. But it was more than an instant rage for him. He wanted to get you in the worst way he knew how. Had you dealt with him before?"

Brynn closed her eyes briefly, then said, wearily, "We were kids together."

Simeon was surprised.

When Brynn finished telling Simeon about her childhood, hers and Claire's, without divulging Claire's mother's involvement, she eyed him. "He hated me for seeing him as he was, even when he was so young. I was only eight when I met him and he was eleven, but I could sense the evil in him. So could Claire. I guess it's true what they say about kids seeing more than adults do in some people. Almost like the sense that animals have when they encounter something evil."

"Had he ever tried to . . ." He couldn't finish the thought.

"No, he never tried to attack me," Brynn said. "It was Claire he was obsessed with." She felt sick when she thought of Claire's mother. "He just hated me because he thought I put on airs and acted like I was better than everybody else. Once he came to a performance and somehow made his way backstage. He scared the devil out of me when he sidled up to me and whispered that I was still nothing but Miss Priss, trying to act like somebody." She shuddered. "Gave me the creeps."

Simeon saw that she was becoming agitated. "Well, he won't bother you or Claire again. He has plenty of time to think and he isn't a happy camper, I'll bet."

He got up and went to Brynn and sat down on the edge of the huge ottoman. He reached into his pocket and pulled out a carefully folded tissue. "How did you know I'd found this?" He handed it to her.

Brynn knew she'd see her emerald when she lifted the folds. She stared at the sparkling gem almost as if it were something mystical. Her eyes met his. "Because it was the only thing that I'd left behind at the club," she said, softly. But her heart ached. *No, I left my whole life there, my career,* she thought.

Simeon saw the sadness that disappeared almost instantly from her eyes, and knew what she was thinking. His hand closed over hers. "Brynn," he said, "I'm sorry." His voice caught and he paused before he continued. "You don't know how many times I've died inside knowing that you were hurt, and I was there. I couldn't get to you in time. When I realized that Claire had not returned and I saw you leave the table, I sensed that something was wrong, but I was too late. I'm responsible for what happened to you. I should have suspected something was up with both of you leaving the set. I would have gotten there sooner."

"You couldn't have known," she murmured. "No one could have known what that madman was going to do. Besides, you didn't even know he was there, did you? Claire and I had never spotted him."

"It was crowded. I was playing." He looked miserable and helpless.

"It happened," Brynn said. "You're cutting yourself up for something that was beyond your control." She lifted the stone from the tissue and held it in the warmth of her hand. "Beyond anyone's control," she whispered. She lifted it up to the light, mesmerized by the sparkle. "I should have known," she whispered.

Simeon watched the strange look come over her face, as she seemed to be entranced with the stone. "Known what?" he asked quietly.

"I'd had a feeling and ignored it."

He watched her run her fingers over the emerald. "It means a lot to you, doesn't it?"

"Yes," she answered. "My father gave it to me when I was sixteen. I wear it often." Suddenly not wanting to talk about her strange feelings and her father to this man who was so concerned, she said, "Do you think that there's any chance that you'll be allowed to open the club any time soon?"

Changing the conversation from her father and the emerald was not what she'd planned, Simeon thought. He'd seen the pain enter her eyes and knew that she was hurting.

"Tell me about your father, Brynn," he said softly. "And the emerald."

"It's my talisman. My father had an interest in gem lore, and some of the things he told me about stones were fascinating. I developed an interest but never pursued it like he did. I much preferred to spend my free time in my own little world of dance. Claire and I ate and slept dance until our mothers would chase us out of the room if we couldn't talk about anything else.

"My father said the emerald promoted creativity. He wanted me to wear it when I danced but of course that wasn't allowed onstage. He told me he could see me becoming a legend in modern dance and he talked about other properties of the stone like faith and hope, and he didn't dwell on the more disturbing myths like psychic power and immortality." She smiled at Simeon's skeptical look. "The stone would loosen and hurl itself from its mounting if someone was in danger of becoming ill. I didn't take stock in any of that, though, because I simply loved the beauty of the stone and the fact that my father had given it to me."

"What happened to your father, Brynn?"

"I was dancing my first lead with the Albert Prince Dance Company. I was nervous, excited, and thrilled to be the star of the night. The night before the opening, he was shot in the stomach in an armed robbery. The internal bleeding could not be stopped. We stayed with him through the night. He was conscious and sensed that he was dying, but he instructed me to dance for him the following night. To dance as though he were sitting in the second row, center aisle seat, beaming proudly as he usually did at my shows. He'd be with me. He died that night."

Simeon didn't let go of her hand as she clutched his.

"I danced," Brynn said. "I wore my emerald to the distress of the artistic director, who cautioned that it would be a distraction, but I was determined. My mother sat next to the empty seat that would have been my father's. I remember it as if it were yesterday. My father's spirit enveloped me and I danced as I never had before."

"That night the dance world learned your name."

Brynn looked in surprise at the man who'd spoken so quietly and in earnest. As if he'd known. "Yes. Two months later I won a role in a long-running Broadway musical. It was the beginning of my career."

"That night at Storeyland when you were hurt, you wore the pendant."

Brynn grimaced "Yes. I-I had these strange feelings and wearing it helped me to feel close to my father. I hoped for that faith that would make everything okay. I didn't anticipate a catastrophe happening, but I took extra care that day to watch my footing, careful not to trip over anything." She gave him a rueful smile. "I didn't leave the house until Claire picked me up in a taxi. You should have seen me walking ever so gingerly down the stairs, as if I were walking on a carpet of eggshells."

"And then your fears were realized in the form of Buddy Randolph. At my club."

A moment passed before she answered. "Yes," she mused. "Although I feared that someone close to me might fall ill, deep down I prayed that nothing would happen to my legs. I was thinking only of myself."

Brynn gave him a hopeless look. "I guess I'm paying for my selfish thoughts."

"No one would intentionally wish harm to themselves, Brynn. Sending yourself on a guilt trip like that is not where you want to go."

They were silent, each wondering about the unexplainable in all things.

Brynn shifted her weight and lifted her leg to the floor. "I think I'm getting molded to this chair."

"Would it help if you stretched out on the sofa?"

"That helps a lot. It's just that I spend so much time lying down, it's downright boring."

Simeon observed her encased foot. "How long before you lose that?" he asked.

"Probably in a couple of weeks."

"What about physical therapy? How soon can you start?"

"I believe right away," Brynn said. "Three weeks after the surgery and not before. Certain surgeries require a delay in any activity and starting too soon would be detrimental." Her eyes darkened. "To what, I don't know." She choked up, not wanting to fall into another morose mood with this man who was so caring.

Simeon knew what she was thinking. He stood and reached for her hand, pulling her up. "Come on, let's take a turn up the hall and back. Loosen up a bit. After that you can get comfortable with a cold or hot drink. Whatever your pleasure."

Brynn leaned on him until she adjusted herself. "With the wind sounding like a gale I think I like the idea of something piping hot, thank you. That unbelievably cold fall that we had certainly was an indication of this winter we're having." She made a face. "I just don't want any tea or coffee. After that . . ." She shrugged her shoulders as they walked to the kitchen.

"Well, if you don't mind my taking a peek in your

cupboards and your fridge, maybe I'll come up with something inventive," Simeon said.

"Okay with me. Ruth pretty much keeps everything she needs. She hates to be in the middle of preparing something and has to stop to go to the store. It's not like the market is a hop, skip, and a jump from here."

She watched with interest as Simeon opened and closed cupboard doors, amused when he made faces at certain things and nodded in appreciation at others. "Ah-hah," he said.

Brynn looked curious. "What?"

"Don't know why it didn't pop into my head right away," Simeon said as he opened a jar of cinnamon sticks and sniffed, then reached for some other spices. "My sister turned me on to this years ago. She was always making up strange concoctions in the kitchen making our nanny tear her hair out."

"You had a nanny?"

"Yeah, guess I'm guilty of that." He shrugged it off. "We got over it though." He poured some apple juice in a small saucepan, dropped in some of the sticks, allspice, a few cloves, a dash of sugar, some lemon juice, and stirred. After bringing the mixture to a boil, he strained the hot liquid and poured it in tall ceramic mugs and stirred. "You'll like it and you definitely won't confuse it with coffee or tea." He took the cake top off the dish, sliced two pieces of plain pound cake, and put them on plates. "In here or there?" he asked.

"Here is fine," Brynn said, maneuvering herself into the kitchen chair.

"Okay." Simeon placed the food in front of her. "Dig in." He sat opposite her.

"Ooh," Brynn said, her mouth puckering. "Tart and sweet. You made your own apple cider."

"You like?" Simeon scrutinized her, happy to see the haunted look gone.

"Delicious."

Later, instead of lying prone, Brynn was sitting on the sofa with pillows behind her head. She had her foot on the ottoman and Simeon was sitting beside her.

"This is better," Brynn said. "I didn't want to stretch out and then fall asleep on you." She adjusted the throw over her legs. "So tell me about your life with a nanny. Were you teased a lot?"

A mysterious smile appeared. "Not too much."

"No? Why?"

He raised his fist. "Knuckle sandwiches weren't so bad in those days."

Brynn smiled. "What did the good doctors do about their brawling son?"

"They gave me as good as I gave my tormentors. Ouch."

Brynn laughed. She liked the way their conversation flowed so smoothly, without any shyness or fear. With their kiss they'd already crossed a boundary and taken their relationship to the next level that either had yet to speak of. Somehow she knew that there were no words to be spoken. Brynn felt deep down that simply because he was there with her meant they'd already had an unspoken understanding. She was comfortable with that and when she looked over at him and saw the unveiled look of deep caring in his eyes, the warmth she felt had nothing to do with Simeon's homemade apple cider.

Six

Simeon enjoyed the sound of Brynn's laughter and wished that it were not so rare. He wanted to know so much more about her, the way she grew up, what her dreams were before dance. He wanted to know all about the woman who he thought one day would bring glorious interpretations to his music, and now never would. He could feel his anger surfacing again and it took all of his resolve to maintain his composure, but knew he had failed when Brynn cast a curious look his way.

"What's wrong, Simeon?" Brynn asked. He'd gotten quiet and she sensed his sudden change of mood.

He caught and held her stare. Rather than reveal his bitter thoughts, he said, "I like this." His voice was low and serious. When he saw her lashes flicker he knew she understood. "You know what I mean."

"Yes," Brynn answered. "I'm glad you're here."

"When I knew I was coming I didn't plan on being here for more than an hour, two at the most," he said. "It's nearly eleven and I don't want to leave you."

"I feel the same," Brynn said softly. Her hand was still in his long slender one. It was a nice, comfortable feeling.

"I told myself that when you went away on tour I would be okay with that," Simeon said, husky-voiced. "That when you returned, I would call, we'd go out a time or two, and that would be that." He stopped moving his thumb around in circles on her hand. "But that wouldn't have happened, would it?"

Brynn shook her head. "I don't think so," she whispered. "I knew that I would regret not calling, seeing you, doing things together when our schedules didn't clash."

"Then you thought about me too?"

"Yes, very much so."

They were quiet for several moments.

"And now?" Simeon asked.

She gave him a questioning look.

"You're here because of the actions of a madman. There's no returning from a tour to begin to wonder if we should start where we left off. What might have been put off is here and now."

Though her heart ached, Brynn concealed her pain. "No," she said quietly. "There's no tour. There's now." She gripped his hand. "I want you here with me, Simeon. I—I want that too."

He couldn't miss her solemn look. "I know," he said. "It's pretty heavy, isn't it?"

"Yes."

He leaned over and kissed her lightly on the mouth. "We'll deal with it, take this heady stuff slow."

Almost as if a weight had been lifted, they simultaneously relaxed and eased into more relaxing positions, as if before, their bodies touching would have been inappropriate. He put his arm around her and Brynn shifted until her head rested on his shoulder.

"Simeon?"

"Hmm?"

"Something you said before has made me curious."

"What was that?" Simeon played with her loose curls and mused that he'd never seen her hair so long.

"That night that I danced for my father's spirit, you

said that was the night the world learned my name."
She paused. "That was true. But I was sixteen. How did
you know that that was the beginning of my career?"

"I read it." A little feeling of insecurity made him
hesitate. How would she feel hearing that he knew all
about the public side of her?

"Really?" Brynn said. "That was so long ago. It must
be an old article."

He went for it. "That one was," he said. "There are
hundreds of articles about Brynn Halsted, and many
of them more often than not mention that fact. Everyone who sees that performance on video, or everyone
who was in the audience that night when you were so
young, isn't too surprised that they were watching a
legend being born. When *Princessa* happened, those
same people were smug in their earlier predictions."

Brynn lifted her head. "You have them all?"

He felt her shiver and tweaked her nose. "Don't be
frightened. I'm not a stalker." He felt her relax. "Ever
since that day Merle called me in to play for you, I've
never forgotten it. Or recovered from the experience."
He breathed in deeply. "I envisioned you dancing to
my compositions. You were like a dazzling bird, moving
so blithely, yet so powerfully, leaping as if to touch the
ceiling. You lulled, caressed, then lured us into your
lair, attacked, and had us all mesmerized before you
released us and let us see the sweetness of the rebel-
lious young princess, maturing into a beautiful woman.
You captivated every soul in the house. There's no wonder that it's become your signature piece."

Brynn listened in awe feeling at once elated and
then, thinking of her future, deflated.

Sensing her feelings, he tightened his hold. "I wondered if Merle would pull my coat after the performance. More than once I had to put myself in check

while I was playing for you and I wondered whether he noticed if something was wrong."

"Was it?"

"You might say that. I was so tempted to start playing my own composition. The one I was writing for you."

Brynn pushed herself upright. "For me?" Her eyes widened. "An original score?"

"Yes," Simeon said, meeting her startled gaze. "For you. I had started it several months before that night."

"I—I don't know what to say." She could only gaze at him in disbelief. "That was more than four years ago!"

"It was." He remembered all too well.

Brynn thought. "That was the night that I . . ." She blushed.

Simeon nodded. "That was then," he said softly. "This is now." He brushed her lips with his and tensed. Realizing he wanted more than the tender kisses they'd shared, he moved away. He wasn't denying that his reaction to her was one he hadn't felt in a very long time. His feelings went beyond sexual desire. His heart was getting involved and he needed to make damn sure that this was what he wanted. And he had to be certain where her head was in this whole thing.

"Have you finished it?" Brynn felt suddenly strange and almost shy. So long ago, he'd had those thoughts of her, thinking that she was some kind of beast. Yet, she realized that he'd only been thinking of her, writing music for her. She was embarrassed. No one had ever presented anything like that to her before. When Merle had created other ballets including *Princessa* for her, that had been different. She'd worked for months with him. They'd struggled through every phase, every step, every move of each finger. She'd *known* what was expected. But, somewhere there had been a stranger, composing music for a woman whom he didn't even know, or even whether she would ever dance for him. Her throat burned from holding back the tears.

"No," Simeon answered quietly, watching her. "I started working on it again."

"After we met in the park." She remembered his angry face.

"Yes."

"You'd put it away four years ago." Brynn lifted her hand to his cheek. "I'm sorry, Simeon," she whispered.

He shook his head. "Remember, this is now," he said softly.

"Yes." Brynn's voice wavered. "I'll never dance to your music, Simeon."

"Who was it that said 'Never say never'?" He tried to hide the raw emotion.

She swallowed. "I'm afraid I don't have James Bond tricks up my sleeve."

"One day your ankle will heal. You're going to walk as normally as before." He cupped her chin. "Who knows what will come after that?"

Brynn stiffened. "Don't!" She spoke sharply. "Don't *tell* me that I will dance again. I . . . I don't want to hear lies, or the falseness that comes with those words. I already know!" Her voice descended to a whisper. "Dear God, I already know."

Simeon's heart cried with her, and he prayed for forgiveness for what he was thinking about the man who'd put those tears in her soul. When he felt her breathing return to normal, Simeon stayed away from the subject that renewed her agony. "This is a great space you have here," he said, looking around the big room. "Do you share it with your mother?"

"Not anymore," Brynn said, grateful that he'd changed the subject. "Six years ago, my mother moved to Roensville, North Carolina, my father's birthplace. It's where I spent the first five years of my life. When

I was born my young parents were overwhelmed. Neither had good jobs and they threatened to break up until my grandparents stepped in and took me, promising to give me up whenever my parents were ready for responsibility. I was truly loved by my grandparents, who never tried to replace my parents. I grew up knowing and loving my mother and father. When they came for me, they vowed never to let me go again. I think they were sorry about those first years, missing my growing up. They showered me with love and affection, tempering all their gifts with more love. I think my father was very emotional having me back. He said given the chance to do it all over again, he'd never let mc out of his sight. We were very close."

Simeon listened without interrupting, knowing her need to talk. This was one part of her history that had never made it to print.

"When I was seven the young fifteen-year-old girl who watched me after school would take me to her dance classes. I was fascinated by what I saw. I tried to emulate everything the dancers did. I begged my mother to enroll me. My life hasn't been the same since."

"Thank God for your baby-sitter," Simeon said. "If she only knew."

"She did. I joined the same company and we were in ensembles together."

"Do you live here alone, then?"

"No. I rent the upstairs apartment to an older woman. She's been a great help to me since I came home."

"That's good to know that you're not in the building alone." Simeon frowned. He wondered why her mother, who had been so attentive in the hospital, and a fierce defender of Brynn's privacy, hadn't remained in New York knowing that her daughter would need someone at home. What a time to leave her to fend for herself.

Sensing his thoughts, Brynn said, "I sent my mother home. I couldn't look at her face anymore. She was so angry and bitter. I think if she stayed here any longer, she might have gone after Buddy herself."

"No one would blame her."

"It would be nothing but folly. What's done is done." Her voice was hollow. Brynn looked at her foot. "She's promised to come back soon."

Simeon could see her inner struggle each time she looked at herself as she dwelled on what had been taken away. He wondered at leaving her alone, because he sensed that after he was gone, she would fall into a malaise. He felt her stir. "Tired?"

Brynn nodded. She was sleepy but didn't want him to go.

He kissed her forehead. "I'm selfish. I don't want to leave you."

"I don't want you to," she said and then gave him a smile. "But I'll see you tomorrow?"

"I'll be here."

When he kissed her, Brynn clung to him, dreading when he left. It was he who ended the deep kiss that threatened to heat into something that would soon be beyond their control.

Later, Brynn tossed in bed, trying to move her weighted foot as easily as she could, finally letting it hang over the side of the bed, but soon changed positions when her foot began to throb. She lay on her back and propped it up on the pillows placed at the foot of the bed.

It was nearly two in the morning and she had awakened almost as if she expected to find Simeon in her bed. She warmed when she realized that that thought consumed her mind since he'd left, and she'd won-

dered about her feelings. For days now, he had been
part of her waking thoughts and part of her dreams.
Had anyone told her that she'd be romantically involved with the owner of Storeyland, she'd have
laughed aloud. Before running into him in the park,
she'd been her old self, Merle Christiansen's star
dancer, with only her career on her mind. No romantic
entanglements that would keep her away from her passion. Now here she was counting the hours until she
would see a man who'd walked into her life mere
months ago. She hadn't known that she could feel this
way, and a long-hidden secret thought surfaced. Did
she have enough love in her heart and soul to share
with a man? All those years before when she'd dated,
no man had stirred her to the point where instead of
moving to the rhythms in her head when she went to
bed, her body would be writhing in desire for a man.

Brynn couldn't even remember how it felt to lose
herself in the throes of love, that experience being rele-
gated to the back of her mind. It had happened so
long ago that she didn't even recall the name or the
face of the man that she'd given her virginity to. She
smiled at that because her friends swore that you never
forget the first time. But of course she'd never offered
that *that* part of her memory had been erased.

Two nights later, Simeon said, "The duck was cool
but Ruth can do a thing with a hen. You were right
about her."

"Would I lie?" She was on the sofa and he was sitting
in one of the big chairs. Brynn was watching him as
she had been all night. After the duck last night and
his kiss good night, she'd had a flush of desire that had
rocked her soul, and she remembered her restless
night. When he'd walked in the door earlier, she felt

that same rush that made her wonder if he could see the passion in her eyes. She'd stayed far away from him until his intense gaze forced her to look at him.

"Tell me what's bothering you, Brynn." Simeon had sensed her discomfort ever since he'd arrived. One thing that he did know, she didn't want him to leave. There could only be one other reason for her sudden shyness with him. He wanted to love her and she knew it. But dare he? Last night he'd felt her desire and it was all he could do to steel himself from caving in to his own passion.

"Nothing," Brynn answered. "I'm glad you enjoyed dinner."

Simeon gave her an intense look. "Just a moment ago you said you wouldn't lie." Crushed by the shadow that crossed her face, he went to sit beside her. "Tell me."

With him so suddenly close to her, Brynn felt awkward and stifled. She struggled to her feet with a murmured excuse and tried to hurry away when he stood and his hands on her shoulders stopped her.

"Brynn." He waited until she was steady on her feet. "What is it?"

One look into her eyes was his undoing. "God," he groaned and enfolded her in his arms, inhaling her sweet musky scent and her hair that smelled of fresh-cut flowers. He put her from him, then cupped her chin until he was gazing directly into her eyes; then he lowered his head and kissed her deeply. She wound her arms around his neck and leaned into him. When a soft cry escaped her lips, chills went down his spine and he moaned with long-denied pleasure. He devoured her mouth, longing to touch her everywhere. His fingers were beneath her sweater and he nearly drew them back as if they were singed when he cupped her full lace-covered breasts.

It was the first time that Brynn's body reacted as if it had a mind of its own. *She* was usually the one that demanded tremendous executions from it when she danced. Now another was pulling the strings and she loved it and exalted in how Simeon made her feel. She was losing herself, quivering at the hypnotic feel of his lips, his hands, and his erection pressing against her. She desired to be loved by him. When she felt his kisses on her throat, then her bare breasts as he loosened her bra, she bit back a scream of joy when her nipples throbbed inside his mouth. The torture of not being able to feel him was unbearable. "Simeon," she murmured, and reached for him, and gasped at the firmness in her hand. A soft whimper escaped. "I want you," she whispered.

Simeon saw red as he brought himself back from the edge of the precipice. He'd nearly fallen over and taken her with him. *We can't do this,* he thought. It wouldn't be fair to her. He couldn't hurt her. With painful effort he stepped back. "Brynn," he said with a rasp, "we should stop before we can't."

Bereft of his heated body, Brynn felt chilled. Confused, she stared up at him. "I—I thought that we— that you . . ."

"Want to make love?" Simeon could sense her withdrawal. She was adjusting her sweater and he caught her hands and finished pulling it down. He straightened his own clothing, then sat beside her on the sofa.

"I want to love you, badly," Simeon said. "I know you want to love me too."

"Then why . . ."

"Because you're still fragile, sweetheart. I want to love you in the worst way, but I feel you need a little more time." He kissed her lips lingeringly, and then feathered her throat and eyelids. "You're still healing."

"My foot?" Brynn tried to make light of the moment

because suddenly she was uncomfortable and confused. How could she have been so wrong about what they were feeling for each other? *There's something bothering him,* she thought. Something about her and she didn't have a clue as to what it could be.

Sensing her hurt, Simeon wanted to kick himself from here to beyond. He followed her lead and spoke lightly. "Well, I was thinking more on the lines of mental healing, but yes, that too." He tilted her chin. "You wouldn't want me to become a casualty of our lovemaking, now, would you?"

"Perish the thought," Brynn said. She smiled and when he bent to kiss her, strain had usurped passion.

After Simeon left, Brynn sat for a long time thinking about the man that she knew she was falling for and trying to understand his strange behavior. She knew that they would have made exquisite, passionate love right there on her sofa had he not stopped them. Brynn no longer believed that she was the reason, as he'd wanted her to think.

Simeon was the one who was hurting, she suddenly guessed. A deep, bitter hurt that was tearing him up inside. He'd been hurt before and *she* was on the receiving end of that failed relationship. She was giving her heart for the first time in her life and the man she chose was guarded against *his* heart being broken again. Bemusedly, Brynn said, "How ironic."

Frowning at the strange call he'd just received, Simeon hung up the phone. Although he and Merle Christiansen had known each other for years they were never more than casual friends. There was a genuine liking but because of their dedication to their separate lives, they had never become bosom buddies. As everyone does when they meet continually at various occa-

sions or events, they promise to call and hoist a few,
but never do.

Because Merle was on his way to visit, Simeon knew
that something momentous was about to happen. Although Merle didn't make every city of every tour, he
still had his finger on the pulse.

It was after one-thirty in the afternoon when Merle
rang the doorbell. Almost as if he had second thoughts
about standing on Simeon's doorstep, he took a slight
step backward.

"Hey, man," Simeon said. "Come on in." He held
back the surprise he felt when he saw Merle. Although
Merle was dressed in a bulky ski jacket and his familiar
black clothing, Simeon could see the man's loss of
weight. He hung the jacket in the hall closet and led
the way into the first-floor living room where he entertained guests.

"Something hot or something cold?" Simeon said
when they were seated. "Lunch to go with it?" He observed the slight flinch around Merle's mouth at the
mention of food and Simeon tried not to speculate.
"Won't be a problem," he said.

Merle shook his head. "I had something a while ago,
but you go on. A hot coffee would hit the spot,
though."

"I've eaten but I'll get that coffee." It didn't take a
wizard to see that the man was carrying a heavy weight,
Simeon thought as he moved around the kitchen.
Merle was a big man at six-feet, strong body, powerful
arms and legs. He exuded strength. The man that was
sitting in his living room appeared to have shrunk and
there was a weight loss of at least a good twenty pounds.

"Here you go." Simeon set down a tray. "Fix your
own."

"Thanks." Merle added milk and three teaspoonfuls
of sugar. He warmed his hands around the mug and

lifted his gray eyes to Simeon. The usual smile that made his eyes twinkle was absent. "You saw Brynn last night."

"Yes." Simeon didn't voice his surprise at the statement.

"Good. Yesterday was pretty hectic and I didn't get a chance to call. I usually find a minute every day to shout at her." He smiled, and there was a brief sparkle when the smile reached his eyes. "Not literally, you know."

"I know. She says you have the voice of a wolf."

"So you two have been talking about me, huh?"

"Among other things."

"I'm glad you're there." Merle paused. "That's only because your spot is closed though. Sorry about that, man." His eyes filled with disgust. "Do you think he's going to beat this?"

Simeon's eyes flickered. They both knew that Buddy Randolph was the "he" in question. "Not if I have anything to say about it. I'm on top of things and it doesn't look like he's going to walk away from this one."

Merle nodded. He looked around the room as if to avoid speaking what was on his mind but then looked squarely at Simeon. "She's very tender, you know. Many people don't know that. They see this powerful dancer onstage and an elite head-held-high persona, off. Aloof, some say." He shook his head. "Brynn's very tender and all alone." He coughed and sighed heavily. "Except for me and Claire."

"Her mother? Grandparents?"

"So far away. She needs someone here with her, when—she breaks." In a lowered voice, he said, "It may come soon. I can hear it, the things she doesn't say when we talk. Soon," he repeated. "And she needs someone strong to help her through the hell that's coming." Merle speared Simeon with a penetrating look. "You haven't seen any evidence?"

"Once. The first night I went to visit. I thought the dam had burst then." Suddenly Simeon felt uneasy. What had he missed all these days and nights they'd spent together? "What did she say to make you think that she's not making a brave effort to pull through this?" he asked.

"Nothing I can verbalize," Merle answered. "I know Brynn."

"Enlighten me."

"She has always shown a tough exterior, but that's not who she is, not really. I met Brynn when she was fifteen at the Albert Prince school. Immediately I knew she was going to be a star." He got a faraway look in his eyes. "I knew that she would be *my* star dancer one day." He smiled. "Man, you should have seen her that night when she was sixteen, dancing *Ruby's Dream*. Unforgettable!"

"You were there?"

"Was I!" He grinned and his eyes lit up. "I was assistant choreographer. Albert Prince, our artistic director, had his compunctions about giving an unknown that piece, but the choreographer and I convinced him that it would be criminal not to let her dance. The movements, the music, everything about it screamed her name. As you know, it made history. I remember struggling with it, and she would timidly give her ideas on a certain movement or step while Albert and I said no, it wouldn't work. Brynn would say just let me try it this way, and voila! Her ideas worked beautifully. That was when we knew she had a natural talent, a sixth sense for choreography. From then on she became bolder, encouraged to express her ideas. Many ballets have her signature on them although she doesn't think about that or even claim any credit. To her it's all part

of the theater. When she joined my company I let her use her creativity uninhibited." He sat back in the chair, musing. "She's a natural," he murmured.

"I saw that in Claire Jessup's solo," Simeon said. "*Élan*'s some work." He could still hear the thunderous applause for Brynn that night. He threw the reflective man a curious look.

Merle met his stare. "Brynn needs a cushion," he said quietly. "But she's not going to accept or even admit that she needs one. I want her to become my choreographer." He blinked, and then characteristically pushed back his long bushy hair. "And eventually if the board sees it my way, take over as the artistic director of the Merle Christiansen Dance Company. She's young but she has the talent and the training and will have the support and expertise of my assistant. The board will realize that."

"Eventually?" Simeon said. His gut told him that there was something wrong.

"I have pancreatic cancer."

The two men locked gazes.

"God."

Merle grinned. "That's what I said." The old sparkle shone in his eyes before they darkened. "Months ago, I had wanted to broach Brynn about taking over for me." He waved at the air. "Oh, I used to make jokes about it from time to time, tease her, you know, just letting her get used to the idea of doing something other than taking the stage every night herself. But she always laughed it off, and her mind would turn to her art. She never even gave serious thought to the proposal. So I kept my thoughts to myself for the most part. When I found out about this—this thing growing inside me, I was knocked for a loop. I ignored what was coming. Until I couldn't ignore it anymore. If not for the great condition of my body, I'm afraid I'd be much worse off than I am now. But time is a-hastening, as my mother would say," he said grimly. "Things are beginning to spin out of control."

"No treatment?" Simeon said quietly.

"After a fashion," Merle answered. "I waited too long. You know the deal and the old whine, 'it can't happen to me', et cetera, et cetera." He shrugged. "I'm managing it. But I can't operate effectively for very much longer. I have to turn the reins over to someone soon." He winced. "I can't see my company folding. Worked too long and too hard for that to happen. I want it to survive, become legendary, and feed the hunger of all the new dancers yet to come."

Simeon could feel the man's hurt. "You knew all of this even before Brynn's accident, so what did you expect her to do? Stop dancing?"

"No. Wear two hats like many artists do."

"But you knew she would be resistant to it, so how did you expect her to react?"

"I don't know."

"What do you plan to do?"

Merle blinked. "She needs to face the reality and get on with her life, without waking up every morning preparing to dance, but to prepare others to dance and to become the future stars. She has to know and accept that."

"Would you?"

Considering Simeon's question with a pained look, Merle answered, "It would be hard. Brynn has an undying passion for her work and won't even think beyond now. But she has to be made to think about it or I fear that she will lock herself up in a world that no one else would be able to penetrate."

"What is it that you want me to do?"

"Finish your composition for her." He gave Simeon

a knowing look. "That is what you're hoping for, isn't it? That she will work with you?"

"I had that in mind," Simeon replied.

"Trust me, Simeon." Merle speared him with a look. "She needs that. When that brace comes off and she begins to walk normally, she'll think that she can dance again. She'll try. When she fails, she's going to fall and fall hard. You will be there to make her see that her life is not over. She can turn to her second talent and do it successfully."

"I didn't know how or just when to broach the subject. I've been wondering about her working on that foot. Will she be able to demonstrate the steps herself?"

"That much she'll be able to do," Merle answered with conviction. "Her foot will heal as good as yours and mine. She just won't have the strength needed to return to finessing steps. The execution won't be there."

Simeon thought of how the bile rose up in his throat when he thought of her never dancing to his music, bringing it to life. How was he going to convince her to create a beautiful piece only for Claire or some other dancer to perform? How could he bear to see his music danced by another?

"I know what you're thinking," Merle said. He was remembering a time a few years ago when Simeon had spoken of his music and Brynn all in one breath as if the two were synonymous. And now? He drew in a sharp breath. "You can do this," he said. "You have to do this for her, to save her life."

A long moment passed in silence.

"Do you plan to tell her?" Simeon asked. Each knew he meant Merle's illness.

"I've put it off for as long as I can," Merle answered. "In a couple of weeks the brace will be removed and she'll be steady enough on her feet. I'll tell her then."

"And about choreographing for the company?"

"I'll do that in the same breath." Merle saw the look of apprehension. "What's bothering you?"

"You can't deny something is wrong. She'll know just by looking at you."

"I'll continue to visit by phone until I'm ready to tell her." Merle stood. "Will you help a man save her life?"

Simeon walked with Merle to the hall. He watched him shrug into his jacket, and then turn to him with a look. "I never thought to do anything else," Simeon said in a quiet voice.

Seven

Two weeks later, Brynn gripped the phone. "Not coming, Ma? You said you'd be here. What's wrong?" Brynn was suddenly deflated, as if someone had punched her in the belly and knocked the air out of her. Her imagination threatened to throw her into a panic but she forced herself to calm down. *Everything is fine.*

"Papa needs me here to help with Noonie," Wenona said, crossing her fingers and toes at the blatant lie. One that could be so easily checked, but Wenona had sworn Brynn's grandparents to secrecy. There was no need to worry Brynn about the surgery or the ensuing radiation treatment she was taking every day.

"But I thought Noonie was coming along," Brynn said, speaking of the grandmother that she loved. "I spoke to her the other day and she told me that her hip was healing fine. And Papa told me not to worry."

"And he was right. Don't worry, we're handling things okay," Wenona said.

"Ma, I miss you," Brynn said with a catch in her voice. Then, "I wish you were here."

Wenona's heart wrenched. "I know, baby," she whispered. "I hope to get there as soon as the worst is past for Noonie. It all happened so quickly. And you know

your grandfather isn't much help lately. He's been getting more and more forgetful."

"Suppose I can't walk normally? Suppose I limp?"
Brynn shuddered with the thought. "What will I do?"
Her heart skipped a beat as she dwelled on her future.
"What will I become? I wish you were here with me."

"Don't do this to yourself, Brynn." Wenona spoke
firmly. "You can't dwell on the negative when you don't
even know what is to be. You must wait until you hear
what the doctor has to say. Otherwise you'll make yourself sick with worry."

Ma, it's too late. I am sick! Brynn hung up the phone,
after promising to call that night. She lay in bed for a
long time, unwilling to start the day. Her mouth became dry at the same time her hands became wet with
sweat. So many mixed emotions were swirling through
her brain that she couldn't—wouldn't—think about
this afternoon. She grimaced. How could she not? At
one o'clock today she would know just how bad her
future was going to be. And wondered if Simeon would
still want to be a part of it.

With great mental effort she pushed aside the covers
and sat on the edge of the bed. Ruth would be there
soon to help her bathe and dress. Brynn had longed
for the day when she could soak for hours in rose-
scented water, soaping herself with sweet-smelling free-
sia gel. This afternoon when she returned home, she
would indulge herself, shamelessly. Odd, she thought,
that her dearest friends, Claire and Merle, couldn't be
with her, especially Merle. Claire had an emergency
dental appointment, but Merle hadn't returned her
call. Curious about Merle, she wondered why he hadn't
been as frequent a visitor as he'd always been in the
past. He'd always raided the refrigerator for some of
Ruth's leftovers. But it was Simeon, the newest person

in her life, who would be taking her to keep her appointment.

Brynn finished brushing her teeth and then stared at her face in the mirror. She didn't know what she expected to see other than her own familiar features. She guessed that she would be looking for what a woman in love looked like. "It doesn't show," she murmured. Then she smiled at herself.

Weeks ago she'd known that she was in love with Simeon. Ever since that night when she'd learned his secret. They'd never spoken of that time yet they were still affectionate and their kisses had grown more passionate with each passing day. But always they stopped before reaching that point of no return.

Simeon double-parked his black Infiniti Q45 and went around to open the door for Brynn. "Careful," he said, helping her out of the car and up the stairs. Determined to walk unaided, she refused to use the cane.

He studied her face. She had been quiet since they'd left her doctor's office on West End Avenue and Seventy-ninth Street. Traffic had been at the usual snail's pace and it had taken longer than usual to make the thirty-minute drive uptown to her brownstone. After a few attempts at light conversation, he'd stopped, letting her have her moments of contemplation. But that would stop once they were alone. He'd be damned if he'd allow her to settle into a funk.

"Let me do that, Simeon." Brynn took the kettle from his hand, filled it with water, and put it on the stove. "See, I can stand just fine. I can even stand here long enough to put the dishes in the washer."

"Don't, Brynn." *She needs someone there with her—when she breaks.* Merle's words sounded in his head. Simeon didn't want to coddle her but he couldn't let her fall into the depression that was coming. For weeks he'd watched her face this day's approach, but like every other human being who didn't want to run head-on into bad news, she had sloughed it off. As if she were a kid who waited for Christmas and when it came tried not to show her disappointment in what Santa didn't bring.

Brynn stepped away from the stove and sat down at the kitchen table. It felt strange not to have to favor her foot. And to be able to wear matching slippers for the first time in months. Both feet were planted on the floor. They looked the same, she thought. No swelling. The doctor said there would be no problem that he could foresee. A wan smile played about her lips. *No problem. For you, Doctor.* She felt Simeon's intense gaze but refused to meet his eyes.

"Want to talk about it now or later?" When she ignored him Simeon said, "I'm not leaving you here alone until after we talk about how you feel."

She looked at him. "You don't plan on leaving tonight, then."

His eyes twinkled. "Is that an invitation?"

"No." The kettle whistled and she was the first up to prepare their mugs of tea. She placed them on the table and began to sip. "I want to be alone. I'm going to have a hot bath. I'll probably be in there for hours. And then I intend to sleep the night away." She drank some tea. *Please go, Simeon, please.*

Simeon appeared to mull over her words while drinking the tea. He crossed his long legs at the ankles. "I'll wait until you do all that," he said. He bent his head and looked at her foot. "You seem to be walking okay, but I'll stick around just in case you get a little wobbly climbing in and out of the tub." He raked her with a long, seductive look. "If you need help reaching your back, I can accommodate you."

"I think I can manage on my own, thanks." *Don't do this. Please,* she pleaded silently.

"Are you shutting me out now?"

She felt the guilt rise up in her belly. All these weeks he'd been so attentive, so caring, seeing to her needs, being a friend and trying to keep her from falling into a depression. Was she just ungrateful?

"I—I appreciate all that you've—"

"Stop! No thanks necessary." He glared at her. "Do you think I'm here for your gratitude?" His eyes glinted with anger.

"That's not what I mean. You know that. I—I need to be alone now. I have to think about what I'm going to do with . . ."

"The rest of your life?" Simeon said. His eyes softened as he watched her lips tremble, saw the eyes mist. He couldn't leave her now. The minute he was out that door, she would fall apart. He sensed it as sure as he could feel his own skin. He reached across the table and caught her hand. As always the heat that roiled in his gut whenever he touched her boiled up until it seared his fingertips. She was so smooth, so tender, and he wished that she would let him in.

He got up and walked around the table, pulling her up and against his chest. He put his arms around her and held her tightly. "Let me stay, Brynn," he whispered against her hair. "I'm here because I want to be, because I care. You know that."

Brynn leaned into him and her heart beat wildly against his chest. "I know, Simeon," she murmured. "I know that, but it's hard." Her throat constricted as she wound her arms around his waist and buried her head in the hollow of his shoulder. "I thought that I had settled this in my mind. Made peace with what is to be.

But when I saw my foot, it looked so natural, like nothing was wrong with it. I look at it and wonder why I can never dance again. I want to talk to it as if it can hear me, obey me. I can wiggle it, turn it, and twist it. Why can't I dance with it?" She closed her eyes tightly, refusing to let the tears fall. She couldn't. If she did she'd never stop, feeling sorry for herself for the rest of her life. But how was she going to get through this? she wondered. She knew the answer. With the man who was holding her so tenderly: the man who was falling in love with her but wouldn't tell her.

He held and rocked her, whispering in her ear. When Simeon felt her body relax against him, the shivering gone, he stepped back, put his finger under her chin, and tilted her head up. His heart leaped at the misery and pain he saw in her eyes. If he had thought about giving in and leaving her alone, that idea dissipated.

"Would you like that bath now?" he said, watching her closely. He felt the deep sigh course through her and her hold on him tighten.

"That sounds heavenly." Brynn didn't want him to leave. "Would you stay?"

"I said I would, sweetheart." He kissed her forehead.

She lifted a hand and touched his face. Her finger traced the most perfect V she'd ever seen on a man's lips. She stood on her toes and kissed them. So soft, yet so firm. "I'm sorry about—"

"Shh," Simeon said. "Nothing to apologize for." He kissed her back, letting his lips linger over hers, and then drew her tongue into his mouth. When she responded the warmth engulfed him and he wanted more. More than the heated kisses that they'd shared these past weeks, and that had threatened to turn into something that would beg for the truth between them. He wanted to love her madly. And he could feel her need for him. But for now, he took her kisses and lost himself in them. She wanted him. And when she was ready, he would love her. He would not—could not resist any longer. She was the woman he loved and, he knew now, worth the risk he'd been unwilling to face all these years. His heart was hers.

"Heaven," Brynn murmured as she lay her head against the inflated pillow, breathing in the violet scent that perfumed the bathroom. "Mm, scrumptious." She soaped herself again for the umpteenth time, loving the feel of the loofah against her skin. She must have been in the tub for an hour, warming the water and pouring in more scent, the perfumed bubbles tickling her face and floating over her head. She luxuriated in the feeling of wiggling her toes and moving her ankle to and fro. No pain, no twinges of discomfort. The agony and moroseness that she expected while she was alone escaped her. At least for now, she thought. The sounds of smooth jazz, Count Basie and Joe Williams, drifted to her ears. She heard Simeon in the kitchen, the slam of the refrigerator door, and she guessed that he was warming dinner.

Once she heard the music die, and she knew he was listening for sounds coming from the bathroom. She smiled at his concern. True to his word, he wasn't leaving her, at least not until he satisfied himself that she was making it through the night. Almost reluctantly, Brynn pulled the plug and as the water gurgled down the drain, she climbed out of the tub.

Simeon looked up when Brynn entered the living room bringing with her the sweet smell of flowers, warm skin, and freshly shampooed hair. She was dressed in a calf-length mandarin-collared, blue silk paisley robe. He was by her side.

Noticing the intensity of his gaze, Brynn said, "No need to worry." He opened his arms and she walked into them and was enfolded in a warm circle.

"Sure?" Simeon held her close, burying his head in her hair, inhaling deeply. He felt the curve of her breasts beneath the silk and he squashed his sense of urgency to love her. He would wait.

Snuggling even deeper into the burrow of his arms, Brynn said, "Yes."

They stood for several seconds, finally breaking apart when Brynn tilted her head. "Something smells good," she said. "Is that Ruth's stewed chicken and biscuits?"

"You know it is. I thought I would have to come in there and pull you out. I'm starving." He tweaked her nose. "What about you?"

"Me too," she admitted. "I didn't have much appetite this morning thinking about, well, you know what was on my mind."

He kissed her forehead. "Ready for something now?" When she nodded, Simeon said, "Let me handle this. Everything is already warmed. You can get the butter out of the fridge. I'll do the rest."

She watched as he deftly filled their plates and poured chilled merlot into their glasses. Always when she watched Simeon, she marveled at his hands. They were long and slender and one would never think of the strength that they possessed. She loved the feel of them especially when they roved over her body, manipulating her breasts, bringing her nipples to glorious attention.

"What did you just think of?" Simeon buttered his biscuit as he watched the wondrous look on her face.

Brynn blushed. "Your hands," she admitted truthfully. "They're deceivingly powerful."

"Years of wringing out of them what I can when I can," Simeon said. He looked amused. "Much to the disgust of my brother and sister when we were kids. I think I abused their ears, forcing them to listen to my creations. My parents bravely suffered in silence, encouraging me though every once in a while I glimpsed the pained smiles." He chuckled at the memory.

She was touched by his story. The affection he felt for his family was in his voice. "How was it growing up with siblings?" she asked. "Claire is the closest thing to a sister I've ever had."

"I've noticed. Growing up with a brother and a sister had its hairy moments. We all had different interests and we got on one another's nerves more often than not." He lifted a shoulder. "We survived intact, though, largely because of my mother and father and their hands-on parenting."

"As busy, successful doctors, that must have been a feat." Brynn was thoughtful. "You've spoken about Asha. Has she always wanted to be a TV journalist?"

"No." Simeon chuckled. "She thought she was going to be the next Alfre Woodard or Viveca Fox. She changed up after her first year in high school when she performed in the school play *The Wiz*, cast as the good witch Glinda. She got the message before the first act ended."

"Oh no. Did she bomb?"

"With a va-room," he answered, solemnly "But she came through it like the proverbial trouper. She found her comfort zone by the time she graduated and enrolled in Spelman." His eyes twinkled. "She's still onstage though before millions nightly. So I guess you can say she got her wish."

"She's great," Brynn said. "Looks comfortable and at home in front of the camera. And Conrad?" she said. "I know you mentioned he lives in Pennsylvania and is a designer but you never said of what?"

"Women's fashions. Bolo."

Brynn arched a brow. "Really?" Every woman had a Bolo suit in her closet. "Was his an early talent also?"

Simeon nodded. "That I can say is the truth. He experimented on all of us and some of his school friends. He was avante-garde in the tenth grade."

Brynn reflected on all he'd told her. She'd never missed having a brother or a sister. Lavished with love from her parents and the strong friendship she had with Claire, she was never sad. Dance took up the rest of her life. Her eyes clouded.

He saw the shadows and reacted, standing and taking her hand and pulling her to her feet. "Come. I think we'll be more comfortable in here," he said, leading her into the living room. It was seven o'clock and the gray sky had turned to night. Brynn turned on lamps and then sat on the sofa where he joined her.

"Claire never spoke of siblings," Simeon said. "So it was the two of you against the world."

"As far back as I can remember."

"I'm glad you had each other."

"Me too." Brynn reached for his hand and held it in hers, unconsciously smoothing his knuckles. She loved the feel of him and was not surprised at how easily they both fell into the comfort of being near. As if it had always been. As snug as two old married folk, she thought. A sudden thought made her warm all over. They'd never made love. She knew she wanted him as much as he wanted her, and knew that if she only said the word they'd be lovers.

But now she wondered about the future. She didn't feel like the person she'd been when they first met. Who was she and where was she going? What did he expect from her now that she was no longer the diva of dance?

Simeon felt her change of mood and gently brought

her back. "No regrets not having those sibling squabbles?" he asked softly. He squeezed her hand.

"No. I was a happy kid," she said. "I—I've told you about my father and me. He spoiled me. So did my mother. But my father had a sadness in his eyes. I'd catch him looking at me sometime and when he caught me, he'd look away and when he turned to me again the look was gone. I asked him about it one time."

"What did he say?" Simeon heard the catch in her voice.

"He said that he missed those first five years of my life. Said if he had to do it all over again he'd give up his life first. He told me that he dreamed of holding his baby granddaughter in his arms so tightly that she'd scream for mercy. He wanted to hear her teething cries. To see the first tooth, then the second, then all the rest come in until she had a devilish smile. He wanted to hear her say 'Granddaddy,' or 'Papa,' as he called his own grandfather. He wanted to see those first toddler steps and to feel her little arms hug him tight." Brynn swallowed. "He only wanted all the things he'd missed having with me." Her voice fell. "He didn't know that he had so little time left."

Simeon didn't have the words to comfort her. His parents had had all those things with three children. They still smiled and chuckled over the videotapes made of their kids from birth on. He could only imagine the anguish that Brynn's father felt for those lost years. He saw Brynn finger her emerald. He noticed that it was an unconscious habit.

"The emerald," Simeon said. "He must have taken great delight in giving it to you."

"He did." Brynn smiled. "It was symbolic of strength and creativity, he told me. He reminded me that its wearer was to always keep faith and hope in his heart."

"You are strong and creative," he said firmly.

"I'm none of those things," Brynn murmured.

"That's not true. Don't be hard on yourself."

Brynn shook her head in disagreement as she looked into Simeon's eyes. As always the light in them excited and ignited the deepest parts of her. She took a deep breath because she wanted to talk, not love him, at this moment.

"Simeon," she said, "do you believe in premonitions?"

Feeling the intensity of her question, Simeon said solemnly, "I've never experienced one, but that doesn't mean that they're not genuine in others. Have you?"

"Yes. When I was twelve years old."

"Want to talk about it?" he asked quietly.

"I believe I saved our lives," Brynn said in a soft voice. "We were walking toward the house after my father parked the car, having a serious discussion about the movie we'd seen. I stopped when we reached the gate, balking at going inside. My parents stopped teasing me after they saw that I was frightened out of my mind. I kept whispering that something was wrong in there and not to go in. My mother stopped laughing when she saw that the light she normally left on was out, leaving the downstairs in total darkness. When she saw the upstairs was dark too, she felt my fear. They rented to an elderly man who lived alone and at that hour they should have seen a light in his apartment. My father hesitated but cautiously opened the gate and started up the stairs when a shot rang out. He pushed us aside. Two men came flying down the stairs toward us, fired again, and then ran through the gate and disappeared."

"Damn," Simeon said. "Were you hurt?"

"No. The bullet missed my mother, who was hunched over hugging the breath out of me. Later we found where the bullet had singed her long thick hair as it fell over her shoulder. My father found the old man brutally beaten and left for dead."

"They were on the way out of the house but were surprised by your return," Simeon stated.

"Yes. They were in the dark vestibule. If I hadn't stopped us from going right on in, we would have been hurt, maybe killed."

"Has it ever happened again?" He was thinking of her foot.

"Once. Before my father was shot. But never again." She looked away and then caught and held his gaze.

Merle was sick. Simeon began to wonder if she'd had a premonition about someone getting ill. "Are you sure?"

Brynn shrugged. "I didn't want to believe. But a few weeks after I had this strange feeling, I got hurt at Storeyland."

Simeon's jaw tightened. His place. His responsibility. He'd never forget or forgive himself for not being more observant.

Brynn felt the constriction of his chest. "There was nothing you could have done that night, Simeon," she said in a soft voice. "It happened."

"Maybe," he said tightly.

"No, I know I'm right." Brynn gave him a wry smile. "I've lived in constant fear of losing my career, Simeon. All my life I've never wanted to do or be anything else but a dancer. I was living my dream." She splayed her hand. "I'm no longer a dancer," she whispered. "Unable to create. To tell beautiful stories with my body." Her gaze caught his. "I'm not me anymore and I don't know what to do with me."

Her voice wavered. *At last,* Simeon thought. *Merle was right.* "You *are* you, Brynn." He tightened his hold around her shoulders. "The same bold and beautiful woman the world has known and loved." *And the woman that I love!*

"Not anymore," Brynn whispered. The thought of what she once was and what she was now was too much for her to think about. She was trying to look at her future out of the eyes of someone who'd never been the popular diva of the dance world. New York's darling. What was she going to do to earn her living? The bleak-looking future was too much and before she could stop herself her eyes filled and her shoulders began to shake. "I—I don't know what to do." She gulped in air and slowly the sobs came.

Simeon tightened his hold on her shoulders. "Let it out, Brynn," he murmured. "Don't hold back. I'm here with you. Go on." As if his words were what she'd been waiting for, her soft sobbing turned into a plaintive wail, a keening cry. She began to rock back and forth and her arms slid around his waist and gripped him hard. He felt his shirt dampen and he crushed her to him as he rested his chin on her head. He caressed her back and smoothed her arms while crooning to her as he would a baby. As quickly as it had started, she stilled and the sobs stopped, but she didn't move from his arms. Although he loosened his hold, he held her close. It was a long while before either stirred.

"We're a mess," Brynn said, shifting herself in Simeon's arms and running her hand over his wet shirt. Her hair was damp and mussed.

"Oh, I don't know." Simeon adopted a puzzled pose. "There's something to be said about messes, isn't there? Thought I heard that somewhere."

Brynn smiled. "I don't know from where." A loud sigh escaped and her body shuddered. "But whatever, I think I lost something that was weighing me down." She looked at his shirt. "And it looks like I dumped it all here. Whew!"

Simeon brushed her damp eyelids, and then kissed them. "You get what you ask for, I guess."

"What?" She was the puzzled one now.

"You cried me a river."

"Ooh," Brynn said. "You didn't!"

A loud laugh erupted from his gut. "Couldn't help it." Simeon planted a kiss on her damp cheek. "That happens once in a while," he said.

"What does?" Brynn traced the outline of his lips and, unable to resist, tilted her chin and kissed him.

"Acting a ham." He nibbled at her mouth, as she was about to pull away. "Kiss and run? Uh-uh." He captured her lips again lingeringly as if time was of no importance. He savored the taste of her while envisioning her naked in his arms. She parted her lips and when her tongue darted inside his mouth he weakened. His kiss became savage in its intensity as he devoured her mouth. He kissed her throat, her cheeks, her eyes, the tip of her nose. He wanted to taste her everywhere.

"Simeon," Brynn murmured as she surrendered to his burning kisses and when his hand touched her bare thigh, she jumped. Oh no, she thought and pulled away.

The sound of her voice and her abrupt departure from his arms brought Simeon up short. Breathing heavily, he rasped, "Brynn, I want you. You know that, don't you?"

"Yes, I do," Brynn said, "but—"

"I know, don't say it." Simeon smoothed the hair from her forehead. "But we have to talk about it—soon."

Brynn nodded and wondered why she had stopped them. Wasn't he what she wanted?

They were silent, both with thoughts of their own.

Speaking on another matter, Simeon said, "Brynn,

what did you think that you would do with your college education? Your liberal arts degree?" He stroked her arm. "You must have given it some thought at one point."

She saw his concern and her heart felt full. He loved her. "I was fooling myself."

"What do you mean?"

"I was a fraud. The whole time." Brynn moved out of his arms and rested her head against the back of the sofa. "My passion was for dance so I knew there could be nothing else for me." She shrugged and splayed her hands. "Nothing else."

"That must have been pretty boring and a little hard for you to sit through those classes."

"It would have been except for the dance classes!" Brynn answered, rolling her eyes. "Thank the Lord for nontraditional college and computer classes! I thought I would always be the professional student. It took me more years than I care to tell to finish up all my credits! Embarrassing! But I knew how much my mother wanted it for me. She was a firm believer in a backup system. 'You never know,' she used to say all the time." Brynn grimaced. "How right she was, and 'never' finally happened."

"And what now?" Simeon said softly.

"I don't know," Brynn whispered.

"Wrong answer and I think you're fooling yourself."

"What do you mean?"

"I think you already know."

Her eyes narrowed. "Teach?" She almost spat out the word. "There's no passion in me to teach others. Every great dancer is not always the best teacher."

"Not teach." Simeon tapped a finger against her forehead. "Create." He touched the emerald. "You have the creativity this is believed to instill. You have the vision to create powerful, impressive dances." He had her full attention. "Inside here"—he tapped her chest—"in your heart, you know the truth. Your choreography is something to behold. You knew and believed when you created Claire's *Élan*. She, Merle, and the whole world knew it. There lies your future."

"Choreography? For the rest of my life?" Brynn looked skeptical.

Simeon saw the flicker of interest in her eyes and he dared to hope that he'd lit a spark of fire. "A legend in the making. Mentioned in the same breath as Alvin Ailey," he said, watching her with all the intensity of a sharp-eyed falcon.

"Alvin Ailey?" Brynn said almost reverently.

He nodded, not breaking their gaze. "Yes." Simeon knew he had her full attention. "You know you can do this," he said. "You're intelligent, practical, and the consummate artist. No matter what you turn to, it will revolve around dance. Dance is part of your soul. Do you believe that?"

Brynn nodded, too filled to speak. She bent her head.

"Yes," Simeon said. "I know you do." He put a finger to her chin and turned her face toward him until their gazes locked. "I want you to work with me."

"What?" Brynn's brows arched. "At Stoneyland?"

Simeon's look was steady and his voice firm. "I want you to dance for me."

Eight

Brynn's eyes widened, then narrowed with anger. "What are you saying?" Her thoughts spun. *What is he doing to me?* she wondered. Her gaze was drawn to her foot. She wiggled it in a circle almost with fascination.

Simeon saw and gave her a stern look. "Brynn, don't go there." He spoke in a low tone. "I know what you're thinking."

"You do?" Her eyes still blazed. "If that's true, how can you ask me to dance? And dance for you? Only you?" She laughed. "Am I to be your own personal sideshow?"

Angered, Simeon caught her shoulders. "Stop that," he said brusquely. He waited until his anger subsided before speaking. "I want you to help me get this music out of my head. The music I'm writing for you. I need to see you bring it to life, Brynn. You."

Dance for me. The words had hung in the air. She'd felt as if time had stood still, never expecting to hear those words applied to her. *He wants me to dance to his hauntingly beautiful music.* Once when she'd visited his home briefly he'd played some of what he'd written for her. The melody ran through her head and she automatically began to attach dance steps to certain strains. She could see herself pirouetting and leaping, her feet hardly touching the floor as she whirled about. Abruptly, she stopped, bringing herself back to the present and reality. With such facility and so naturally the choreography came to her, she thought. She remembered Merle's words. *Dance is in your soul. You can never be away from it. You've a natural, innate talent.* She heard her name and was pained at the look in Simeon's eyes as he stared at her. Her lips trembled. "How?" she whispered. Her eyes pleaded with him.

Simeon wanted to take her in his arms and hold her close but he sat back, looking at her intently. "Together." When she closed her eyes, he said, "With me."

"I only wish," Brynn murmured. "I could see myself, Simeon. Your music was swirling around in my head and I just started to move to it. I could feel it." She touched her breast. "In here." She saw the flare of hope in his eyes. "But it's one thing to be in my head and another to execute on this." She looked miserably at her foot.

Simeon was careful not to show his excitement. "Shh. Don't dwell on that. Don't think of dancing for an audience, the public, the reviews. Forget about the director. You're just putting one foot in front of the other. A step here and a step there."

"Baby steps."

"Just like that."

"Oh, how easy it all sounds, Simeon." She was nearly breathless. "So easy."

He took her slender hands in his. "No. Not so easy."

Brynn thought of the music. "You have wanted this for a long time, haven't you?" She loved the feel of his hands on her and suddenly she wished he would handle her all over. Her breath became short.

"Years," Simeon said simply. He saw the soft look come into her eyes and her lips part. He wanted to taste them again. But he held back, not wanting to distract her from her moment of decision.

"But what about your business? The club? How will

you do both? When you reopen I would think that you need to expend all your time and energy in bringing it back to what it once was."

"I've been thinking about that," Simeon said thoughtfully.

Brynn didn't miss the look of anger that briefly shadowed his face. "What?"

"I'm not reopening."

Her heart thumped. Because of her he'd lost his business. "I'm sorry. It's all my fault." Her eyes downcast, she stared at her foot. "If not for me, you'd have your club. Continue to do what you've always wanted."

At once, Simeon felt the pain of her guilt and it stabbed him in the heart to see her hurting. "Nothing is your fault, sweetheart. If I could take your pain and make it mine, you don't know how fast that would happen. If I could turn back the hands of time, there would have been no such man as Buddy Randolph to cause you harm." He felt her grip tighten on his arm. "My troubles started long before you set foot into Storeyland. The assaults, the thefts, the planted drugs. That was all Buddy's doing and I was too ignorant to catch on until he'd done his damage." His lips twitched in anger. "Yes, the club was a dream I held. But I've had that and it was a good thing for me. And now?" He shrugged. "It's not like I'm financially desperate," he said.

"The silver spoon." Brynn remembered his wealth.

"Something like that," Simeon said. "But my big concern was the staff. The closing was so abrupt that without adequate planning it messed up a lot of lives. I'm glad I could help see them through the rough. Everyone's finally employed elsewhere."

Sincerely thankful for that, she murmured, "That's good." She still thought about her involvement in the whole mess.

"Now that I don't have the club, I can pursue another dream," Simeon said. He stroked her arm. "I have nothing else on my mind but to compose music. That's what I want now."

"It must be wonderful to be able to make one's dreams come true," Brynn said.

He stared at her with uncertainty. *Bitterness?* he wondered. "I am who I am," Simeon said quietly.

"That was uncalled for," Brynn said. "I—I don't know why I said that."

"Yes, you do. It's a natural reaction to what you're feeling inside. Don't repress the anger, Brynn."

She sent him an intense look. "You really believe in me, don't you?"

"I do."

She smiled. "That sounds like a promise."

Simeon was unsuccessful in hiding his emotions. It had been many months before he'd had thoughts for only one woman. He knew that he was in love with Brynn. He felt pretty certain how she felt about him. But he had to be sure. He had to know if her feelings were genuine, because if they weren't . . . Disturbing thoughts from his past invaded his brain.

"Simeon?" He'd drifted. When she had his attention, she said, "There was someone."

"That was a long time ago."

She heard the pain behind the words and knew that she'd guessed right. "You were in a failed relationship and you think the same thing might happen to us if we become intimate." Her words were blunt but she saw no reason for holding back. Not now. Especially when she was about to give him her heart.

He shuttered his eyes against the pain he saw in hers. How could he answer her?

"What is it that you fear from me?"

"Dishonesty."

Her eyes widened. "What are you saying?"

"I want you. Not your gratitude. I want honest feelings between us."

"Gratitude? Honesty?" Brynn was bewildered.

He breathed in deeply. "I know these last months have been traumatic for you and the last thing on your mind was starting a romance with a stranger. I was there for you and I'm thankful that you wanted my friendship and didn't push me away, especially because you were injured in my establishment." He stared at her. "We've shared kisses and tender moments like this and it was with monumental control that I didn't take you each and every time. Like now," he rasped, and caressed her cheek with his knuckles. "But, I want more than a close friendship with you, Brynn." His voice dropped to a whisper. "I want to love you madly."

Brynn caught her bottom lip between her teeth almost as if to keep herself from speaking. *Friendship?* she thought. *My God!* She wanted to make wild love to him where they sat. "Simeon," she whispered, "I—I want that too. It's just that I-I thought that you didn't want me like that, that you were befriending me out of . . ."

Simeon's eyes blazed. "Guilt?" he rasped. When she only looked at him, he said, "For God's sake, Brynn, you thought that? I had to leave this room and go to the bathroom to jump in your shower and stand there under the icy water before I came back in here. Each night after leaving here I had to open my jacket and walk in the freezing cold to get myself back to normal. Friendship? Yes, I want that too, but I want to love you as my woman." Her lips parted and he groaned. The heat in his loins made him glance down at the telltale sign of his desire for her.

Brynn followed his gaze and blushed at his erection. "Simeon," she murmured, as she caressed his cheek. "I want you too."

"Lord," Simeon rasped. The fire that he sensed in her was evident in her smoldering gaze as her eyes held his. He caught her in his arms and crushed her lips to his. "Brynn, sweetheart," he murmured against her sweet mouth. His tongue traced the soft outline of her lips and then thrust inside her mouth to capture hers. With a hunger that didn't surprise him he explored the sweet recesses. She kissed him passionately, and he became drunk with the sensation that heated his body from head to toe. Her hands were on his chest, underneath his sweater, and the heat of her fingers was excruciating. She squeezed his nipples and joyous pain shot through him like an electric jolt.

Brynn was lost in his kisses. She had only imagined how his hands would feel all over her bare skin and now her nipples responded as if they'd always known his touch. He unbuttoned her robe and pushed it off her shoulders. He caught his breath and she blushed at the fire in his eyes. "Simeon, love," she whispered. She knew without a doubt that he *was* her love. She was in love with him.

"Yes, I know," Simeon said as he sensed her need. His kiss became more intense as he bent his head and took one tender nipple in his mouth and was ecstatic when it hardened against his tongue. He was on fire and he groaned his pleasure as he devoured first one and then the other of the sweet buds as if they were succulent berries. He inhaled her womanly scent that smelled of heated sex and perfume. He was nearly over the edge when her fingertips touched his flesh, exploring his chest and back and then teasing his nipples again. He heard her moans of pleasure when she extricated herself from his arms and bent to kiss them, her teeth nipping and her mouth suckling.

Under her ministrations, Simeon was wild with desire for her. "Brynn, let me love you," he managed through gasps.

Brynn lifted her eyes to his. "Please," she murmured.

Simeon voiced his desire with low groans of delight when she stood and slipped off her robe letting it slide to the floor. She wore white lace panties and when she slipped her fingers under the elastic and drew them over her hips he stared in awe. Never in his wildest dreams had he imagined that Brynn Halsted would be standing before him naked asking him to love her.

"You're beautiful," he managed, wondering how he could think lucidly. He let his eyes drink in every inch of her, marveling at the smoothness of her honey-colored skin. He caught her hips and slowly slid his hands down her satiny thighs. "You're beautiful," he repeated in a hushed voice. She tugged at his hands and he stood up.

Brynn could not keep her hands off him while he slipped his sweater over his head. With a speed that left her breathless, he shed shoes and clothes and stood before her naked. She looked at his pulsing sex and warmed all over when she lifted her eyes to see the raw desire in his. The dampness between her thighs was no surprise as she was ready for him. She leaned into him and the sudden contact of flesh against flesh sent a current of electricity between them that could no longer be denied. "Simeon," she pleaded.

As one they sank to the floor, Simeon's kisses smothering every inch of her body, his tongue sliding over her delicious curves, lingering in the valley between her legs, then gently probing inside as she moaned and writhed to his touch. His fingers found her moist center and slipped inside her, touching the tender buds of her womanhood. Brynn's body jolted at his invasion and her whimpers of pleasure rocked him senseless.

"Simeon, stop. Please, please, I want you inside me."
She caught his throbbing shaft and was stunned when
he drew away from her and fumbled for his pants.
When he returned to her he was sheathed in a condom
and when he eased himself over her, her legs reflexively
wound around his hips, capturing him. She arched her
body and nearly swooned when he entered her. "Ooh,"
she murmured. "Oh, yes!"

Her cries appeared to unleash raw passion in Simeon
and his thrusts became turbulent at every moan she
made. At first he was puzzled, and hesitated at her almost virginal tightness. But she clutched his neck and
rose up, silently asking him to fill her completely. He
was lost when she whispered his name and he knew
nothing else but to embark on the wildest journey of
his life.

Delightful was the only word that came to mind
when Brynn let go with abandon, letting herself soar
on the magic ride, writhing her hips to meet his thrusts.
They were in perfect rhythm and she was in awe that
this was what was meant by the rhythm of love. She was
heady with the power she had when with just one arc
of her body Simeon went wild with passion and loved
her madly.

Just as quickly as it had started, with a jolt, she felt
herself sinking, the highs of the last minutes settling
over them like a heated cloud as they lay atop her robe,
panting and sated. Her breath was choppy and
Simeon's chest rose and fell on her breasts as he put
the bulk of his weight on his forearms.

Simeon eased himself to her side, and lay looking
up at the ceiling that wouldn't stop spinning. He closed
his eyes and murmured, "Incredible."

"Yes, you are," Brynn whispered in his ear, then
kissed his eyelids. When he looked at her she kissed
his lips. "Simply incredible."

"I meant that for you, sweetie," Simeon said. He propped himself up on one elbow and stared into her eyes. "You are out of this world, I want you to know."

A soft laugh escaped and Brynn's eyes twinkled. "It sounds like we're both in agreement on something here."

"You're right about that." Simeon bent his head and kissed her hard and fast. She was slick from their love-making, and her warm, musky scent intoxicated him. "You're doing something to me, Brynn," he whispered in her ear. "Mm, mm. Let me get you up from here or I won't be responsible for what happens next," he growled.

Brynn grinned as he stood and pulled her up. "In our business isn't that called an encore?" she teased. She leaned into him and moved her hips provocatively. He started rising against her.

Simeon jumped as she touched his erection. "Damn right," he rasped, and held her close. "Brynn," he rasped, "I want you again."

"Love," she murmured, "isn't that what encores are all about?" She ducked her head and rained tiny kisses on his chest, his shoulders, and stood on her toes and nibbled his ear. "There's something about encores I simply love. I can never get enough of them."

Her throaty whispers went through him, turning his legs to jelly. Simeon caught her hand and before leading her to the bedroom, grabbed his pants, found his condoms, and tossed the pants on the sofa. "Let's see how many is enough," he said, huskily.

Nightfall had long since come and the street sounds had diminished to a soft hum of rubber wheels over asphalt and the occasional beep of a horn. The bedroom was shadowed in soft light from the nightstand lamp. Simeon sat propped up against pillows as he looked at the sleeping Brynn. He had been awake for nearly an hour, had removed the evidence of their love fest, smiling at the number of encores they'd had, before he'd returned to her bed. She slept soundly like a woman at peace with herself. Only once during the night did she stir when she murmured a name. She didn't wake but flung her arm over her head and settled into a deep sleep.

Simeon's emotions were high as he thought about the exquisite creature beside him. Not only did he want to love her, he was *in* love with Brynn. He knew from tonight that he was the first man in her life for a very long time. After their frenetic coming together, and later, sensing her shyness in the bedroom, he had been slow and gentle. But soon her inhibitions vanished as she freely gave of herself and accepted his loving.

The fact of their intimacy bothered him. Did she really want that kind of relationship? She had given her all to her career and now what was there? Could he possibly replace that one love in her life? Should he try to fill that precious void?

"Did I put that frown there?" Brynn said softly. She had been watching Simeon for the last few minutes and the more she watched the more she became increasingly worried that she was the reason for his deep thoughts. Had he regretted their torrid lovemaking?

He'd never felt her stirring and he kissed her lips. "I was thinking of you," he said, simply.

Brynn scooted up until they were almost shoulder-to-shoulder. She looked at him with serious eyes. "That was what I was afraid of."

"Afraid? Why?"

"Was I that bad?" Brynn said softly. "So many frowns."

"Oh my Lord, no!" Simeon said and scooped her

into his arms, cradling her in a tight embrace. He kissed the crown of her head. "Don't think crazy like that, sweetheart," he said against her curls. "You were wonderful and made me feel alive." He held on to her. "I've never had such an experience," he said huskily.

A tremendous wave of relief swept through Brynn, and she shuddered with the release of tension. She pushed herself out of his arms so that she could look him in the eyes.

"It's been a long time for me," she said in a quiet voice. "A very long time, and I was afraid of my performance."

"Performance? You thought you were onstage?" Simeon asked, annoyed at her phraseology.

"Wrong choice of word but you can see where my head is and where it's been." Her look was intense. "Please don't be angry. Simeon, I . . . I've been celibate for years. It was my choice. I . . . I wanted my career above all else. Serious relationships need time and nurturing to materialize into anything meaningful. I realized I had neither the time nor the desire to expend in intimate relationships that meant nothing to me." She drew in a breath and her voice dropped to a whisper. "Until you." She glanced at him. "You knew, didn't you?"

"I guessed it," Simeon said, loving her more with each word she spoke.

She nodded. "I knew I was right. I felt your hesitation the first time. And when I awoke and saw your frowns I was afraid that my long self-imposed abstinence only resulted in my inability to satisfy you."

"Sweetheart," Simeon said, tossing aside the blanket. "Does that look like I was never satisfied?"

"Oh," Brynn said and was immediately aroused by his erection. He was naked and with quiet aplomb he let her stare at his pulsating shaft. "Simeon," she breathed.

"I'm here." He watched her intently. He wanted to devour every inch of her but waited for a sign. He knew there were some unresolved issues that needed clearing up. He wasn't certain that she was telling him that their night of intimacy was just that—one night—or whether she was ready to end her state of celibacy. He knew he wanted more and wasn't certain that he could be around her without loving her. He wasn't Saint Jude. But when she closed her hand around him he nearly jumped to the ceiling. He had his answer.

"We need to talk," he gasped. "Later." He covered her mouth with his and was lost.

They sat contentedly at the kitchen table over second cups of coffee. It was nearly noon. After making love they'd loved some more and then showered. Brynn had made the breakfast that they ate hungrily, with Simeon swearing that he wanted cinnamon and apple pancakes for dinner too.

Brynn sat back and rubbed her stomach. "I feel like saying oink, oink," she said. "I was just plain greedy."

"I believe I ate more than you, so what are you calling me?" Simeon narrowed his eyes.

She laughed. "You said it, not me." She ducked and the pinch meant for her cheek landed on her neck and her skin tingled from his touch. His eyes were laughing and his beautiful lips curved in a smile and she wanted to feel them on her all over again. Brynn didn't know that being in love made one light in mind and body, and right now she felt as wispy as a dandelion.

"What are you thinking?" Simeon asked. "You went from the barnyard to the house because now you look like the cat that has a secret." He cocked his head. "Want to share?"

She lifted her shoulders lightly. "Not right now," she demurred. She brushed spidery fingers up and down his arm. "Maybe later?"

"Ouch." Simeon shuddered and caught her hand. "No fair." He nearly groaned with the effort not to take her where they sat, but he knew it was time for unfinished business. He stood and pulled her up from her chair and, arm around her waist, walked slowly with her to the living room. He sat opposite her on the sofa.

"You want to talk to me." She was accustomed to his changes of moods and facial expressions. He was serious.

"I think it's time," Simeon said. She showed simple curiosity as she waited for him to speak. "I need to know. How do you feel now about your celibacy? For months I've wanted to hold you in my arms and love you, and now that you've made fantastic love with me, I have to know if you want more. Or does our intimacy end now?" A shadow crossed his long features. "Even though you've yet to give me your answer, I don't know if I can stand working with you professionally, knowing that I can't have you in my bed again. Watching your glistening body move, and me wanting to kiss you dry; knowing that being so near, that I have to keep my hands to myself. That's outright torture, just plain cruel and unusual punishment." She had looked away from him and was staring out the window through the sheer curtains. His heart thumped, as he awaited her answer.

"I love you." Brynn turned to see stark happiness leap into his eyes.

"I love you." Simeon could barely speak the words.

Both sat where they were as if their admissions had turned them into pillars of stone.

"I want you in my bed," Brynn said softly almost as

if in awe. "I want the intimacy that I've never experienced with another man. I want you."

Simeon knew that she spoke the truth because her eyes shimmered with her love. But he didn't go to her. Not yet. He breathed deeply. "I think I started falling in love with you even after that first day we met," he said. "When I saw you come into the park, I affected my disdain because I didn't want to make a fool of myself."

"Oscar-nominated performance," Brynn murmured.

"Tell me now," Simeon said. "Because you won't be dancing for the stage, is your love for me just a fill-in for the love that you've lost? Your lifelong passion?"

Brynn heard the anguish in his soul spill from his mouth and her heart wrenched. She wasn't surprised at his question. Were things different she would have expressed the same thoughts and experienced the same doubts. He had every right to know her feelings. Long before she'd made the physical connection with him she had accepted him into her soul and wished him to become a part of her life.

"I love you, passionately," Brynn said quietly.

Simeon went to her and she opened her arms to him. He caught and held her close, unwilling to break the silence disturbed only by their beating hearts.

After a while Brynn untangled herself and sat up. "I'm glad we were friends first."

"Me too, sweetheart." Simeon slid his knuckles over her cheek. "During the night you fretted and called a name. Are you worried about something?"

Surprised, Brynn asked, "What did it sound like?"

"Noni, or Nonnie?"

"Noonie. That's my grandma." Her forehead creased. "She's been incapacitated, that's why my mother isn't here with me. My grandfather isn't in the best of health and can't offer much in the way of care so my mother is doing her best to help them out." The frowns increased. "But she promised that she would get a nurse to look in so that she could come up to be with me for a few days. I know she wants to."

"When was she supposed to come?" Simeon had thought it odd that her mother would stay away when her daughter could use a lot of moral support.

"As a matter of fact I was supposed to call her last night, but I guess I forgot." She nuzzled Simeon's neck and he caught her mouth and kissed her. "I was distracted."

"Mm, in another world," he mumbled, trying to catch her fleeting tongue. He felt her body go limp. "What is it?" How quickly he sensed the changes in her.

"My mother. Something's not right, Simeon."

"What do you mean?" He straightened up as she did.

"I can't put my finger on it, but even when she was here, I sensed that she wanted to talk to me." Her eyes widened. "I remember thinking that, but I was too engrossed in my own problems to ask if anything was wrong."

"Don't, sweetheart." Simeon's voice was quiet but firm. "You don't need to send yourself on a guilt trip for a whim of a thought."

"But what if I'm right?" She thought about her premonition when she was a child.

"There's only one way to ease your mind. Why don't you do it now?"

"You're probably right." Brynn got up and went to the bedroom to make the call.

Minutes later, Simeon heard her enter the room. "Everything all right?"

"Her machine answered." Her brows knitted.

"That's the third time in a row that I've called and she didn't answer right away. She always calls back within the hour."

Thinking that strange, he kept his thoughts to himself. "Probably nothing to worry about," he assured her. He stood and put his arm around her waist and walked toward the hall. "I have to leave, sweetheart. Meeting with my lawyer later today. I want to get started on the legalities since I've decided to put the club up for sale."

"Call me later?"

He pulled her into his arms and kissed her intensely. "You need to ask?" he said huskily.

The phone rang before Simeon was down the front steps, and Brynn hurried to answer it. "Ma? Where were you?" Brynn asked.

Wenona caught her breath. "Brynn, is anything wrong?" She winced as she switched the phone to her good side.

"You sound out of breath," Brynn said. "Are you always outside when I call? What in the world could you be planting this time of year? And it must be cold down there. Are you sure you're okay?"

"Everything is just fine, honey," Wenona said as she eased into the armchair. "I'm sorry I haven't gotten there yet to be with you."

"Ma, how's Noonie? She's been on my mind. Whenever I call, she doesn't stay on the phone for very long, as if she's rushing me off. Doesn't sound like someone who is housebound. You're not keeping anything from me, are you?"

Wenona crossed her fingers. "No, of course not, honey. Stop worrying about us down here. It's you we're all worried about." She paused. "How are you really, Brynn? Have you thought about what you will do now?" She held her breath, unable to keep from feeling her daughter's pain.

"Yes."

Startled, Wenona said, "You have?"

How easily it came to her, Brynn thought. "Yes, Ma. Simeon and I have been talking and I'm making plans. I'll tell you all about them when I see you."

"Simeon?" Wenona frowned. "The owner of the club where you were hurt?"

"Storeyland. Simeon Storey is the owner, Ma." She hesitated. "He—he's been there for me."

"Humph, and as he should be," Wenona huffed.

"It wasn't his fault," Brynn said softly. How could she make her mother understand? "He tried to get to me and Claire in time but he and the others were too late. It happened, and I'm trying to get past it now. Really trying, Ma." Her voice trailed away as she closed her eyes against the future. She couldn't have this conversation. Not now when her feelings were still so raw. Loving Simeon. Their plans to work together. All so brand-new.

Her daughter sounded different and Wenona could almost guess the reason. A tall drink of water with honey-colored eyes, and a sculptured face with a chiseled jaw. *How dare he seduce my daughter at the most vulnerable point in her life?* she thought. If she weren't in so much discomfort and had to stay to complete her treatment, she'd be on the first plane to New York.

"I'm sorry, honey, what did you say?"

"I have to go, someone is at the front door. Call me tomorrow, Ma, hear?"

"I will, honey. Stop worrying and take care of yourself. Everything's going to work out fine for you."

"Bye, Ma."

Brynn hurried to the door and was surprised to see Merle huddled against the doorjamb to escape the cold breeze. "Hey, come on in. What was the name of that wind that blew you to my door?" she teased. She stepped back and Merle sailed past her and walked straight to the kitchen, shedding his jacket as he went. Brynn couldn't help but notice his hunching walk. *Pain?* she wondered.

Merle sat down at the table and vigorously rubbed his hands together. He eyed the coffeepot. "A cup of that hot stuff would hit the spot."

"Have you eaten?" Brynn sent him a skeptical look over her shoulder as she poured a cup of coffee and put it in the microwave. "You've lost weight. Has it been that long since I've seen you?"

"Not really," Merle said quietly. "I daresay, you've had other things on your mind." On the brink of her becoming legendary, her career as a dancer was ended. But maybe, just maybe, if she would only listen, and see past her hurt, she could carve another formidable niche for herself. There was little time left for her to give him an answer.

Brynn sat in the opposite chair and really scrutinized him. He didn't use that tone of voice unless he was holding a *serious* meeting with his dancers. His bright gray eyes were a washed-out sickly hue and his hair had lost some of its bushiness. It struck her then.

"What's wrong with you Merle?" She couldn't help but remember her strange feelings.

He gave her a weak smile, guessing her thoughts. "You were right, honey."

"You're ill!" So it *had* been Merle!

For once in his life Merle could not think of a witty comeback line to those words. He'd always been the one to father and mother his dancers, beat them over the head when they needed it, console them and cajole them until he achieved the perfection he desired. If he were any judge of talent for selecting and training his teachers, his company would live on in the hordes of new students eager to embrace his aggressive stylized movements. And the one person who could keep his dream alive was sitting before him ready to fold when he spoke again.

"I have cancer." No matter how he tried to make it sound less than what it was, the words sounded ominous even to him and he had been living with them for almost a year since his doctor's pronouncement.

Shocked into speechlessness, Brynn could only stare at the man who over the years had become her father, mentor, teacher, big brother, and all the rest that came with growing into womanhood without a male presence. All except her lover.

Merle inhaled as he watched her world go flatter than it already was. An innate sense told him that she was stronger than he thought and stronger than she even knew. At that moment, somewhere deep inside he knew that his company was going to survive. Helmed by his female principal dancer, the fabulous Brynn Halsted.

"H-how bad?" Brynn faltered, unable to quiet the pounding in her chest.

"I've known for longer than I care to admit. Almost eight months." Just a little lie!

"Oh, Merle, how could I not have seen? That long?" Brynn was devastated. Had she been so self-absorbed that she couldn't see his pain? He must have suffered keeping the news to himself for all those months!

"Don't fret, honey. You know I convey what I want when I want. You always told me I was half sphinx. So don't beat yourself up over it. Had you guessed, I wouldn't have admitted it anyway." He grinned weakly. He could see the next question coming and shrugged. "All this time I let nature do its thing. I didn't want to be incapacitated, so I experimented with alternative treatments. But as I said, I ignored the initial problems too long for anything to be of any help now. I'm taking drugs if only to relieve the pain. Can't move these old bones the way I want to anymore so I might as well."

"Merle," Brynn whispered. She gripped her mug with two hands as if to hold on to something real. The whole world was going crazy and she felt helpless and angry. What else was going to happen to her? she agonized.

"I'll be going in for treatment once a month. From what I hear, it takes days to recover from the mess before I start feeling good and then it starts all over again." His face clouded. "So I won't be of much use to anyone."

"D-did they say when . . ."

"Uh-uh. No predictions on how long I'll be around and I don't want to know either. Just let me do my thing with these drugs and when it's over it's over."

There was such finality to his tone that Brynn shuddered. It was almost as if she could see him dead already. Was he really so accepting of his fate?

"Isn't there anything that they can do?" She spread her hands helplessly. "There's so much new technology around, you hear of something miraculous almost every day. Did you ask, Merle? What does your doctor say?"

He smiled and reached across the table and patted her hands. "You weren't listening. I waited too late, honey. Whatever might have helped early on is useless in my present state."

"Why?" Brynn was angry and her eyes welled. "Why did you do that to yourself? You have so much to live for. To give to the world! You're not finished yet!" The tears fell and she swiped them away to no avail because they fell with abandon.

Merle reached for a paper napkin and handed it to her. She took it and wiped her eyes and blew her nose but her lips were trembling. He pushed away from the table and taking both their mugs filled them and heated the coffee in the microwave. When he returned he saw she had dried her eyes and he knew she was coming to terms with his news. "Here. Have another swig." He sat down and studied her face.

Brynn hiccupped away the residual sobs and sipped the bitter brew. What was to become of the company that he'd so painstakingly built with his sweat over those early grueling years? She was staring at him and he was speaking and when what he said finally penetrated she scalded her lips.

"Wh-what did you say?" she stuttered.

"You heard me right, Brynn." Merle refused to let her scamper inside herself when her eyes slid away from his. She invisibly held herself. "I want you to manage the Merle Christiansen Dance Company. I want you to become its resident choreographer, and later, its artistic director. When I'm gone, my style will endure. I know you'll see to that." He paused. "I've made my wishes known to the board and they'll seriously consider my request. They'll know when you're ready."

"No, no, stop that!" Brynn cried. "Don't talk like that. You're not going anywhere, Merle. Nowhere!"

"Shh, shh, shh," Merle crooned as he gripped her hand across the table. She held on, her nails digging into his palm. When she opened her eyes she stood and he rose and caught her as she flung herself into his arms. "Shh, honey," he said. "We're going to be all right. You'll see. Everything's going to work out just fine." He rocked her back and forth until he felt the shivers leave her body and she went limp.

"Feel better?" They were in the living room and

Brynn had curled up in her big chair, hugging her arms while Merle was sprawled in one corner of her long sofa. Silent minutes had passed. He knew the worst of the shock had run its course and now it was time to talk.

"As well as I can at the moment," Brynn answered. She stared at him from head to toe seeing now what she'd missed for months. "Does anyone else know?" she asked in a soft voice.

"The board, of course, and I told Claire this morning. I asked her not to call you."

She nodded. "Understandable." Brynn knew that Claire was devastated. She adored Merle and was grateful to him for being hard-nosed with her early on, pulling the best from her and making her the fine dancer that she was. For the first time Brynn saw the old twinkle in his eyes. "What?"

"I think you two ladies are going to have a lot to talk about," Merle said. "And it ain't gonna be all about old Merle."

"What do you mean? She's not leaving you?" Since the tour, other companies were trying to woo Claire away to become their principal dancer. "She wouldn't!"

"It ain't all about dance, honey." Merle laughed. "But I'll let you two talk about that." He put on his serious face. "I want you to think about what I asked, Brynn. It would mean a lot to me. But don't take too long. I want to know that things are in place when the time comes." He looked at her. "Will you do that for me, honey?"

A lump made it hard for Brynn to swallow. Not trusting herself to speak, she managed a small nod.

"Good." After a pause he caught her eye. "I saw Simeon not too long ago. He said he's been by a few times." He paused again. "The guy is all bent out of shape about what happened to you in his club, Brynn. I think he's going to carry that monkey for years to come."

"I told Simeon that that wasn't necessary. What could he have done?"

At the tone of her voice, Merle's eyes brightened. *So that's how it is,* he thought. He prided himself on recognizing the signs of a woman in love. Then he smiled. Yes, his two divas were going to have lots to talk about. "He's a good guy."

"Merle," Brynn said, "Simeon has asked me to choreograph to his music."

Thank God. Merle knew then that she was going to be all right. He also said a silent prayer for Simeon Storey. *He did it! She's thinking about moving forward with her life.* Suddenly he knew that she wouldn't turn him down. The Merle Christiansen Dance Company would survive.

"What did you tell him?"

"I—I never really gave him a definite answer. But I know I will," she said. "I think I'll be able to do it."

"Of course you will. I have no doubts." He looked at her with pride. "I know what you can do and are capable of," he said. "And you'll be able to do it even with your new job." He held up a hand, then laughed. "I mean potential job." He stood and she rose and after retrieving his jacket they walked to the door hand in hand. "You'll be a smash at whatever you do, Brynn Halsted. You spin nothing but gold."

"Now I have the Midas touch?"

"You always have," he said solemnly. "I'll let you know when I have the staff meeting to tell them about—well—about what's going on. Will you come?"

Brynn nodded. "You know I will." She hugged him and when he was gone, she stood for a long time, her back against the door. She felt so alone and bewildered, and wondered what untapped emotion was going to slam her next, knocking her into a world of unreality.

Nine

Claire met Brynn at exactly five-thirty as they'd planned. Meeting like this in Sylvia's was a rare treat for them. The hectic past few months meant that they were long overdue for some downtime together. Claire had been on an emotional high for weeks. In the past she would have unwound with long discussions with her friend who always saw things clearly and put them in their proper perspective. Brynn saw the world as it was and not in Technicolor cotton candy. Claire had respected her comments and sound judgment for most of their lives. But she had never seen Brynn like she was when her world had come to a screeching stop. Claire had been shaken to her core when it was learned that Brynn would never dance professionally again. It was all she could do with a Herculean effort to complete the tour, dancing as she had never before in her life. It had been her most successful season ever. She knew that man's mortality had a lot to do with her thinking and the decision she'd made. Life was too short and not promised to be filled with satin sheets and decadent ice cream cones. Fluff that could disappear in a heartbeat. Nothing was promised. She realized that with a thud the first night that she had danced without her friend watching her from the wings. Each time during the tour that she had danced *Élan*, she had thought of Brynn, its creator. And each time she had won rave reviews.

Claire's decision came hard after the crest she was riding, but she decided that she wasn't going to look back. Today her heart was heavy. Merle's news had felled her as if she'd never known one of life's truths: no one lives forever. After her crying session all alone in her apartment, she knew that she was more determined than ever to follow through with her plan. She turned at the murmurs that arose and she knew that Brynn had entered. It had been weeks since Brynn had left her home to venture out alone and had almost not come, but Claire had quietly insisted. It was time to get past the inevitable stares and pitying remarks.

The two women hugged and clung to each other for a brief moment. They sat in a quiet corner, and after the hum of the restaurant returned to normal, the friends eyed each other.

Brynn saw the evidence of Claire's distress, as she well knew Claire was eyeing her own tear-swollen eyes.

"I can't swallow another bitter pill." Brynn's voice sounded weary.

"My insides won't settle down. I hope I can get through dinner without an emergency," Claire replied. Her lashes fluttered as she fought to hold the tears at bay. "It's so hard to accept."

"I know." Brynn paused as she and Claire gave the waitperson orders for cocktails and without a menu ordered their favorite roast chicken. After the young woman left, she studied her friend. "We never dreamed, did we, when we had thoughts about him?"

"No," Claire agreed. "Whenever Merle disappeared for long periods, it seemed perfectly normal. Except for a few times when he suddenly stopped in the middle of an instruction and never returned. We all thought it was the usual fund-raising meeting or some such. You, me, no one ever guessed."

"He was suffering."

Each had a moment of reflection after which Brynn sighed deeply. "Merle asked me to choreograph." The words came hard, and she looked away briefly. "After he—he, well, he's asked the board to consider me for artistic director . . . eventually." Claire nodded. "You knew?" Brynn asked.

"He told me this morning before he offered me the position as the assistant director to the young adults."

Brynn looked blank. "Assistant?" Baffled, she said, "What of your career? Merle wants you to stop dancing?" Suddenly, she *knew* the world was going absolutely nuts. Claire not dancing was equivalent to watching a woman drown!

The incredulous look on her friend's face made Claire smile. "It's not what you're thinking. It was my decision," she said softly. Now that the words were spoken for the second time that day she felt an enormous sense of freedom. "I'd decided last week after mulling it over for months. After the tour I was convinced that I was going to stop."

"Not dance?" Brynn honestly didn't know what she should feel or say. Her choice to dance had been taken from her and her friend was sitting across the table telling her that she'd made the *conscious* decision to end her career. Almost resentfully she asked, "Why?"

"Brynn, I know what you're thinking. Listen to me without judging, okay?"

Their drinks had come, and both women sipped in silence for the next few seconds.

"I've had a wonderful career in dance, performing all over the world, traveling with my best friend and my other family. I've loved every minute of it and wouldn't have asked for a better way to spend the first thirty years of my life."

"Until now?" Brynn was mystified. Claire wasn't the least bit remorseful about her decision.

"Right." Claire paused. "I'm going to marry Art Chessman. He proposed before I went on tour and I gave him my answer when I returned. It wasn't a snap decision. It's what I want now."

"Has he asked you to stop dancing?" Brynn asked quietly. She could write a laundry list of acquaintances who'd traded their passion for a man.

They made room for the dishes that were set before them.

"Never." Claire was emphatic, as she tasted the corn bread and apple stuffing. "I love Art for the kind man that he is. He's logical, fair, and wants me to do whatever will make me happy. And I'm lucky that Merle has offered me a job because before that I didn't know what kind of work I would have been looking for. Plus, I don't know that I would have been content in the corporate world. I want a job that will enable me to spend bunches of hours with my husband and kids. That's my passion now."

"You sound like you've been thinking about it for a long time," Brynn said.

"I'd given it careful thought," Claire answered. Her eyes clouded. "Before we left Storeyland that night, I was going to tell you what was on my mind. But after what happened, well, I just couldn't."

"I don't know what to say."

"Say you'll be my maid of honor and wish me all the happiness I can stand."

"Yes, and I do." Brynn smiled for the first time since she sat down. "I really mean that." She signaled the passing server and ordered a bottle of champagne. When it came she toasted her friend. "To eons of happiness." She grinned devilishly. "I want two nieces and two nephews." She winked. "Soon."

Claire sputtered over her drink. "You sound like you want to start your own little star-bud ensemble." Her look became serious. "So will you become choreographer for Merle? He wouldn't want anyone else, Brynn. As for artistic director down the road I can't think of anyone else we'd all want."

In a split second all the years she'd spent with Merle flashed before her. "I—I won't turn him down, Claire. I couldn't." Brynn still found it difficult to think in terms of the company without Merle as its life force.

"I knew you wouldn't walk away from him." Claire caught Brynn's hand. "I'm glad we'll be working together again." She leaned back and heaved a great sigh. "I'd been so worried about you . . . what you planned to do with your future. I felt so helpless and couldn't offer you the slightest idea." She raised a brow. "Had you begun to think about it at all?"

Brynn nodded. "I was planning to choreograph with Simeon. After that, well, it was up in the air."

"With Simeon?" Claire was surprised. "His music!"

"Yes."

"How great that will be! Oh, that's wonderful, Brynn." She caught her breath. "How'd that come about?"

"It just came up," Brynn said, suddenly shy about mentioning his name. She'd yet to reveal their new relationship to her friend. Yesterday was still fresh in her mind.

"Uh-oh." Claire scrutinized her friend's face. "I think you have something to tell me?" At the look on Brynn's face, Claire nearly shrieked her pleasure. "You've fallen for him!" she said in a stage whisper. "Come on, tell. I know it!"

Brynn laughed. "Look at you. You're squirming in your seat like a third grader."

"Well, what do you expect? Of all places to find out that my girl is in love!" Claire moaned. "How can I get the skinny in here?"

Primly, Brynn said, "Who said you were going to get it anywhere?" She couldn't help but be tickled at the expression on Claire's face.

"Well, after all these years, it's finally happened." Claire's voice softened. "Is it love?"

Asked that question months ago, Brynn would have scoffed at the inquirer. But now? "Yes," she answered. "For the first time in my life." She smiled. "Do I look like you when you were talking about Art?" she teased.

"Did I look like I was dazed?"

"Uh-huh."

"Then you've got the look, my friend." Claire chuckled. "Come on, let's eat so we can get out of here. We need to kick back in private. Your place or mine?"

"Yours."

Shortly after, patrons in the restaurant stared at the two famous dancers walking arm in arm and smiling like two giddy schoolgirls as they hurried out the door.

Simeon was more relaxed than he'd been in months. He knew it was not only the decision he'd made about the club but had everything to do with Brynn. Not discounting their incredible lovemaking for his feelings, he couldn't help but grin like a lovesick, trail-lonesome cowboy.

After coming home from his meeting, he'd changed expecting to go to her after he'd called to say he was on his way. He'd gotten her machine and was surprised to find her gone but was elated that she'd finally ventured out alone. For weeks he'd gently suggested that she needed to get out, to face the public, but she'd always demurred. Wondering whether she'd get home in time for him to take her out for dinner, he'd given up that idea when she still hadn't returned by nine o' clock and there was still no word from her. At ten, he began thinking in the negative. Where was she? He wished he'd had Claire's number or even had the number for Brynn's upstairs tenant. Suppose she'd fallen, injured herself, and needed help? Mentally making a note to get that information, he picked up the phone again when his doorbell rang. Swearing at the unexpected visitor he looked through the glass of the outer door, then flung it open, relief washing over him like a tidal wave.

"God, Brynn," he said, pulling her inside and crushing her to his chest. She smelled of fresh air and strawberries and he couldn't get enough of inhaling her scent. He slipped his hands beneath her coat and wrapped his hands around her waist so that he could feel her body. "Don't do that to me," he said gruffly.

Brynn clung to him, basking in his tender concern. She loved this man with every fiber of her being and still marveled at how long it had taken her to realize it even from the first day they'd met.

When he finally released her, Simeon looked down at her. "You scared me, sweetheart. I didn't know what to think when I couldn't reach you." He couldn't help but notice the brightness of her eyes and something else that he couldn't recognize. A sadness that he hadn't seen since her accident.

"Oh, Simeon, I'm sorry I didn't call," Brynn said. "But, I had a glorious time!"

He cocked his head in mock hurt. "Without me?"

She pinched his waist. "With Claire. We had dinner at Sylvia's and I just left her place. We talked for hours." They'd walked upstairs to Simeon's apartment and she flung herself on the long burgundy couch. Her eyes twinkled. "You were there."

"Ouch," Simeon said. "Should have felt my ears burning, huh?"

"You should have." Brynn gave him a seductive smile. When he sat beside her and kissed her lips, she clung to him and kissed him passionately. She'd missed him in the space of a few hours and wondered if that was how people in love felt. Feeling spoiled and loved she admitted against the crush of his lips, "I missed you."

"Is that a fact? Care to show me just how much?"

Brynn sat up and looked around, a frown on her face, then shook her head.

"What's wrong?"

"I can't do that. Not here," she demurred. "This is a gorgeous couch but so, so inadequate for . . ."

A low growl tore from Simeon's throat as he pulled her up. "So it's space you want? Sweetheart, come with me."

Brynn lay in Simeon's arms in his king-size bed. She was still awed by the past couple of hours. Such exquisite lovemaking. She hadn't dreamed that they could surpass their passion of the day before but indeed they had! She blushed as a tiny smile parted her lips. Eighteen months short of her reaching the ripe old age of thirty, for the first time she was spending the night in a man's bed and wondered if she were some kind of relic or throwback to an ancient age.

Simeon felt her snuggle closer and glanced down at her face. "Is that for me?" he asked, tracing her smile with a finger.

"Uh-uh," Brynn answered, looking up at him.

"Uh-uh?" Simeon frowned. "I've got a woman in my

bed, looking quite satisfied, *love* satisfied, I might add, and that contented look on her face is not for me?"

Brynn shook her head. "It's for Tremaine."

"Who the hell is Tremaine?"

"Oh, someone from my past," Brynn said airily.

Simeon started. "Your past?" Suddenly jealous, he thought, well, of course there had been someone in her past. But she had to think of him now?

"Yes," Brynn said, feeling ashamed of herself for teasing him. "He was my imaginary Prince Charming when I was in seventh grade. Claire's was named Lamont." She giggled at the breath Simeon expelled, then yelped when he grabbed her in a bear hug and pulled her atop his belly.

"Don't do that to me," he growled. Then he captured her lips and kissed her thoroughly. "Now tell me that this won't send Tremaine packing forever." He slid his hands along her hips and cupped her smooth, naked buttocks. She squirmed and his arousal pressed against her but he exerted powerful control not to give in as his screaming body ached for relief. Slowly, he trailed his fingers toward her center and was further excited by her telltale moist readiness for him. Her soft moan weakened him, but bent on his mission, he slipped a finger inside, gently teasing the warm, throbbing essence of her pleasure. She strained into him and murmured his name that brought a smile to his lips. "Good-bye, Tremaine," he whispered in her ear and proceeded to bring her to climax. When she screamed his name again as she sank limply against him, he had a wicked smile on his lips.

"Good-bye, Tremaine," Brynn echoed. She purred like a sated kitten as she slid beside him. She leaned over, and peered into his eyes. "You're a hedonist," she whispered.

Pleased with himself for a superbly accomplished

mission, he raised a brow. "Didn't I tell you? That's my middle name."

Brynn kissed his twinkling eyes and then his smiling lips. "Let's keep that our secret," she murmured, and then laid her head contentedly on his shoulder. "I won't be responsible for my actions if I find some other felines sniffing around, seeking your pleasures."

"No chance of that, my love." He fondled her still-taut nipples and thinking that she was ready to drift into sleep, he flinched when he felt her warm mouth close over his nipples. "What are you doing?" he gasped.

"You gave me dessert before the meal," Brynn said, sultry-voiced. "I'm still hungry. Aren't you?" In excruciatingly slow motion she moved her hips over his erection in circular fashion.

Simeon was on fire. "Brynn, honey, I'm not prepared."

Brynn stopped. "To love me?" She looked hurt and curious at the same time. "Oh well, I thought . . ."

With a guttural cry, Simeon reached to his nightstand and with the speed of light was sheathed. "Tease me, huh?" he rasped. "What was that you said about a meal?"

Timidly, Brynn said, "Are you, ah, hungry?"

"Starved." Simeon positioned her hips over his and held her firmly in place, his hands caressing her smooth skin. He moved his hips as slowly as she had done, holding her close to his thickened shaft. He nearly burst but held himself in check. Brynn tried to part her legs to let him inside, but he held her tight. "Sweetheart?" he said through clenched teeth.

"Wh-what!" Brynn gasped.

"Are you still hungry?"

"F-famished!" Brynn managed.

"Good. Get ready for a feast, my sweet." He entered her and thrust upward.

Brynn swooned.

"Mm, that smells scrumptious." Brynn entered the kitchen and immediately went to the stove where Simeon was stirring a pot. "Just what a starving woman needs," she said, licking her lips like a greedy cat at the simmering grits and browning sausages.

Simeon affected a hurt look. "And I thought I had taken care of that last night," he said.

From behind, Brynn hugged him around the waist. "That was for my body, love. This is sustenance for later."

"Well, all right," a mollified Simeon said. Brynn set the table and poured the juice and while she moved slowly but gracefully around his kitchen he gave her surreptitious glances. There was no sign of the tears she'd shed when during the night she'd awakened him with her sobs. It was then she'd told him about Merle's visit. They'd talked for a long time about her life of dance and how she'd met Merle when she was fifteen. This morning they'd showered together, made love again, and slept some more. It was almost eleven-thirty and they were just now having breakfast.

"Delicious," Brynn said as she ate some more of the tastily prepared grits. "You do a lot with those magic hands of yours, huh?"

The wicked look in her eyes and the devilish smile on her lips made his stomach do cartwheels. "Unless you're prepared for the consequences I warn you not to talk like that before you've gotten your strength back," he growled.

"Or else?" she teased.

"Or else," Simeon said firmly. A warning look leaped

into his eyes as she deliberately spooned more of the food into her mouth, twirling her tongue around the fork and slowly flicking the pink tip around her lips.

"Brynn!" Simeon was already hot and she was driving him to the brink. If she didn't put that tongue of hers back in her mouth, he swore they would never leave this house today. Even her throaty chuckle after she obeyed drove him insane. He was on fire.

"What's wrong?" Brynn asked innocently.

"Would you get me some ice water please?"

"But *you're* closest to the refrigerator."

He looked to the ceiling. "I—can't—walk," he managed between clenched teeth. "Would you mind?"

"Well, all right," Brynn said, getting up. "If you insist." One of his hands was hidden and she made a production of getting the water and giving it to him while trying to peer into his lap. Before she sat back down she bent and blew in his ear and hurried away as Simeon yelled and nearly fell out of his chair.

Nearly doubled over with laughter, Brynn quickly swallowed some orange juice to clear her throat. "Ah, sweetie, I couldn't help that. Forgive me?"

Simeon cut his eyes at her. "I'll think about it," he growled.

Somehow they managed to finish eating without further distractions.

Impressed as before by the vast space in the upstairs music room, Brynn walked to the black grand piano that took up a major part of one corner near the windows. Thin beige miniblinds allowed the light to filter through the room. Like her work studio the room held the bare minimum of furniture. A sofa, a table, music stands, and a few chairs against the wall. She'd been in the room before only long enough for him to play some of the music that he'd written for her. He'd seen her looking wistfully at the dance space, had stopped playing, and led her back downstairs. Now she sat down at the piano and leafed through the sheets of music with penciled notes. She looked up at Simeon, who was watching her intently.

"There's so much here." She looked somberly at the sheets, some of which had her name written at the top. "So long ago." Her voice was sad as she looked at a date almost five years ago.

Simeon stared. He was leaning against the piano with arms folded.

So many thoughts swirled through Brynn's head that she momentarily felt a sadness sweep over her. If only he'd approached her before. Had she really been so stuck on herself, head in the clouds, not acknowledging those around her? If only he'd stopped her backstage that night after he'd played for her. Who knew what could have come from their meeting? She'd have new repertoires and his music would have become known. All these years he could have been fulfilling his dream of composing his music. She felt Simeon's touch on her shoulder.

"There's no time for what-ifs. There's only now." His voice was firm yet quiet and not scolding. He sat down beside her. His hands touched hers as he leafed through the sheets of music. "Let's see what you think of this one."

She slid off the bench to give him room and watched as he settled into a comfortable position and began to play. Brynn listened to the intensity of the music and was instantly captivated. She turned her back and closed her eyes, feeling the rhythm that caused her body to sway slightly. The tempo was slow and hypnotic as she unconsciously began to envision movement. She shifted her weight from one foot to the other in preparation for a step. Oblivious of the man who played, she found herself walking about the room using the space to bring to life what she was feeling. She positioned herself to jump, a move that was second nature. The music stopped and she opened her eyes.

"Brynn, don't." Simeon's voice was a soft command. She looked at him dazedly.

"It's too soon," he said.

Brynn followed his gaze to her foot. She'd forgotten. The doctor had said no strenuous exercise outside of normal walking and her therapy for the first few weeks.

Simeon was moved that she'd become so uninhibited that she'd been ready to execute to his music. He went to her. "I shouldn't have brought you up here."

"If not now, when?" Brynn shook her head. "I can't hide from what is." Feeling oddly exhilarated she turned to stare out the window. It had come to her so naturally, the rush to move so readily to the music. Movement coming to her like it was always to be, and that there had been no interruption of her natural propensity to dance. She knew that she had the gift to choreograph, to create ballets. That this was something that she could do and do well. It would become her new livelihood. Merle believed in her enough to give her the run of his company when the time came, but she hadn't wanted to believe that that would be her second calling. She'd only wanted to dance forever. When she'd choreographed *Élan* for Claire, it had come from her heart and she thought it to be a once-in-a-while happening. But now, she knew that she could do this. And she would love it!

When she turned to him, Simeon started at the light in her eyes. He'd suspected that because of him she'd fallen into a morose mood and was kicking himself for starting something that he'd be sorry for. For the first time he saw contentment on her face and it was evident in the lift of her shoulders. Relieved, he said, "Never to hide, Brynn. Accepting and moving forward. You've taken the first step."

She put her arm around his waist and squeezed, then steered him back to the piano. "Yes, I have," she said softly. "Play some more, please? We have to get this partnership started."

Brynn was worried. After two weeks her mother was still in North Carolina. For the first time, Brynn suspected that her mother was lying to her. Something was very wrong. Her mother would never have stayed away from her this long unless she was unable to travel. There was no job she had to report to and no other obligations other than her church committees and choir. And she knew that her mother was a staunch volunteer in the literacy program at the library. The frequent calls, only to be left to record a message, were becoming irritating if not frightening. Brynn was ready to hop a plane and go to see just what was up in Roensville, North Carolina. Calls to her grandparents were equally disturbing and noninformational. Once, her grandfather had said that her grandmother had gone out.

Since that day in Simeon's studio Brynn had been caught up in choreographing. Not physically but she'd actually become her own notator, transcribing human movement to paper, and her visions and ideas were endless. More than once Simeon had to caution her from demonstrating her movements. Frustrated, she could only wish for the time to pass quickly. She was diligent in attending her therapy sessions and her progress was excellent. Secretly, she was pleased and couldn't wait to begin executing some of her ideas.

It was January and the dead of winter but Thursday

was the mildest day the city had seen for more than a month. It even smelled springlike. Appropriate, Brynn thought, because she felt that she was starting life anew. Except for the cloud in the back of her mind concerning her mother she felt right with herself and her decisions.

Claire had already eased from the dance company's performing schedule and was working in a many-hats role until her new position became available in the fall. She wore many hats including rehearsal director and administrative assistant. Brynn could hear and see the excitement in her friend's face.

Brynn was also busy. She was at the school meeting and discussing the upcoming spring season with the present director, choreographer, costumer, and other personnel involved in the planning of the well-run company. She still felt uneasy even to think of taking over as the company choreographer but her dance family welcomed her with encouragement and admiration for the monumental undertaking. They were supportive and caring and made Brynn feel as if she'd never left the company as its star. In their eyes she was still the principal dancer and they could only learn from her vast store of knowledge and creativity and looked forward to the new and exciting dance pieces she would plan for them.

She knew that without the love and support of Simeon she would never have reached this point alone. She feared that she would have had a complete collapse without his levelheaded thinking, always ready to pull her back when she hovered near the precipice of despair. Almost anything lent her pause to think about what she'd lost. A TV movie. A careless remark made by an insensitive TV talk show host. The unkind articles she came across in the media rags. One particularly nasty article called her the spoiled new kid on the block

usurping her predecessor and using her former clout
to demand a meaty position with Merle's company.
That had cut her to the quick. What the vituperative
reporter didn't know was that Merle's choreographer
had given notice nearly a year before. His wife, a prima
ballerina with the Suisse Moderne, was ecstatic that he
had applied for and was accepted as master choreographer with her company. People just never knew the
backside of a story, Brynn thought. They preferred to
do the devil's work and keep trouble brewing.

When she left the school she was happily tired, but
not too tired to spend at least two hours every other
night working with Simeon. She loved the music, the
piece that he was composing for her. She ached to
dance it. On one of his sheets he had scribbled *strings*
and when she'd inquired he told her that he was writing music for the violin and the oboe. She heard the
sound in her head and knew just where he would insert
those instruments. Excited, she told him the sound
would be wonderful. She hadn't seen him for the last
week because he'd worked in his studio with the musicians, pulling the piece together. She missed him, but
refrained from interrupting his session just because she
was lonely.

Only a few days ago, Brynn had met Simeon's family.
Jemma Jamison Storey and Thomas Storey were genuine in their welcoming of her into their home. As the
evening neared the end, Brynn saw the exchange of
looks between the two astute doctors and she knew that
she'd passed whatever test they had secretly put her
through. She felt warm inside about her acceptance
and wondered if they would become her New York family. The thought had made her tingly because although
her relationship with Simeon was so new, she knew that
they were both in for the long haul though neither had
mentioned marriage. Asha Cunningham was a delight,

privately telling Brynn that she wasn't the snob she appeared to be. Astonished at her forthrightness, Brynn could only laugh and afterward could feel that the two were going to have a new-girlfriend type of relationship. Conrad was quiet and had a witty sense of humor that made his round face crinkle in smiles and his rich brown eyes twinkle. Just as Simeon had said, that perfect V was an affliction of the Storey men. Amongst the three males, Brynn was just too biased in thinking Simeon's lips were the most exquisite.

After the visit, Brynn and Simeon had made good love and when he left she'd gotten lonely. She wished for her mother to be here so that she could meet the man in her life whom she hoped one day to marry.

At close to nine, Brynn was in the living room sipping hot tea when the phone rang. The number showed unknown and Brynn was surprised to hear her mother's voice.

"Ma? What's wrong with your phone? And you sound awful!"

Wenona said, "I'm using a phone card. Everybody's been having trouble with the lines." She went on hurriedly, "Just caught a little cold that's trying to turn into something big, Brynn. I'm taking care of it though so no need to worry." Wenona coughed spasmodically and when the spell was over, said, "I'm taking a foul-tasting tonic to rid myself of this cough too. Nothing like that stuff settling on your chest."

Brynn frowned. "You sure don't sound too good. What does your doctor say? And how long have you had it?" *More excuses for not coming?* she wondered.

"Just a few days ago it came down on me like an anvil was slung into my chest. But it's going away, thank God." Wenona paused. "How are you doing?" Brynn was finally sounding like her old self and Wenona had to wonder if it was going back to the company that did it or Simeon Storey. In any case she was happy to note that her daughter's voice was void of the listless hopelessness she'd heard in the last few months. *Thank you, dear Lord.* She whispered the silent prayer.

"I'm fine, Ma," Brynn said. "It's you that I'm worried about."

"Don't, I'm doing okay." She was hesitant to ask, but no sense in avoiding the painful topic. "How's Merle doing? Is he still working?"

Brynn was slow to answer because thinking of Merle always gave her pause to wonder about the mysteries of life. A man so young, in his prime at forty-five, who should have had many years left to create masterworks, was slowly disintegrating before her eyes. Merle must have lied to them all about when he'd discovered his illness because he was showing the debilitating effects long before he said he would.

"He-he's weak, Ma," Brynn said softly. "He comes in when he can and tries to be the big bad wolf but we can see he's making a heroic effort. He won't stay home and rest, says that will get him no place because he has things he needs to do before he . . ." Brynn choked on the words.

Wenona was sad. She'd met Merle the same year her daughter had and had liked the tall, talented man on sight. He'd let Brynn's parents know that he saw great promise in their fifteen-year-old daughter and put them on notice that she was going to become one of the world's great dancers. Now, Wenona thought sorrowfully, he was struggling to stay alive, fighting the demon that had laid claim to his body. It was a struggle that Wenona knew all too well but hers had a miraculous ending. She was thankful that she was calling herself a survivor. Her daughter's solemn voice interrupted her thoughts. "I'm here, Brynn." She started to cough again.

"Ma, I'm going to hang up so you can stop talking. Take care of that cough and I'll call you tomorrow."

After Brynn hung up, Wenona sat up in her hospital bed for a long time, thinking about the continued deception. But it was so much easier to keep Brynn in the dark. And less painful for her. Next time she saw Brynn, her treatments would be finished and everything would be much easier to explain. She still harbored the unnatural fear that she would die, leaving Brynn alone. Wenona knew that she and her husband Joseph had spoiled Brynn. Had doted on their daughter, and given her her every little heart's desire. They'd spent all her life making up for those first five years that they'd given her up. But they'd prided themselves on tempering their love with discipline so that she understood that she wasn't the only little girl in the world. They had become quite proud of the little person as she grew. She was genuinely kind-hearted and sweet. But she had a tenacious spirit and showed fierce ambition to accomplish her goals. It was Joseph who saw that drive and helped channel it into positive lanes where she would not become a blindly selfish woman who lacked respect for her peers and who had no humility.

Wenona was torn that Joseph had not seen the woman his daughter had become. He would have been bursting with daddy pride to see his baby's success. Brynn's heart had been broken and Wenona knew that she would never be as proud of her daughter as that night when she'd danced for her father. No one else could see her pain but Wenona had felt it with every step and leap that Brynn had taken on the stage all alone. At the end when she'd taken her bows, she'd stared at the empty seat, tears streaking her cheeks as she caressed the emerald her father had given her.

When their eyes met, each knew that Joseph had been there all along.

After all these years, Wenona still missed her husband with a passion. She'd stayed in New York until Brynn was on her own and well established in her career. When the time came, Wenona left her job to live in Joseph's small-town home near Raleigh. She loved his parents and they welcomed their murdered son's widow with open arms. She knew that she was running from life, but she had come to hate the place where she'd loved her husband, because that same place had taken him from her. She needed to feel a kinship to someone who had known him in life. It was here where she'd finally begun to heal inside, to face up to what she'd lost.

But Wenona would never return to live in New York. Even visiting Brynn in the old home was hard on her, the memories of her passionate life with Joseph haunting her. And if she hadn't had her surgery, she would have been hard put to find a plausible excuse not to visit her daughter in Brynn's hour of need. She was happy to know that her friends had been there for Brynn. At the same time, Wenona was both perplexed and worried about Simeon Storey's entrance into Brynn's life.

Wenona had long ago given up the idea of having a son-in-law and children. Brynn's lover was her career. She worried. If this man was serious, had indeed fallen in love with Brynn, she knew that it had to take a special kind of man to help Brynn through her personal tragedy. To lose the one passion in her life was a trauma to be reckoned with and it was not for the lighthearted or fickle-minded. A man would have to want more than sex from the beautiful woman. He would have to be willing to sacrifice. His integrity would be put to the test.

From what Wenona had observed of the man when he'd tried to visit Brynn at the hospital, he appeared to be a stern, no-nonsense figure who didn't seem to play games. Although she hadn't been in the mood to entertain his presence she had seen that much. If she was right about his strength and honesty, Wenona welcomed his presence in her daughter's life. He would be the strong shoulder for Brynn to cry on once she found out about her mother's cancer. Wenona knew the thought would be in Brynn's mind that yet another tragedy would touch her life: her only parent would die. Wenona prayed that Simeon Storey was the man she thought he was.

Ten

Brynn woke the next morning feeling disoriented and realized that she'd had a disturbing dream. She couldn't remember much except that she had heard her parents' voices and in place of the nebulous gray and white figures and shadows, she'd seen vivid red and orange hues. What did it mean? she wondered. She sat on the side of the bed, a frown marring her features. Her dreams were frequent but never had she awakened so disquieted.

By ten-thirty she'd eaten, spoken to Simeon, Claire, and Merle, and had called her mother and left the usual message. There was no static, nothing to indicate line trouble. Perturbed, Brynn made a decision. She was going to Roensville. Something was going on and she was going to find out just what it was that was keeping her mother from coming to New York and why she never answered the phone. Even if she was screening her calls, why didn't she pick up when she heard her daughter's voice? Why was she lying? But Brynn had a dilemma. What of her work at the school? And she needed to continue her therapy. Should she just postpone everything?

Claire picked up the phone in her office. She was surprised that Brynn was calling again. "Aren't you coming in today?" Claire asked.

"Yes, later," Brynn answered. "I—I think something's wrong in Roensville," she blurted. "I'm going there."

"What?" Shocked, Claire gripped the phone. What more could happen to her friend? "I-Is it your mother?" she breathed, fearful of what she'd hear.

"That's just it. I don't know." Taking a deep breath Brynn carefully explained her feelings over the last few weeks, the strange conversations with her grandparents, and how Noonie always sounded so pleasant instead of acting like the righteously grumpy patient. "They're keeping something from me, I know it."

As much as Claire didn't want to believe something was wrong, she couldn't help but think that Brynn was right. There was nothing in the world so important as to keep Wenona Halsted from her daughter. She loved that girl to pieces and would do battle for her until her last breath. She'd always wondered about the absence of Mrs. Halsted after the first few weeks of Brynn's injury.

"You agree with me," Brynn said flatly. Claire's silence told her plenty.

"It could be nothing at all," Claire replied slowly.

"You're not convincing me."

"So when do you think you'll leave?" Claire asked quietly. "Have you told Merle yet?"

"I've just decided," Brynn said. "There's so much to take care of here first. Merle knows that I'll be back and he can count on me to do anything he wants. I have to know that my mother is okay."

"Tell me what you want me to do."

"You have so much on your plate," Brynn said.

"Tell me." Claire was firm.

"Okay." Brynn sighed. "This really needs to be taken care of; otherwise I wouldn't ask. You know I appreciate it. It's the young adults. I've just begun working with them and they're all a little skittish." She went on to map out the instructions and when she finished she exhaled. So much depended on the students feeling comfortable in their new roles, especially if they were going to be ready to perform in the spring. "That's it," she breathed.

"Got it." Claire perused her notes, and then questioned one point. Satisfied, she said, "Don't worry about a thing. I'll see you later."

After she hung up, Brynn made several other calls, getting her house in order for at least a week's stay away. Ruth would come by to clean out the fridge and Ms. Morton would keep an eye on the house. Most important to Brynn was her physical therapy. She had to continue it no matter where she was and made a mental note to get a recommendation once she got to Roensville. She needed to be one hundred percent when she fully assumed her new role in the company, and if she wasn't, what price would she have to pay?

The travel arrangements had been simple enough to make, she thought with a scowl. On such short notice all it took was a pocketful of plastic money. Her plane was scheduled to leave on Sunday morning and she'd arrive in Raleigh before two P.M. There were two more calls she had to make.

After listening to Brynn for the last five minutes, Merle felt that he understood her anguish. He'd thought that something had to be wrong. Mrs. Halsted's actions were not normal. At least not for the woman he'd always known.

"Everything will be fine here," he said. "You go and look into what's going on. And tell your ma for me not to stay away so long." He paused. "I'll be waiting for you, Brynn."

The last call she had to make was going to be the hardest, Brynn thought. She didn't want to leave Simeon. Not now. They'd grown so close and beside the fact that they were in love, they were friends. He was as close to her as she'd been to Claire since their childhood. They spent long hours talking and sharing stories of their adolescent years, when they became teenagers, and finally complex young adulthood. When Simeon learned that Brynn had never been to Six Flags Great Adventure in New Jersey, or worse, Coney Island, he'd been bug-eyed with awe and had called her a deprived child! Not to have eaten a foot-long hot dog, slathered with the works at the now decrepit Nathan's Famous, was akin to mortal sin for a New Yorker. Every teenager at least once in his life had made the trek to the once world-famous amusement park to scream in terror on what was at one time the tallest Cyclone ride in the world. He'd penciled in the date on her kitchen calendar. Memorial Day weekend they were going adventurously into a unique part of Brooklyn that she'd never seen before. It would be a day she'd never forget!

Simeon sagged against the kitchen cabinet. "What did you say?"

"I have to go," Brynn said. "There has to be something wrong."

Still trying to absorb her words, Simeon found it hard to control his emotions. In a level voice he said, "Have you even asked your mother if there was a problem, Brynn? Does she know you're coming?" He held himself rigid against the support of the cabinet. He missed her already.

"Yes, I've asked and no, she doesn't know I'm coming," Brynn answered.

"Are you sure you don't want to think about this?" Simeon asked. "You can't go into a situation that you might not be able to deal with alone." After a second he said, "Would you like me to go with you?" Had she even thought of asking him? He felt strangely alone behind that thought.

Brynn heard the steely-voiced question behind the question. "Simeon, you're working so hard. I can't ask you to drop everything that you've begun."

"Aren't you?"

"But I'm only staying a week," Brynn said softly. "Simeon, she's my mother and I'm worried."

"And I'm worried about you." Simeon closed his mind against what could happen if Brynn walked into a heavy situation.

"Brynn," he said in a low voice, "I know you're a strong woman and you've fought your way back to normalcy after what happened to you. Now is not the time to venture into an unknown situation that might cause you more pain."

"I hear every word you're saying." Brynn took a deep breath. "But you must see that this is something that I have to get off my mind so that I *can* function normally. Not going to see for myself that she's okay will eat at me and be a greater distraction. And my mind must be at rest if I'm going to be of any help to Merle—and to you. I—I can't fail."

There was a short silence before Simeon spoke. "I want to be with you."

His husky whisper stroked Brynn's inner being. "I want that too," she murmured. "But there's so much to set in place before I leave. Claire has agreed to help me. And I—I want to see Merle."

Only tonight and tomorrow and then she'll be gone. "I'll meet you at the school," he said with resignation. "You'll finish early?"

"Earlier," Brynn whispered. "I'll be outside at four." She heard his sharp breath. "Simeon?"

"Yes?"

"Do you like leftovers?"

"You know I do. Why?"

"Because I don't want to go out for dinner," Brynn said softly. "I want you to bring me right home. Okay?"

"Done," he breathed.

"I'm missing you already," Simeon said, enfolding Brynn in his arms once again.

It was after eight o'clock, hours after they had arrived at Brynn's home, made love, eaten leftover baked ham, and made love again. They were in the living room cuddled on the long sofa.

At his words, Brynn felt a pang of loneliness. Years ago she'd experienced a void in her life when her mother moved from New York, leaving her with only Claire and Merle for her close family. "I'm going to miss you too, love," she whispered, and then sighed. "I just know the week's going to drag, making it seem like an eternity will pass before I see you again." She tilted her head and planted a soft kiss on his chin. "But I am anticipating my first look at you when you meet me at the airport." Her eyes twinkled. "Unless you have other plans for the following Sunday at four o'clock."

"All I know is you'd better not miss that flight." His kiss was long and deliberate and to neither of their surprise sparked electric currents through them. They succumbed to their passion.

They hadn't spoken for some time, thinking about the time when they would part and days would go by before they were together again. Brynn roused herself from Simeon's arms and looked at him earnestly. "I wish you could meet my mother," she said softly.

"We've met." Simeon thought about the angry, frightened woman he'd seen for a hot minute by Brynn's hospital door. He wasn't certain that that same woman would welcome him into her home.

Brynn saw his closed look. "I mean *really* meet her,

love. The woman you saw was not the one I want you to know." He had told her of his brief meeting with her mother. "That lady you saw that night had other things on her mind. Me." A grim smile touched her lips. "Always me." She closed her eyes briefly. "It was always like that, you know, for all my life. They gave me everything I ever wanted or desired. They were always there, watching over me, making sure that my needs were taken care of so I wanted for nothing. My father was working that second job because of me. He used to joke sometimes when he came in late and found me up. I could see the weariness in his eyes. He would wink and smile and say, 'One more sequined sleeve paid for.' I would go to bed happy that my needs were taken care of."

Simeon heard the anguish in her voice. Sensing her need to talk, he put an arm around her shoulder and squeezed, encouraging her to continue.

"I wonder how many times in my life that I ever thought of the sacrifices my parents made for me," Brynn said quietly. "Before my father was killed it wasn't many. I learned that when I heard my mother muffling her cries at night. For weeks after the funeral she would console me, trying bravely to hide her own pain to keep me from falling to pieces. She knew the special relationship that I'd had with my father. I thought she was so strong and brave, going about keeping the house, seeing that I did what I needed to do, going to school, to rehearsals, studying, and making performances. She went back to her demanding and chaotic job as a public housing manager at the Manhattanville Projects. You know where they are."

Simeon nodded. He'd lived in Harlem all his life and had friends who'd lived in the housing projects that dotted upper Manhattan.

"She used to walk to work sometimes," Brynn said.

"I know she did it because she was remembering him. They loved this neighborhood and we would walk all around it when I was younger. They pointed out the different architecture. They never tired of stopping and examining the Romanesque work of St. Martin's Episcopal Church, right around the corner on One Twenty-second. When I got too busy to join them they'd go together. They were so in love and I never really knew how much until after he was gone. She missed him and it was tearing her up inside." Brynn's gaze swept the room. No longer done in the sleek contemporary look her mother loved, it was dressed in an eclectic style with shawl-draped chairs and oriental rugs over the hardwood floors, a look that was all her own. "She couldn't stand being here without him." She shrugged. "Not just here, in this space, but the whole town bothered her. I know that's why she left New York."

"He was born in Roensville?" Simeon asked.

"Yes. He loved it and often spoke about retiring there. The house my mother is living in is the one she and my father planned and built together. They were going to use it as a getaway place until they both retired." Brynn made a helpless gesture with her hands. "But I think my father had only stayed in it once or twice before he was killed."

"Have you ever been there?"

"A few times, but not enough to get a feel for the place. I always wanted to get back home."

"It takes time to call a place home," Simeon said as he hugged her close. He kissed her forehead. "Most people say it's where you are. Your heart was always here in New York. The company is your family."

Brynn nodded in agreement. "I knew that years ago. I don't know how things will be in my new role." She looked up at him. "I'm frightened, Simeon." Her breath escaped in a soft sigh. "Just plain scared that I'll fail."

"Shh," Simeon comforted. "Yes, Merle has placed a tremendous responsibility on your shoulders. You're so young and I don't know that there are many people your age with such a big undertaking. But you've been in the business since you were seven years old. That's over twenty-one years of know-how! Even so young you were racking up experiences. All of that knowledge and learning can only help you now. You'll be surprised what will come back to you."

Brynn was quiet as she absorbed his words. She thought that those years were her whole life. How fast time went. She didn't look at her age as being a factor in whether she could do the job. She just felt that she could do it simply because she was so passionate about dance.

"And Merle has taught me well," Brynn said. "He was the driving force behind the company but he saw to it that his well-trained dancers learned from the best of the best. He encouraged us to study and develop our own unique talents wherever they lay. His students are now teaching in companies all over the world. Some have formed their own companies and visit as guest artists or choreographers. They bring such a unique mix to Merle's dance concerts."

"He's a giant."

She stirred in Simeon's arms, sitting up and staring at him intensely. "You will continue to write our music?" she asked in a low voice. "You won't put it down again just because I'm not here?"

Simeon chuckled. "You're only going for one week, honey." He winked. "That leaves me with lots of uninterrupted time to *really* get some work done."

Her eyes widened. "What do you mean? You haven't

been working with the guys? I thought you were making such progress."

"Yeah, I am," Simeon admitted. "It's just that I get my knuckles rapped once in a while to bring me back to what's happening. I've been accused of daydreaming."

Brynn laughed. "That I would love to see. I can't imagine you being the one to mess up. *You're* the taskmaster." She skimmed her fingers over his long slender hand. "I hope I'm never the cause of you not writing again," she murmured. "Promise me you'll never stop."

"I never will," Simeon said simply. "It's what I do now. But yes, I promise you."

Sunday night, Simeon was upstairs in the music room. He'd finished working and was sitting on the sofa, drinking a beer. After he'd driven Brynn to Queens to LaGuardia Airport that morning he'd returned to Manhattan where he'd eaten a light brunch at Dede's Café and afterward visited his parents. He'd stayed for dinner but left early once his mother continued her probing of his relationship with the new woman in his life. Besides he didn't want to miss Brynn's call.

Simeon missed Brynn and her abrupt departure was still eating him up inside. He couldn't talk about her, especially not to his mother, who when she looked at Brynn saw a beautiful bride and grandkids. In all their close talks, neither he nor Brynn had ever mentioned marriage. Simeon knew in his heart that she was the woman he would ask to be his wife. But he'd never touched on it for fear of her answer. So much was happening so quickly in her life that he dared not upset the balance she was trying to bring to her world. Sometimes old thoughts would surface, that he had been in the right place at the right time. That he was the buffer that she'd needed to help her get through her pain and the horror that came with the realization that she would never dance professionally again. He wanted her to love *him,* and not just the comforting source that he'd been. At other times he felt that his thinking was skewed. She was a passionate lover and he couldn't imagine her giving so much of herself only because she needed comforting. No, he was certain that she loved him but he felt that she needed more time to settle into her new life before he hit her with another major decision to make. And he had to be certain that *he* wasn't making another mistake.

Since he watched her plane take off that morning, he'd had a gnawing feeling in the pit of his stomach that he was losing her. But he quickly squelched that thought. He couldn't imagine living his life without Brynn in it. Not now. Every morning when he awoke, she was in his thoughts. All day, no matter what he was doing, her bright smile and luminous eyes would appear and he'd get that warm feeling that was ever-present when he was near her.

He glanced at his watch again as he'd been doing since he got back home. Brynn should have called him by now. More than enough hours had gone by for the reunion between mother and daughter. Surely, she would have had some time to place a quick call to him only if to tell him that she'd arrived safely. He frowned, wondering if he should use the number she'd given him. If she hadn't arrived, his call would only upset Mrs. Halsted. If he tried her cell phone and she didn't answer, then he would be worried out of his skull. Not given to pacing, Simeon sat where he was, drinking his beer and watching the clock on the wall.

* * *

Brynn drove her rental car with caution through the unfamiliar streets of the small town where her mother lived. Her grandparents' home was the equivalent of nine blocks away and she passed their neighborhood on the way to her mother's street. It was only three-thirty in the afternoon yet the streets were deserted and only a few cars passed up and down the main street that was appropriately named Roen Boulevard. Her mother lived on Pruitt Drive and when Brynn turned into the quiet street she recognized the small white house that was only one of two that sat on the same side of the road. Across the road was a big sprawling house that took up most of the land down to the corner. There was no one around and Brynn had an eerie sense of impending doom. She shook off her nervousness and called herself silly for thinking the worst. It was just a quiet Sunday afternoon and families were inside eating, taking naps, or had gone back to church for evening services.

Brynn used the unfamiliar key that her mother had given her years ago and unlocked the door. When she pushed it open and slid her luggage inside, she knew that something was wrong. The house was quiet. There was no smell of a delicious Sunday dinner warming in the oven. In fact there was a sense of lonesomeness that abounded throughout the neat house. Without going to look, Brynn knew that her mother was not there and had not been for some time. But Brynn walked through anyway, with the silly thought that of course there would be no note of explanation. Her mother didn't know she was coming.

In the bathroom the toothbrush bristles were dry. There were no damp washcloths or towels flung carelessly over the bathtub. The shower stall was bone-dry.

Brynn walked to the bedroom and looked in surprise. The bed was unmade. A dresser drawer was open and a nightgown hung over the top. Brynn's heart pumped when her glance fell on a bottle of ibuprofen on the night table, a stale glass of water beside it. Painkiller? Slowly she walked to the bed and sat down, perplexed. Brynn looked around the room and chillingly guessed where her mother was. Almost in slow motion she picked up the phone and dialed a number.

When her grandmother answered, Brynn said, "Noonie, what hospital is my mother in?" She knew she sounded rude and cold, but she felt betrayed by them all and wasn't in the mood for hugs-and-kisses talk. How could they?

"Brynn?" Anne Halsted gasped. "Where are you?"

Hearing her grandmother's surprise, Brynn felt her heart drop. She was hoping that she was wrong but Noonie's response told her the truth. "I'm at Ma's," she said. "What are you all keeping from me, and why, Noonie?"

Anne Halsted didn't miss the anger in her granddaughter's voice and she couldn't blame her. "Your mother's at Rutland Memorial Center on Granby Avenue," she said softly. There was no animosity in her voice. She was sorry that she had helped deceive her granddaughter at Wenona's fierce insistence. "I'll let Wenona explain. Get a pencil, honey, and take down the number and the directions. After you see your mother, please come by so that we can talk. I'll have dinner waiting for you. Okay?"

Brynn took a deep breath before entering her mother's hospital room on the third floor. She stood at the door looking at her mother, who appeared to be sleeping. It was a two-bed room and the occupant near the wall had the curtains drawn so Brynn couldn't see whether the person was asleep or not though the television near the ceiling was on with a very low volume. Brynn walked to her mother's bed and pulled up a chair and sat quietly, never taking her eyes from her mother's face. Her presence must have been felt because Wenona opened her eyes.

For a moment, Wenona thought she was dreaming when she saw her daughter sitting at her bedside. The anger that flashed from her beautiful dark eyes was fierce. Wenona hadn't seen that look in many a year since Brynn was a teenager.

"Brynn. H-how did you know?" Wenona said in a froggy voice. "You never told me that you were coming."

At the sound of that weakened voice so unlike her mother's normally rich deep sound, Brynn's anger dissipated, and she went to her and bent to kiss her cheek. "Ma, what's wrong with you?" she whispered. "Why are you here and why didn't you tell me you were sick?" She brushed the long black hair from her mother's cheek, vaguely thinking how thin it had gotten, and when her mother reached up to hug her the blanket slipped away. Brynn saw the uneven chest. The flattened hollow beneath the nightgown was unmistakable. Brynn fell back into her chair. "Ma!" Her gaze fastened on her mother's chest and then searched her anguished face. Brynn looked in horror.

Wenona filled up inside. She didn't want her daughter to see her like this. She'd done all she could to prevent her knowing. It was too soon for her. "Brynn," she murmured. "It's all over now."

"All over? What's all over?" Brynn whispered, watching her mother through a bleary haze. "You had a mastectomy and didn't tell me? Cancer! You had cancer and kept it secret?" She was fearful and angry. Did they get it all? Merle. Her mother. What was happening? "Why are you here now? Did it spread and they're removing the other breast?" Her own words rung in her ears and scared her silly. Was her mother dying too?

"No, Brynn," Wenona managed with a small smile. "The cancer was removed when they took my breast over six weeks ago. As far as they know, it hasn't spread. I caught pneumonia and now that's all gone. I'm being discharged tomorrow."

Brynn found it hard to speak. Her mouth was dry and her thoughts were wild. She could only stare at her mother in disbelief. "I'm your daughter, and you kept me in the dark." Her eyes were accusing. "You were going to hide this from me for as long as you could, weren't you? And my grandparents. They were in on the deception. But, why?"

Her daughter's cry of despair wrenched Wenona's heart and her eyes welled up. "You'd had enough pain and sorrow, you didn't need to carry my burden too," she said. "Before you had your accident, I was all set to tell you that I'd found the lump and was going to look into it. I postponed the biopsy. With the state you were in I decided not to tell you. There was no need to worry you."

"Worry me?" Brynn was astounded. "*You* were the one with the cancer and you were worried about *me?*"

"You were losing your career, baby." Wenona frowned. "I would have been foolish to tell you what was going on with me right then and there. Sometimes you have to weigh decisions, and not telling you was mine. Your doctor said that you were in a bad way and he thought that any more bad news would—well, there was no need to disturb you further."

"*Disturb* me! I don't believe this! Did you both think that I was suicidal? Is that it?" When Wenona dropped her eyes, Brynn bristled. "Was I such a complete basket case?"

Wenona nodded. "Yes, you were. We were all scared for you. The doctor said the length of your stupor wasn't normal."

"Unbelievable!" Brynn fell back in the chair. She thought back to that horrible period in her life. Her unresponsiveness to her mother, Merle, Claire, and even her doctors, who'd hinted that her career was over. Miserable, she slumped down and dropped her forehead in her hand. *What's wrong with me?* she wondered. Her mother could have been dying and she would never have known because she was being sheltered and protected as she had been all her life.

Wenona reached over and touched Brynn's hand. "Don't do that to yourself," she said firmly. "It was my decision to make. I still think it was the best thing to do. Look at me, Brynn. Don't let all that I've done be a waste. I didn't mean to leave you out of my business. I only wanted to shelter you from more hurt. I knew that when you were stronger I would have shared everything with you. Didn't we always do that?"

Brynn opened her eyes and caught her mother's hand. "Yes," she whispered. "Always."

"And we will from now on." After a pause Wenona said, "You know, Brynn, I was lonely."

"What?"

"And scared," Wenona confessed and heaved a great sigh. "I'm glad you know. I wanted to talk to you so many times, to ask you to come so I could unburden myself and to give me strength. To hold my hand like you're doing now."

"Ma." Brynn was filled with anguish.

Wenona sighed deeply, then said, "That was a lonely journey I took and I would never do it again. I didn't want the support of strangers though they offered their counsel. How could they know what I was feeling? They didn't know the person I was, so how could they love *me*? Noonie was a good listener as much as she could be and I love her for supporting me. Especially in deceiving you. Sometimes I would stand before the mirror staring at myself knowing I was going to lose a part of me. If I'd been in an accident and in an emergency they took an arm or a leg I would have had no choice in the matter. But I was walking in whole and walking out less than myself. I wondered if afterward, would my body lean? Would my clothes hang lopsided? Would I get those knowing, pitying stares? Lying in the hospital bed after the surgery was the loneliest time of all. I wanted you here. Then I remembered. And so I cried until they sedated me."

Wenona frowned. "After, I still couldn't come to you because I had the radiation therapy sessions. Five days a week for seven weeks. I had to be here." She grimaced. "It's all over now. I thank the Lord that I'm still here. But I was so scared and lonely." She hesitated. "So I wasn't as strong as I thought I was after all."

Through blurry eyes, Brynn whispered, "You're the strongest woman I know. I love you, Ma. So much."

Wenona's eyes were damp and she kissed her daughter's cheek. "I love you too, baby." She sighed and her eyes became heavy.

Brynn saw. "You're tired," she said, sniffing back the tears. "I'm going back to the house, so you can sleep." She kissed her mother's cheek. "Is Papa picking you up tomorrow?"

"He'll be here before noon."

"Then I'll leave those plans alone," Brynn said. "I'll be at home waiting for you. Do you think that they'll put you on a special diet?"

"No, I can eat anything." Wenona made a face. "Just as long as it's got some kick to it, I'll be fine."

Brynn kissed her again. "I'll take care of that." Her mouth grew grim. "No more secrets, Ma. Okay?"

"No more," Wenona said before closing her eyes.

As soon as she got back to her mother's house, Brynn made a call. "Noonie," Brynn said to her grandmother, "I won't be over for dinner tonight but thanks for keeping it warm for me. I was too exhausted after leaving Ma and I'm going to turn in early. I'll call you in the morning, okay?"

Brynn sat down on the bed in her mother's bedroom, still bewildered and trying to make sense of the whole thing.

"Am I so selfish and obtuse not to have known that my own mother's life was in danger?" Her voice was conversational as if she were speaking to another. Agitated, she got up and left the room and went to the guest bedroom where she lay on the bed fully clothed, looking up at the ceiling. Like a videotape she played and replayed the past few months in her head. No, the last few years of her life. Why had it been necessary for her mother, her grandparents, to shelter her from the hard truth? She was fragile by no means. She was as strong as the next person, even more so. Then why? Had her passion for her career made her so insensitive to the world around her? To those who were closest to her and who loved her? And to the point that they would rather lie, deceive, and suffer in silence rather than to *disturb* her? Brynn shivered. "What kind of person am I?" Surely not the kind that deserved the love of a wonderful man like her lover. She wondered if Simeon or Claire and Merle had seen her flaws, shortcomings that they overlooked because they loved her! She closed her eyes against the not so pretty image of herself.

The phone was ringing insistently. When Brynn shed light on the darkened room she saw that it was past nine o'clock and realized she'd slept the evening away. She picked up the phone. "Ma?" she breathed.

That one word brought his fears to life. "This is Simeon," he said quietly.

Eleven

The unexpected sound of his voice was unsettling and it was seconds before Brynn composed herself enough to speak.

Simeon heard the tiny gasp of surprise and patiently waited, but his stomach was in knots.

"I—I thought it might have been the hospital calling this time of night," Brynn finally managed.

"Your mother," he said as calmly as he could. "Is that where you found her?"

"Simeon, she's sick. She's had cancer all this time and she never told me." All of a sudden the words gushed from her like an angry geyser. "All these months when she wouldn't come back to New York, visiting me by phone, she was sick. She found a lump in her breast just before I got hurt. When she came to New York to see me in the hospital, she'd put off having a biopsy. When she finally learned she had to have a mastectomy she still didn't want me to know. She didn't want to *disturb* me!" Her cheeks flamed at her period of self-examination the night before and what she'd thought. "She had everyone lying to me. Noonie had never been ill. It was all excuses and lies so that I wouldn't be *disturbed!*"

"Brynn." Simeon called her name softly. He guessed that she was alone in the house. "Calm down," he said more firmly, but he clasped and unclasped his hand.

He knew she was blaming herself. He called her name again.

"I'm here, Simeon." She wished that she were hundreds of miles from here back home in his arms. This house that was so new and unfamiliar to her, without her mother's presence, it was not home.

"Take your time and tell me what happened when you saw her. Your mother had the mastectomy. Is she hospitalized now because of complications?" he asked.

"She has pneumonia. That and her radiation treatment were what prevented her from coming up these last months," Brynn answered, her voice rising again. "She's being released tomorrow. I should have guessed that there was something, Simeon. I'm her daughter! She wasn't acting like herself and I should have known!"

"She didn't want you to know, Brynn. You can't blame yourself for not realizing what was going on."

"That's no excuse." Her mother's words reverberated in her ears. "I was so selfish and vain that all I could see was my own pain. Just *my* needs over my mother's suffering. I should only have *looked* at her face to know." Her voice was bitter.

"Brynn, listen to me," Simeon said in a careful tone. "You were lying in that hospital bed never knowing but secretly guessing that you were never going to dance professionally again. You didn't need to wait to hear it from your doctor. You were losing the one passionate thing in your life. To you, the future was bleak, a grayish void that you dared not confront. Your mother saw all of that and protected you."

"As she did all of my life."

Simeon was silent, at a loss on how to comfort her. She was agonizing over the new waves of pain and guilt. He wondered about her backsliding, losing herself in that deep funk that was like a huge black hole. And he was so far away. He took a deep breath. "Brynn, I can be there in a matter of hours."

She was quiet, thinking about where she had to start to make things right. And she knew that she had to do it alone. No more buffers.

"No, I'll be all right. Please stay and work. I don't want to be the cause of you putting everything on hold. I'll be fine here. My mother will be home tomorrow and I'll be taking care of her."

Simeon felt a pain in his belly. Her words held such finality and he thought about the feelings he'd had when her plane took off. *Was* he about to lose her? "Will you hire someone to look in on your mother when you leave in a week?" he asked.

A week, she thought. There wasn't enough time in the world to make up to her mother for her selfishness. "I—I'll think about that when the time comes," she said.

When the time comes? It sounded like light-years, Simeon thought, and because she was the woman he'd fallen in love with, he knew what Brynn was thinking. She was extending her stay.

"Simeon?" She listened to his uneven breathing. "I feel so used up. I—I just can't explain it and still make good sense. Empty is the best description I have right now." She hesitated. "Can you understand?"

"I think so." He wanted to fly to her the second they hung up but knew that wasn't what she wanted. Not now. "I'll call you in the morning, but I want a promise from you."

"What?"

"I want you to get in bed and go to sleep. Not later," he said firmly. "I don't want you sitting up all night, kicking yourself for something you had no control of. What's done is done and you can't criticize your mother for doing what she thought was right. And you can't browbeat yourself." He inhaled. "Do I get that promise?"

"Yes," Brynn said.

"Good." He exhaled.

"I love you," Brynn said softly. "I want you here with me but there are some things I have to resolve with—"

"You don't have to explain to me," Simeon interrupted. "I understand. All I want right now is that you keep your promise and go to sleep. No thinking about what's going to happen tomorrow. Okay?" When she wearily agreed, he said, "I love you, Brynn."

The room was silent once again, except for her anguished breathing. Bone-tired, Brynn undressed and slipped beneath the cool sheets. Simeon knew that the best panacea for her right now was sleep. Blissful sleep that took away all the pain and hurtful thoughts. At least for a little while.

An hour after he talked to Brynn, Simeon was still restless. For the first time in weeks he thought about where he used to spend his Sunday nights. Storeyland was the place to be for all those work-weary New Yorkers who tried their best to prolong their weekend at the supper club. Toward the closing hours he would frequently join the band and they'd play some funky Thelonious Monk jazz. Often he would start one of his own creations and the sidemen would immediately pick up where he was coming from. What followed was a rousing, satisfying end to a perfect Sunday and the crowd left feeling ready to tackle another workweek.

After he'd closed Storeyland he had gotten feedback that his loyal patrons sorely missed the Harlem club. There were few quality nightspots left to serve the crowd who wanted to stay uptown. Traveling downtown was what they'd all hated to do just to hear some great jazz. Even his sister Asha doubted that he'd made the right decision. She'd hinted that if he was doing it for the love of a woman maybe he'd better rethink his actions. Love is a sometimey thing, she'd told him.

"Not this time, sis," he said, raising his beer glass to the ceiling. "I've got the real thing." He grimaced. Conversing with his sister in absentia was not good but he gave one more salute.

His thoughts were still on the woman he loved. The awful guilt she must be dealing with twisted his heart, and he wasn't there for her as he'd been before. He thought about Mrs. Halsted and the decision she'd made to spare her daughter any more pain. He wondered if she now had misgivings, seeing the effect it had on Brynn. The irony of it all was that Brynn could never have been spared learning the truth and was now left to deal with it all alone.

Simeon squeezed the image of a hurting woman from his eyes and prayed that Brynn would dig deep and cull that strength he knew was there.

Wenona was sitting on the living room sofa dressed in gown and robe. She watched her daughter watch her with anxious eyes. Since she'd gotten home from the hospital around noon, Brynn had made her undress and go immediately upstairs to bed. All protestations fell on deaf ears as Brynn shepherded her mother until she was satisfied that Wenona was resting comfortably. Then she went back downstairs to finish dinner. By eight they'd eaten and had been watching television for half an hour when Wenona picked up the remote and clicked the off button.

"Brynn, I know what you're doing and I want you to stop," she said. Her dark eyes flashed with impatience and her voice was no-nonsense serious. "Don't look at me so surprised. You're far from being obtuse."

Hurt by her mother's sudden outburst, Brynn

looked pained. "I'm sorry but you'll have to explain, Ma. Exactly what is it that I have to stop?"

"Trying to make up for not being a dutiful daughter all these years. Being so solicitous of my every move and sound. You don't give me a chance to tell you if I want something, you *decide* what I need." Wenona gestured at herself. "I don't need to stay in bedclothes. They sent me home because the pneumonia is out of my body. I'm fine!"

Taken aback by the accusations, Brynn sat stunned. What she couldn't do was to deny every word. She stared helplessly at her mother. She'd never felt lonelier in all her life.

It pained Wenona to see Brynn's crumpled face, and unwilling to exact further punishment on her daughter, she held out her hand. "Come here." She patted the seat cushion next to her.

Confused at her mother's changed expression and soft tone, Brynn crossed the room and sat beside her. She grasped the hand that slid into hers.

"I thought about you last night," Wenona said in a calm voice. "I saw how you reacted and I felt so bad that you were here all alone dealing with what was going on inside your head." With one finger she tapped her shoulder above her remaining breast. "Come, put your head here like you used to." When Brynn hesitated, she said, "It doesn't hurt. Make yourself comfortable."

"Ma, I'm so sorry," Brynn whispered.

"Sorry for what?" Wenona said, as she combed her fingers through her daughter's growing hair that she wore pulled back behind her ears.

Brynn closed her eyes and settled into the softness of her mother's breast. She used to love to have her hair brushed while she sat on the floor by her mother's knee.

"Sorry doesn't live in this house." Wenona smiled.

Brynn laughed. "I know. Daddy used to tell me that all the time."

"Only whenever you batted your lashes at him trying to get out of a punishment after you'd been bad. That was when your 'I'm sorry' didn't work." Wenona remembered how she would make eyes at Joseph from across the room, trying to hold the giggles in herself. Later, in the privacy of their bedroom, they would crack up at their daughter's antics.

"Brynn, you have been the best daughter a mother or father could ever dream of having. So get out of your head that you were uncaring, selfish, you name it, all those other adjectives you claimed for yourself. And besides, how selfish can a woman be who year after year funds her own private charity footing the bills for those expensive costumes for some deserving students?" She chucked Brynn's chin. "If Joseph had heard you just now, you know what would have been in store for you."

Brynn smiled at the so-called punishment her father meted out. "Yeah, no pointe shoes but left with everything else in my room." After a smart rap on her backside he'd march tall and straight to her bedroom and remove all her dance stuff. She was left with all the other entertainment features that adorned most every middle-class kid's bedroom—cassettes, TV, phone—as, serious-faced, he'd close the door, leaving her to ponder her behavior.

"Everything we did, the way we raised you, was just exactly what we wanted. If there was ever any sign of those negative attributes we would have cut off the heads of those ugly monsters. As a result, we have a beautiful, kind, gracious, and talented young woman for a daughter." Wenona's voice dropped. "And Joseph got to see the woman in the making at sixteen. He knew what you were and what you would become."

Brynn's throat constricted as she felt a giant weight lift from her shoulders. "I was so angry with you, Ma. I couldn't believe that you were willing to bear all that burden by yourself. Staying here alone with all those thoughts."

"I wasn't alone, honey." Wenona patted Brynn's cheek. "Noonie was here. She stayed with me that first week, bless her heart. And she's in a lot of pain with her arthritic joints. But she wouldn't take no for an answer."

"Noonie?" Brynn blushed at her angry thoughts toward her grandmother.

"I think you owe her an apology. I heard your cold tone when you spoke to her over the phone today." Wenona clucked. "And your granddad was pretty puzzled by your rush to get him out of here. You hurt their feelings, sweetie."

Her cheeks burned. "Ma, I was horrible to Noonie yesterday when I got here and found you gone." Brynn pushed herself up straight. "I felt so deceived!"

"I know," Wenona agreed. "They were so flabbergasted at your arrival that they didn't know what to tell you. Especially after I swore them to secrecy. You know that they would never do anything to hurt you. Don't you know you were their own little girl? I think if your father and I hadn't come to get you when we did, we would have had a court battle on our hands later."

"I remember." Brynn shook her head ruefully. "Shame on me," she said. "I should have known that you made them promise." She took her mother's hand in hers. "I think you have such a wonderful relationship with your in-laws. Has it always been that way? They accepted you right off?"

"It was like I'd grown up across the street from them.

There was no honeymoon period or daughter-in-law this or that. It was their son and daughter from the beginning." She blinked her eyes.

"That's why you're here, isn't it?" Brynn said, still smoothing her mother's hand. "To be close to Daddy."

Wenona studied her daughter's face. "I needed to be here. I'd thought about it for a long time. Leaving you was hard. But I knew you would be okay with Merle and Claire and your family of dancers. If I'd thought otherwise, I would have stayed. There was something dying inside me little by little. Every day when I walked into that house, slept in that bedroom, I cried inside. It was as if there was no remembrance of the good times we had together. I could no longer hear his hearty laugh or see his gorgeous brown eyes light up when we made good love. Those things never entered my mind after a while. They seemed to have faded, and all that invaded my senses were the horrors." She rubbed her temples. "The night I received the call from the police, the terrifying ride to the hospital, my heart in my mouth. It was almost as if I knew that he wouldn't be coming home to us. And when I thought of you without him I cringed at how I would fix my mouth to tell you that your father was dead."

Brynn shuddered at the memory. How her mother had suffered! "Is it better for you now?" she asked softly.

Wenona smiled, and nodded. "The good memories returned as soon as I settled in this house. For years I've been at peace. No demons nag at me and tear at my insides, making me hateful. It's just that when I—I visit New York, sleep in that house, I get unsettled."

"I didn't know, Ma," Brynn said.

"Of course you didn't." She looked around the room furnished in the sleek contemporary style that she loved. "I'm at peace here."

Brynn stirred, a worried look in her eyes. "You don't, uh, talk to Daddy, do you?"

"Talk?" Wenona was startled and then she chuckled. "I think you're thinking theatrically, like one of those concerts you and Merle dream up." She squeezed Brynn's hand. "No, sweetie. I'm not living with a ghost. I'll never ever forget your father and the love we shared for too short a time. He's buried about twenty miles from here and I visit his grave occasionally. But although he's in my heart, he's not in my head. I'm still alive."

Curious, Brynn asked, "Are you, uh, have you, uh, ever been involved with another man?" As far back as she could remember her mother had never brought a man home.

Wenona's eyes twinkled. "You mean like you and Mr. Storey?"

"Ma!" Brynn warmed to the roots of her hair. "I never mentioned anything!"

"You didn't have to. You're my daughter." Wenona clucked. "Now I may have been a widow for umpteen years but like I said, I'm still alive and still able to see and hear the sounds a woman in love makes."

"What?"

"I heard you on the phone in the bedroom this afternoon. I was supposed to be 'resting' in bed." She cocked her head. "Simeon, is it?"

Brynn's body heat rose. She'd rarely talked to her mother about falling in love. Years ago when she was in her early twenties the subject of marriage and babies came up but Brynn had brushed it off as unimportant and her mother had never asked intimate questions again. "Simeon Storey," she said. "It was in his club where I—I was hurt."

"I remember," said Wenona. "I met him briefly at the hospital. At the time I wasn't very nice to the man whom I held responsible for my daughter's being where she was. I owe him an apology. Claire told me that after he was stitched up he left his hospital bed to go downstairs to see you." She searched Brynn's face. "Do you really love him?"

"I love him, Ma."

"Enough to think about marriage?"

"I—we haven't talked about that far into the future. Not yet."

"I saw a very intense young man that night," Wenona said. "He didn't appear to be one to take things lightly. You're not feeling grateful because he showed concern, are you?"

A smile played about Brynn's mouth as she thought of their passionate lovemaking. Was that just being grateful? She didn't think so! "It's the real thing, Ma," she answered. "I've never felt this way before."

"How could you know? As far as I could tell you've never gone with a boy or a man long enough to sense whether you were in love or not."

She smiled. "There are some things you just can't help but know." She grew serious. "I think marriage with Simeon would be good," she said thoughtfully. "But there is so much that I want to do now."

Wenona saw the sparkle return to her daughter's eyes and heard the rush of breath and she knew Brynn's head was in the dance studio. "You mean stepping into Merle's shoes when he . . . well, taking over?"

The women grieved silently about the time when Merle would no longer walk into the theater, all bluster and business and big heart.

"Yes," Brynn said almost breathlessly. "He's placed so much weight on my shoulders. He feels that when I'm ready to take the reins completely I can build on what he's created in all these years. Merle really thinks that I can do this, Ma. But for now to undertake the role of company choreographer! To plan season after season!"

"That's a big task, honey. But Merle wouldn't have placed such a heavy burden on you if indeed you thought of it as such. He knows that you have the talent and the desire to do it. You have the passion."

"Do I, Ma?" Brynn asked solemnly. "My passion was for dance. To be on that stage performing, making intimate contact with my audience. Telling my story as passionately as I could. I lived for that."

"And you'll live again for the new passion of seeing your stories come to life. Just as Merle did." She looked thoughtful. "So is that your reason to hesitate if Simeon proposes marriage? That you won't be able to have as much passion for him as you will running the company?"

"I think that's it. I know how much it will take out of me." She stared at her mother. "Can you say that it will be easy or even fair to ask a man to compete with that? You know how intense I can be. I may forget that I have a man waiting for me in my bed."

Wenona chuckled. "Nothing you have a passion for comes easy. Think about it. Did you become a dance diva by taking a stroll in the park? Not on your life. You worked your little fanny off to achieve your goals. But you did it because you loved it. Loved the hard work, the sweat, the pain, the aching body, and the sore feet. Loved the way it made you feel so much that you were back at it day after day after day." She paused and her eyes grew sad. "That's the way you'll feel about your other passion. The man in your life, in your bed, as you put it. Because you waited all these years to give yourself to a man, and to admit that you're in love, you know it's what you want as much as anything. And you'll do all in your power to make it work. A day with the company will become your nine-to-five, so to speak.

Looking forward to an evening at home with your husband will be just an extension of your passion."

Brynn listened carefully to her mother's words that were full of love and common sense. She knew her mother was thinking of her own years of working hard and spending evenings with her husband. Evenings that had been few, once he began his second job.

After a moment, Wenona said, "You'll know what to tell him when he asks. Just be true to yourself." She noticed the unsettled look on Brynn's face. "Is there something you're not telling me?"

"No, nothing about that," Brynn answered slowly. "I just don't understand."

"What?"

"You. All my life I watched you take care of your family's health, seeing that we stayed fit with vitamins and regular checkups. You insisted that I do monthly breast self-exams and I know you were doing your own. At least you used to. What happened? Why did you chance a catastrophe? You were playing with your life!"

Wenona shifted with unease at her daughter's accusing eyes. "Fear. Stupidity," she finally said. "You know I have cystic breasts. After a while I stopped doing the self-exams."

"But why? You had a friend who died from breast cancer! Didn't you think of Mrs. Harrow's suffering toward the end?"

"Maybe I was thinking of her," Wenona said. "Then maybe it was because I felt like a fool running to see about a lump that wasn't there the month before only to find that it was just another cyst that had moved around! The doctor would just look at me with impatience."

"Then you should have changed doctors!" Brynn said through clenched teeth. "Of all the nerve!"

"No, don't blame anyone else. I'm responsible for

my own health. I was afraid of the future and what it held for you if I fell ill and died leaving you alone. There's no one left for you but your grands, and they're old and sickly."

Brynn grew angry. "Me again. *Why* do you think that I would fold up and wither away because the realities of life hit me? I'm not a weak child to be lied to and coddled because I would feel the pain! You have to stop that, Ma. I've dealt with what happened to me and I'm moving on. So stop worrying about me."

Admiration was in Wenona's eyes as she listened to her daughter. "I realize that. And I also realize how dangerous delaying the surgery was. I thank God that I'm still here, healing, and getting on with my life. I'll never stop being grateful for this second chance." She stood. "Now, I think I could use some rest."

They walked upstairs and Brynn waited until her mother came out of the bathroom, slipped off her robe, and got in bed.

Wenona saw the discomfort in Brynn's eyes. "I was undecided at the time, honey."

"What?"

"Breast reconstruction. Isn't that what you've been wanting to ask me?"

"Yes. I wondered."

"I wasn't so sure about having it done at the time of the surgery," Wenona said. "But I'm comfortable with myself now. The breast removal was necessary to save my life. Cosmetic surgery is not."

"You're certain?"

"There are thousands of women just like me. Comfortable with their own bodies and who they are. I was depressed the first time I saw myself." She paused. Joseph had loved kissing her full breasts, nuzzling and suckling them while bringing her to climax. But she was who she was now. The scar that took the place of her breast was a reminder that she was alive because of God's grace and man's medical technology. She was at peace with that.

Brynn kissed her mother's cheek. "I love you, Ma."

"Love you too," Wenona said. "You'll stay a couple of days?"

"A couple? I'd planned to stay a week, but now I think I'll stay for another. Wait until you get a little stronger." She eyed her mother. "That therapy did weaken you. You look so tired. And that bug is nothing to play around with especially after major surgery."

"Oh, Brynn, I'm fine. You have to get back. You know Merle is counting on you."

"I know. But he understands. Two weeks away he can deal with, longer I'm not so sure." She could see his gray eyes darken with anxiety if she extended her stay beyond that.

"I think I'd better get the name of that therapist after all," Brynn said.

"What are you talking about?"

"My foot. I have to continue my therapy, three sessions a week. Since I'm staying, I can do it here just as well."

Trying to talk to her daughter now would defeat the progress they'd made tonight, Wenona thought. Besides she really was feeling weary, and tomorrow would be the best time to talk some sense into Brynn. "I'll see you in the morning, honey. Don't stay up too late. I know you're exhausted."

When she left her mother's room, Brynn went downstairs. She was too restless to sleep though she was feeling sleepy, but she had to assess her priorities. And her mother's needs came first. First thing in the morning she would call the hospital and get a recommendation for a therapist. Then she would visit her grandparents. She felt ashamed at how she'd treated them when all the time they were only doing her mother's bidding. She loved them dearly and would hate to have a rift in their relationship.

She felt happy and rejuvenated, now that the dark clouds of uncertainty had been lifted. But a little pang of hurt still stung her chest when she thought of her mother's deception. The worst feeling came when she realized she'd be away from Simeon for so much longer. A week she could deal with sensibly, but to prolong their separation was agony. Her need to talk to him was great. Brynn dialed his number, then carried the phone into the living room and settled herself on the love seat.

When his phone rang at close to midnight, Simeon knew why Brynn was calling.

"Hello," he said, happy to hear her voice but dreading the content of the conversation that they'd have.

"Simeon. I'm so glad you're still awake," Brynn said. His voice sounded wonderful and a wave of passion swept through her. She thought of her mother's words. "Everything's going to be all right."

He couldn't tell whether she was sounding pleased or relieved. But he did suspect that he was right. She was staying. "You talked?" he asked.

"Yes, and we're fine," Brynn answered. "I was letting my emotions rule my head." Then, "Simeon, I miss you so much," she murmured.

"I miss you too, sweetheart," he answered, and wondered how much longer she'd extended her stay.

"My mother's still a little wobbly," she said quietly. "I'm staying until she's back to her self."

After a moment he said, "For how long?"

"Another week," Brynn answered. "What's wrong? You sound so distant."

"Nothing, except I'll find Harlem a lonely place, that's all."

Brynn felt that there was something he wasn't saying. "I need to be here with my mother, Simeon. Don't resent me." It wasn't in his makeup to be petty and jealous.

"I don't." He hesitated. "Are you coming back, Brynn?"

What a strange question. "What do you mean?"

"I can understand the need to stay until your mother is strong again," Simeon said quietly. "I guess what I'm really asking is whether you're going to stay indefinitely to make up for what you think was poor behavior on your part. Whether you're still beating up on yourself."

She stiffened. "You think I'm doing this out of guilt?"

"You might be," he answered in a solemn voice.

Could he be right? So much had happened in the space of a day that she never stopped to analyze her actions. The only thing that was clear to her was that she wasn't leaving her mother right now. And Brynn refused to set a time limit on her availability to provide love and attention as long as it was needed. She was going to be here for as long as was necessary.

"Brynn, talk to me," Simeon said.

"I'm here," she answered. "I was thinking about what you said, and my answer is no. I'm not feeling guilty. Staying is just something that I must do. It's the most important thing to me right now."

He gripped the phone. "I hear you," he finally said.

Brynn knew immediately what he meant. "This has nothing to do with us, Simeon. We're still in love, aren't we?"

"I am," he answered in a low voice.

"And I'm not because I love my mother and want to be here for her?"

He sighed. "It sounds like you're asking me to choose between our love and your mother."

"There's no choice," Brynn said. "I love you both. I'm coming back home and, I hope, to you, Simeon," she said softly. "I need to be here right now."

"I'll be here, Brynn." He paused. "Just call me and let me know that you're okay."

"I will," Brynn answered. "Simeon?"

"Yes?"

"Please don't stop working. We've come so far and I have more ideas that I can't wait to try. I wish that I could . . ." She hesitated and her heart fluttered. *Dance. Oh, to be able to dance the movements that are in my head.*

"Don't do that, Brynn," Simeon said softly. "I know what you're thinking. I have your notations and I'll be using them when I'm writing. When you get back we'll finish it up. It's going to move perfectly." He closed his eyes against the dream of seeing her in delightful movement.

"I know," Brynn breathed. "I can feel it." She voiced a thought that had been nagging her since she and Simeon began the piece. "I wonder who will dance it?" she said. "Now that Claire has stopped performing, I can't imagine who will do it justice."

His jaw hardened. As if he were ready for another woman's body moving in sensuous motion to his music! For years he'd only envisioned Brynn Halsted, the quintessential modern dancer. *His* woman, now. "I can't imagine," he said quietly.

"We'll get through this, love," she consoled.

"Yes, we will." Simeon's breath sounded ragged as he sought to compose himself. He couldn't let her begin to second-guess her hard-fought battle to gain confidence. If Brynn was accepting of her future, so then must he be as strong and faithful to her new role as she.

Twelve

At the beginning of the second week in her mother's home, Brynn was swept with a sense of contentment. Gone were the self-doubts and self-recriminations. She and her mother had had many more conversations where each shared her thoughts. There was a new mood between them that did not lend to keeping secrets. Each day she saw in her mother the growing strength she required to accept her ordeal and get on with her life without self-pity. She was the best role model that Brynn could ever have asked for at this time in her life.

She gave her mother the once-over again. "Well, now, don't you look ready for something devilish! I thought you were just going to spend the day doing the nails and hair thing. I think something else must be going on, huh?"

Wenona grinned. "Afterward, I'm going to lunch and a movie with friends." She smoothed the boxy jacket of her smart black pantsuit that fit her perfectly. "It's a crisp, gorgeous day and after your therapy session I think that you should do something different too. And don't bother to cook dinner. For the longest, I've had a taste for a huge juicy steak, medium-well, with a roasted potato and dollops of sour cream. I'll bring back some of that delicious peach cobbler you love so much and we both can act like little piggies in the farmhouse kitchen.''

Watching from the window as her mother drove away, Brynn was still amazed whenever she looked at her. She *was* a strong woman.

Preparing for her appointment, Brynn had to admit that the misgivings that she'd had about her treatment were all for naught. She had complete confidence in the therapist, who was expert at what he did and his ability to put her at ease. From the time she'd walked into his office, he didn't show the slightest awe of her celebrity status or ask for an autograph for his kids or commiserate about her unfortunate career-ending accident. She looked forward to the thrice-weekly sessions and on the days she didn't go to him she did the home exercises he'd given her. She was going to miss him after she flew back home on Saturday.

The one sad part in Brynn's heart was her friend and mentor, Merle, who was dying. They spoke often and Brynn nearly cried each time after hanging up the phone. He always sounded so weak and tired, and it was hard for her to imagine him inactive. He joked that he wished that he had the strength to act like one of those instructors who directed from a chair, waving his arms and wagging his head in maniacal fashion to get his point across.

The therapist's office was located in a building that housed several other businesses and whenever Brynn passed the door that read CARMEN'S SCHOOL OF DANCE she was intrigued at what went on in those rooms. The music, the thud of bare feet over wood floors, the groans of impatience from an instructor, all filtered through at one point or another when Brynn was walking by. She'd thought that she would fall into a deep abyss of self-pity but surprised herself that she only wished the best of futures for all those impassioned young dancers. She was proud of herself.

"Ms. Halsted?" Brynn turned at the sound of her name being called as she left her car. She saw a slender tan-skinned woman who was looking at her with uncertainty as if she wasn't sure she should have spoken. Brynn smiled. "Yes?"

As if relieved at the unexpected pleasant response the woman walked to Brynn with extended hand, and a smile of her own. "Hello. My name is Carmen Roberts and I own the dance studio next to the medical offices."

Brynn shook hands. "Hi." The woman, who was Brynn's height, had a firm grip that Brynn liked. Even beneath Carmen Roberts's unbuttoned jacket, Brynn's practiced eye saw that her body was in excellent condition.

"I saw you last week," Carmen said, "but I didn't want to invade your privacy. I'm so pleased to meet you."

"Thank you," Brynn answered as they walked. "I'm glad you stopped me this time. I'm happy to meet you. Have you had your studio long?" She barely looked thirty.

"For about five years now," Carmen said solemnly. "I —I had to stop performing professionally when I was twenty-six."

"Oh, I'm sorry." Brynn suddenly saw her own past. "What happened?"

"Car accident. I was caught between two crazed road rage drivers. They walked away, I didn't." Her mouth tightened. "The settlement enabled me to open the studio." She gave Brynn an apologetic look. "I'm sorry to bring back bad memories for you. I was devastated as the whole dance world was to hear about your accident." She paused. "And your career."

Brynn felt the pain of Carmen Roberts so acutely that she couldn't help but empathize with her. "Thank you," she murmured. "Have you always wanted to dance?"

"Forever. Now I'm involved with it practically around the clock and I wouldn't want to be doing anything else." Her dark eyes sparkled. "Each year when the new classes begin I eagerly look for that quality that will produce the next Brynn Halsted." Realizing her gaffe, she said, "I didn't mean to sound insensitive, Ms. Halsted."

"Call me Brynn, please." She smiled. "I'm not offended. Rather pleased, I think." They entered the elevator. "Don't you remember when you were in class, that your instructor would throw a tantrum at your pliés, swearing that you wouldn't be the next Judith Jamison?"

Laughing, the women fell into an easy camaraderie.

"Or my namesake, Carmen de Lavallade," Carmen said, striking a pose, a la de Lavallade.

Brynn laughed. Since she'd left New York, she hadn't felt so free-spirited with a stranger, always ready to shy away from those pitying glances and whispers. She liked this woman who appeared to have overcome the tragedy in her life. She accepted and moved on, building a future different from the one she'd planned. *Just like me,* Brynn thought. She was so ready to take on full-speed her duties with the company and choreograph to Simeon's scores.

They stopped at Carmen's studio door and the strident voice of a female instructor seeped through. The two women shared a knowing look and laughed, each having been on the receiving end of such scorn.

Brynn was reluctant to say good-bye to the woman she was beginning to like. Her mother had said to do something different, she thought. Why not? Inviting a stranger to lunch was definitely a new venture. Even Claire would have raised a brow.

"I should be finished with my therapy close to lunchtime," Brynn said. "Would you like to take a break together?"

"I'd like that," Carmen said with a bright smile.

The two women parted, and Brynn opened the door of the medical office, feeling that a new chapter was opening in her life. She looked forward to the developing friendship with a fellow dancer, thinking that they had a symbiotic kinship.

On Wednesday, their third lunch date, Brynn and Carmen were seated in the same nearby restaurant. Each enjoyed the fast friendship that was forming.

Brynn discovered that like herself, Carmen had put her love life on hold while she pursued her career. Now, though she dated, there was no important man in her life though she said she would like to walk down the aisle someday when the right guy came along.

"How's your mom today?" Carmen asked. She made a face. "I know she's going to miss you when you take off on Saturday. And so will I." She waved a hand. "Having lunch here won't be the same after you leave."

"Thanks," Brynn said. "I'll miss you too, and I'm going to hold you to your word to call me next time you're up my way. You'll have to visit the company and meet Claire, and Merle. They'll love you." She smiled. "And my mother is doing just fine, thanks, that's why I'm leaving. I think she's getting tired of me underfoot, almost as if she wants me to be gone. She thinks she needs my permission to go to this meeting or that one. I'm getting tired keeping up with her schedule. She's on two choirs, so enough said."

"It's great that she's back doing the things she loves," Carmen said. "I don't think you have to worry about her anymore. I've never met her but she sounds like a strong woman."

"She's the best and I'm glad you're coming over Friday so you two can meet." Brynn winked. "She'll just think I'm planting a guard dog in her backyard, though, to send me reports."

"After the understanding you two have now, I'm sure she won't be keeping such important information from you." Carmen smiled. "If we hit it off, I might drop by every now and then."

"Consider yourself a frequent visitor then," Brynn said. "You know, I've never taken a peek in your studio. I didn't want to disrupt the class. I know how it is getting them back to order. Would you mind?"

"Mind? Of course not! They'd love it. I probably will get flack from my teacher, Leria, but the ruckus will be worth it. Do you want to stop by now?"

Brynn was frowning. "What did you say?"

"Do you want to stop now or later?"

"No, I mean the name of your teacher." Brynn's eyes darkened.

"Oh, it is an unusual name, isn't it? Leria Monserrat. She's been with me since I lost my first teacher to love and marriage."

"I knew a Leria once, but her last name was Dickson." Brynn appeared to relax. "I just never ran into anyone with that same name again."

Carmen waved toward the door, then looked at Brynn. "Well, you won't have to wait too long before you find out if it's the same person. Here she comes now. Probably coming for her afternoon shot of caffeine. Leria, over here," she called.

Brynn turned to watch the woman approach and she couldn't hold back the gasp of surprise. "Leria."

Carmen saw Brynn's reaction but it was too late to address it. She said, "Leria, meet Brynn Halsted. We were talking about your unusual name. Have you two met before?"

Leria Monserrat stared at the beautiful woman who sat watching her with astonished eyes. Her pouty lips curled at the corners as she looked down at Brynn Halsted. "After all these years," she said in a low voice, looking the other woman up and down. "Brynn, what brings you to my humble bailiwick? Slumming?"

"Hello, Leria. It's a surprise to see you too," Brynn said warily. "It has been a lot of years."

"When we were sixteen, I think," Leria said with a wicked gleam in her eyes. "I believe the last night I saw you was the night your father died. No, it was the next night. The night you danced and became a star." The emphatic drawl on the last word was like slow-dripping acid. "I had to leave the company, remember?"

"What happened to you was your own doing, Leria." Though Brynn's voice dripped icicles, her eyes blazed like hot coals. "Yours, alone. You should have realized that after all these years." She clasped her hands in her lap to keep them from shaking. Never in her life had she wanted to slap someone as much as she did the mocking woman who stood before her.

Carmen looked from one woman to the other in amazement. She could see the cold fury in Brynn and the outright hatred in Leria. She didn't understand what was happening but she did know it had to stop.

"Leria," she said with a firm voice, "I think you'd better get your coffee and return to the class, don't you? I'll be up in a little while. You can prepare the students for Brynn's visit. She's going to drop by to say hello."

"Yes, I'll prepare them," Leria said without looking at Carmen. Instead she melodramatically peered around the booth and the floor. "Hmm, no cane, no crutch. How's that foot of yours, Brynn? Not all bent out of shape? I do hope you're at least able to get around on it, if not much of anything else these days." She did a drunken releve, rising on her toes in a wobbly fashion.

"Leria!" Carmen exclaimed.

Brynn watched the woman saunter away, her calf-length dress swirling around her shapely hips. She fell back against the cushioned booth and closed her eyes. *No,* she said to herself, *I won't go back there to that awful place. I won't!*

"Here," Carmen said quietly as she handed a glass of water to the shaken woman. "Drink some." After Brynn drank she gave her a curious look. "I guess you do go way back. I'm sorry about that. It's a small world after all," she said with a rueful smile.

"Yes, it is," Brynn agreed in a raspy voice. She stilled her trembling body.

"Do you still want to go up? I won't blame you if you don't."

"No, I'm fine. Sometimes demons just appear at the weirdest times. And there's nothing in the world you can do about that." She gathered her things. "Come, let's go."

The door to the studio was open and as Brynn and Carmen were about to walk inside, they heard Leria's shrill voice coming from the dance space just beyond the outer office.

Brynn stopped in shock as the words burst her eardrums. She slumped against the door. She was too numb to make her legs take her away from the filth that was spewing from the bitter woman.

". . . and thank God, Brynn Halsted is out of the business," Leria said. "To think that she was inflicting her awful style of dance on young impressionable minds was an abomination. Her leaps looked like an elephant trying to fly! She thinks the whole world is

sad over her career ending so tragically." Leria's laugh
dripped with derision. "What a joke! Poor deluded
thing will probably never know what we *dancers* all
know. Shh, and when she gets here don't y'all tell her!"
She laughed again. "That the dance world is sighing
with relief and overjoyed that it doesn't have to put up
with the spoiled prima donna who hadn't the talent of
a beanstalk! She was just Merle Christiansen's darling
and who knows *what* else, and that's the way she made
it, kiddos." She clapped her hands rapidly for empha-
sis. "Don't ever let me see *any* of you trying to imitate
that style in this room. Or I'll tell your parents to save
their money because you'll never amount to anything
in the dance world. If you need to emulate someone,
pick a real star like Jamison. And when Halsted comes
into this room . . ." She whirled around at the bark of
Carmen's voice.

"Leria! That's enough!" Livid, and shaking, Carmen
motioned for Leria to leave the room and then closed
the door on the astonished teenage students. "Brynn,
I'm sorry . . ." Except for Leria there was no one else
there. Brynn had gone.

A shaken Brynn struggled to start the engine. The
spots before her eyes made it difficult to see and she
backed out of the space narrowly missing a mother and
child who were walking behind her car. "God, help
me," she whispered. "Please."

At home, she rushed inside, thankful that her
mother was still out. She hurried up the stairs, seeking
the solitude of her room. She closed her eyes but soon
opened them when those hurtful words blasted her
ears. Her heart was tripping. What was Leria talking
about? What rumors? What things were they saying

about her? No talent? She and Merle lovers? She tried to laugh at that but only a short gasp escaped.

When she stopped shaking she got up from the bed and walked to the mirror. She stared at herself for a long time. She stepped out of her shoes and slowly began to undress. When she was in her bra and panties she stood stock-still, critically surveying her body in the mirror. She ran her hand over her strong, shapely body, smoothing her generous hips and muscled thighs. Elephant. No talent. Spoiled. Overjoyed? *Who* was happy that she could no longer dance?

Brynn swayed as her emotions gave way. Her throat burned with the tears that threatened to fall. No, she refused to become a victim of a venomous tongue. Nothing that vindictive, evil woman had said had an iota of truth in it. Nothing!

But as Brynn stood there, she posed in arabesque; poised for flight, supported on one leg, the other extended, and her arms in a graceful arc. She closed her eyes and the music she heard was that of her concert piece, *Ruby's Dream,* that she'd danced all those years ago, when she was sixteen and had danced in sorrow for her father who was with her in spirit that night: the night that the critics had discovered Brynn Halsted. "I *was* a star," she whispered.

Brynn moved around the room, remembering the steps, and as each movement became clearer, she danced to the beat that was thrumming in her head. It was almost as if she had gone back in time. The crowded theater. Her mother sitting sadly beside the empty aisle seat, tears glistening on her cheeks. Merle in the wings, encouraging her with signs of approval as she moved. *She was there!*

In the limited space of the bedroom she moved, did small leaps, her feet and the floor a meld. She used the space and danced. Her body felt as light as it had back then. She was young and the world was hers. When she tired, the image of her father's grinning face propelled her on the makeshift stage. "You're doing it, princess!" Those words rang through her head like the ominous clang of an alarm bell.

Brynn stopped. She searched the room as if she expected to see and hear her father. Suddenly limp from exhaustion, and emotionally spent, she sank to the floor as the room spun.

A week had passed since Wenona had come home and found her daughter on the floor, asleep, and her cheeks tear-streaked. Frightened that she'd been injured, she was relieved when Brynn woodenly explained what had happened. Wenona could only hold her fury back until she was certain that Brynn was okay. Then she wanted to get her hands around the neck of that vicious child, Leria Dickson. Wenona could only think of her in that sense since the last time she'd seen the woman was when she'd been a teenage vixen.

But a day after the incident, Brynn had fallen into a depression and had canceled her plans to return home. On the Saturday that she was to leave, Wenona had called Simeon Storey. There was no need to pick Brynn up from the airport, she'd told him. The man had been ready to fly out that day but Wenona had discouraged him. Brynn wasn't receptive to anyone, not even to her.

On Saturday morning, Simeon was brooding over a second cup of coffee. He hadn't spoken to Wenona yesterday and it bothered him. They'd spoken every day for the last week since he'd gotten that dreaded phone call. Whether Brynn liked it or not, he was scheduled to take the two-fourteen flight out of LaGuardia. Annoyed, he picked up the phone. "Hello."

"It's Wenona."

His chest tightened. "What is it?" he asked quietly.

Just as softly, Wenona said, "I think you'd better come." Her voice dropped to a dry sob. "I just don't know what to do anymore," she whispered.

"Is she in her room?"

"For now," Wenona answered. "But she'll start soon after breakfast. Simeon, her foot; I'm afraid. Can you come?"

"I'm already there." Simeon hung up the phone and stared into space. Finally he swore softly and stood. *Brynn, sweetheart, what's happened to you?* he thought. If he never did anything else he was going to bring the love of his life home. He should never have stayed away from her so long.

At six-fifteen the taxi made its way slowly from the Raleigh-Durham Airport. Simeon observed the pleasant landscape of the suburban countryside. Neat homes, deserted streets spoke of calm and unfettered lives. He could think of no better place to come for healing. Mrs. Halsted, Wenona, as she insisted on being called, had the right place in mind to put her own demons to rest. But his eyes narrowed. As hypnotic as it was, this was no place for Brynn. She was dying here. He hadn't rented a car because he was taking Brynn from this place immediately. He wasn't leaving without her.

Poised to ring the doorbell, Simeon could hear the music from where he stood on the front porch. The door opened and he met the worried eyes of Brynn's mother.

"Come in, Simeon," Wenona said softly. When he stepped inside, she kissed him on the cheek. "I'm glad you're here."

He was touched by her gesture, and realized how fast they'd become friends over the telephone. He would never have thought he would have been welcomed in her house after their meeting in New York. Strange, how common goals and problems brought adversaries together, he thought. He returned the gesture and followed where she led him to the living room.

"How is she?" Simeon sat down on the sofa, across from Wenona, who sat in a mauve, contemporary wing chair. He listened to the strains of his music. It was the tape they'd made together when they were working on his composition. His jaw hardened, and his eyes glinted. "Who is this Leria Dickson?" he snapped. Wenona had refused to go into details when she'd first called. "How could someone she hasn't seen in years affect Brynn like this?"

Wenona's mouth tightened as she remembered. "Age-old jealousy and spitefulness. Leria Dickson, now Monserrat, was a student at the Prince dance school along with Brynn and Claire," she said. "Merle was a young teacher there at the time as well as one of the principal dancers. Everyone at the school loved Merle and vied for his attention. The artistic director, Andre Prince, relied on Merle's vision of the young dancers, and gave him free rein in choreographing for them. Leria was one of the favorites in the young adult ensemble. No one could deny her talent. She was an excellent dancer, showing at so young an age the execution of the difficult Horton technique. Prince loved to showcase her and frequently gave her the plum roles. When the new season began, the artistic director's excitement infected the whole company. It was the twentieth anniversary of the Andre Prince Dance Company."

Wenona looked at Simeon pointedly. "As you know, Prince was only second in the city to the Alvin Ailey American Dance Theater and the media critics were waiting anxiously for the season. Prince had already put out news releases pertaining to the surprises he had in store for the New York audiences. He was going to surpass last season's performances." She smiled. "So you can understand the hype that was going on."

Simeon nodded. "I'm aware of what goes on," he said.

"Merle wanted Brynn to dance the new concert piece he was choreographing for opening night. When Leria learned that she wasn't going to be the principal dancer of the evening she was livid. Even Prince appealed to Merle to change his mind and give her the role. Merle refused, insisting that Leria's body shape was wrong for the character in the story he was telling. He said that the critics would laugh her off the stage and her career would be ruined before it got started." Wenona's eyes clouded and she winced in pain.

"What happened?" Simeon felt the older woman's anger.

"For months, Leria begged and cajoled Prince and anyone else who she thought could help her oust Brynn out of the role. She harassed Brynn unmercifully, but my daughter, intense in everything she does, was preoccupied with learning the dance, and pretty much ignored Leria's childish and spiteful remarks and silly schoolgirlish pranks like hiding her costumes and pointe shoes." Wenona rolled her eyes in disgust. "Leria even went after Merle in a woman's way. Sixteen. She was sixteen and tried to seduce Merle! Talk about an old black-and-white movie cliché! Leria knew the ins and outs of the game. Merle, in disgust, stayed away from the company for a week. Prince, ferocious at anything that affected his company, finally intervened. But for whatever his reasons he refused to ban her from the ensemble. He warned her to behave." Wenona laughed. "How do you tell a child-woman to behave?"

"Did she?" Simeon's jaw throbbed.

"Two weeks before opening night, strange things began to happen," Wenona said.

"Strange?"

"Yes. Of course the costumes had been made and were ready for dress rehearsals. Once, Brynn appeared onstage to the immediate laughter of the dancers. There was an indelible ink stain smack dab in the middle of her derriere. Brynn was startled and at first she wondered if her performance was that bad. She was horrified at the prank and as everyone else did, suspected Leria, who innocently denied that she'd ever do such a thing. For once, Prince lost his temper. Deliberately ruining expensive costumes was unfathomable. He warned her that if it was proven that she was the culprit she was out the door, pronto. But that's all he did. Leria stayed."

"What else?"

"Oh, there were other silly happenings that didn't directly affect the show or performances." Wenona looked away and for a moment seemed to drift.

"Wenona?" Simeon prodded.

"The night that Brynn's father was shot and taken to the hospital, Brynn was devastated," Wenona said. "Merle and Prince and the whole company rallied around her. Merle said that he would use her understudy, but Brynn refused. She'd visited her father and he made her promise to dance no matter what happened." Wenona stiffened. "The night of the performance, Leria squeezed herself into the understudy's costume and waited in the wings. Merle was beside himself but there was nothing he could do. The understudy never reported to the theater and since Leria had dogged Brynn's every step, she knew the role. Short of rearranging the program, Prince decided to let Leria dance if Merle gave the okay."

"What happened?"

"Leria was so astounded that Brynn hadn't begged out of the performance because her father had died during the night that she lashed out at her like someone gone mad. Brynn was mentally preparing herself before her cue. She was waiting quietly when Leria walked up to her and laughed in her ear. She told Brynn that she was a coldhearted monster to go out on that stage with her father lying in the morgue. What kind of love was that? she asked my daughter." Wenona wiped her eyes. "She told Brynn that all she cared about was the media hype and seeing her name in the newspapers the next day and she didn't care that her father was dead. Brynn was shocked. Prince, who had heard, grabbed Leria and pulled her away from Brynn. He bodily escorted her out of the building."

Simeon felt himself reliving Brynn's pain. His hand curled into a fist.

"I learned all of that later, because I was already in my seat," Wenona remembered. "But I saw the look of panic on her face when she first appeared on that stage. I knew something other than her father's death had upset her. And I was right." She paused. "She's like she was when she was in the hospital but only on the opposite end. Instead of zombielike, she's almost frenetic in her actions. It's not normal. I know my child, Simeon. She's headed for disaster. That's why you have to get her out of here."

"I intend to." The music stopped and he listened for sounds of Brynn coming down the stairs.

"She's only rewinding the tape," Wenona said. "It's

been like that all day. She hasn't had anything to eat since she stopped for lunch around one. I tried to get her to come down for dinner but she refused. I know she's exhausted." Moments later the music began again. She nodded her consent at Simeon, who stood and strode toward the stairs.

Simeon followed the music and stopped at a door at the end of the hall. He pushed it open. The room had been conformed to a dance space. The rolled-up rug occupied one long wall. Standing in front of it were the parts of the bed and the mattresses. A dresser was beside them.

Brynn's back was to him and she was executing the arm and hand movements that he remembered from their few sessions together. When she slowly began to lift her leg in a graceful arc, he stared in horror. The left foot she raised toward the ceiling was swollen to the ankle.

Oh, dear God. "Brynn." He called her name softly and when she turned to face him, his heart caved in his chest. Her eyes were wild and dark and full of fear. She looked blankly at him. He called her name again and this time her eyes focused.

"Simeon." Brynn looked confused. "D did you tell me that you were coming? I'm sorry, I must have forgotten." She tried to walk to him on her swollen foot and winced in pain.

"Damn." Simeon was by her side. "What have you done to yourself?" He caught her. Her arms went around his waist and he was overcome to tears. What had happened to the beautiful woman who'd left him only weeks ago with love in her heart and a new determination to carve a future? What he saw was only a specter of that beauty. They clung to each other and Simeon rocked her in his arms. Her hair was dampened from his tears that had fallen. Finally, Simeon sank to the floor and cradled her in his lap, carefully extending her leg.

Brynn clung to him, her head resting on his shoulder. "I've missed you, love," she whispered, tearfully.

As Simeon held and rocked her, he vowed he'd never let her out of his sight again. "It'll never happen again, sweetheart," he murmured against her hair. He stared at her foot, wondering how much damage she'd done. His brow was a mass of frowns. Had she injured it so she wouldn't even be able to teach? The horror of that refused to sink in as he tilted her chin and looked into her eyes.

"What were you trying to do, honey?" he asked.

A shadow crossed her face. "Dance," Brynn said almost in a panic. Her eyes darted around the room. "I know I still have the talent. I know it, Simeon," she breathed heavily. "What she said wasn't true. I know it. It's just that my foot wouldn't cooperate, but I did so many things. I performed *Princessa*. I danced *Ruby's Dream*. I did them, Simeon. She was wrong. No one said those hateful things about me. I know they didn't." She looked wildly about. "I even added new movements to our piece. They're beautiful, Simeon. Wait until you see what I've done—"

"Brynn!" Simeon's voice crackled and bounced off the walls of the nearly bare room. "Stop it!" He caught her shoulders and shook her. "No more!" He hated to see her like this. Where was his beautiful, practical Brynn? He stood and helped her up, careful that she didn't put weight on her foot. He walked to the stereo and turned off the music, removing the tape and putting it in his pocket.

Brynn's eyes widened. "What are you doing? You must see what I've—"

"No, Brynn." Simeon's voice had softened but the anger was still in his eyes and his mouth was grim. "Not now. We're going home tomorrow and you need to rest." He led her from the room and stopped at a door. "Is this your bedroom?" When she nodded, he led her inside and made her sit on the bed. "Don't move."

He found Wenona in the kitchen. "Would you fix her something light to eat? She needs her strength for the trip tomorrow. I'll take it up to her. Call me when it's ready." He hesitated. "Her foot needs attention. If you don't mind I'm going to call my father."

Wenona nodded. "Call him. Don't come down, I'll bring up a tray." She looked worried. "How is she?" Wenona could see how shaken Simeon was. He wasn't the same young man that had entered her house. He was like a man living in hell. She knew without a doubt that her daughter would be loved and cared for by this man. For the first time in a week her senses quieted.

"Not good," Simeon answered. "She's hurting inside."

"There's the phone." She turned to the refrigerator to hide her tears.

Fifteen minutes later, Simeon found Brynn still on the bed, staring at her foot. Her eyes met his and relief lightened his shoulders. The wild look had been replaced with one of remorse. He sat on the edge of the bed.

"What have I done?" Brynn whispered, catching his hands and gripping them tightly. "Look at me."

"We'll get the swelling down before we leave," Simeon said, keeping his voice firm. The least bit of tenderness on his part, he feared would send her into a fit of self-pity. "After you eat something, we'll get started on it." He reached down and gingerly ran his fingers over her foot. "You'll stay off of it the rest of the night."

"Leave?" Brynn asked.

"Tomorrow. We have an early morning flight."

Absorbing his words, Brynn nodded. "You came for me."

"And I waited too long."

He put his arm around her shoulders and held her. Simeon looked at Wenona, who was standing in the doorway holding a tray. Their eyes locked in understanding and Wenona sniffled as she set the tray on the bed and left the room without a word.

Midmorning on Monday, Simeon stood in the doorway of Brynn's bedroom watching her sleep. She wasn't tossing as much as she had when he'd first put her to bed yesterday evening. When they'd arrived from the airport late Sunday afternoon, Brynn was pensive and sleepy and wanted to lie down. But he'd insisted on bathing her foot again as per his father's instructions. Later, he'd had to force her to eat a light meal before she fell into bed. Once during the evening he'd spoken to Wenona and assured her that he would stay with Brynn. Simeon had slept beside her. In the morning he'd awakened her and soon after breakfast she returned to bed.

Frowning at the near-noon hour, he realized that Brynn might be using sleep as a barrier against her emotional pain. "Not good," he murmured and walked to the bed.

"Brynn." He sat down and gently ran a finger across her cheek. The featherlight touch caused Brynn to open her eyes. It took seconds for her to orient herself and she looked up at him with puzzled eyes.

"Simeon?"

He kissed her. "Sweetheart, you have to get up," he murmured.

Looking at the concern on his face and then around

at her surroundings, she sat up after glancing at the clock. "Is that the time?"

"You were exhausted," Simeon said. "But it's time to bathe your foot again."

Almost fearfully, she pulled the cover from her foot and stared. "It's fine," she said glumly and hid it beneath the cover.

"That may be," Simeon said, "but we still need to do this." He stood. "I'll get the whirlpool ready."

Brynn scooted up in the bed, listening to Simeon preparing the footbath. She knew that because of his diligent ministrations the day before and last night, the swelling had disappeared. She got out of bed and sat in the chair and waited.

The water was tepid and smelled of wintergreen. She eased both feet into the whirlpool, and then looked at Simeon, who was sitting on the bed, watching her with intent eyes.

"Thank you," Brynn said. She couldn't embellish on her feelings, knowing that she'd choke up. Simeon hadn't left her side since he'd arrived at her mother's house. Because of him, she'd gotten her head back on straight and wondered what would have happened had he not come for her. Her body still suffered from the ravages she'd inflicted upon it as if she'd been set upon by whirling demons.

Nodding his head in acknowledgement, Simeon continued to watch her. "How do you feel?"

"It's soothing," she answered.

"No. How do *you* feel?" Simeon said.

With understanding, Brynn sighed deeply. She looked down at her foot and back at him. "Better," she answered.

"No more crazy thoughts about who you are?" His voice was skeptical.

Eyeing him intensely, she said, "I'm Brynn Halsted,

former principal dancer with the Merle Christiansen Dance Company. Now retired and about to start her new career as company choreographer, and in many months to come, I hope, artistic director." At the last, her face shadowed. *When Merle is gone,* she thought.

Not totally satisfied, Simeon stayed where he was and asked, "None of that nonsense about your talent and star quality and vicious rumors milling about in your head?"

She blinked, remembering Leria's hateful diatribe on the sad life of Brynn Halsted. All these years, that pitiful woman had carried around such hatred in her heart for a young teenage girl, letting it fester until it became a rabid sore. What a bitter, unhappy person she must be, Brynn thought.

"Brynn?"

She shook her head. "Vicious words from a hateful, jealous woman. I allowed that hatred to seep inside me, rendering me emotionally unfit and irrational. Leria was always spiteful and will never change. I should have remembered that when I first laid eyes on her in the restaurant. Instead of feeling sorry for her I allowed her venom to seep inside, poisoning my brain. Now I am sorry for her, but more so for anyone she teaches. She'll always be a vindictive woman. But, I'll be fine," Brynn said quietly.

He wasn't totally convinced but he would accept it for now. "Okay." Handing Brynn a towel as she removed her feet, he turned off the whirlpool. When he returned from emptying the water, he gave the injured foot a critical look. Nodding in satisfaction, he made a sound of pleasure.

Wiggling her foot, and feeling no discomfort, she stood and walked to the bed and propped her feet up. She looked up at Simeon, who was staring at her thoughtfully. Brynn patted the bed beside her. When he was sitting next to her, she snuggled against him, wrapping her arms around his waist.

"Will you stay again?" she murmured.

"I wasn't going anywhere, sweetheart," Simeon said in a husky voice. He kissed her forehead. "Nowhere at all."

Thirteen

For the next few days Simeon stayed with Brynn, leaving only to check his apartment and bring back fresh clothes. During that time, they talked quietly about what she'd experienced. Simeon was still uncertain about her newfound views about where she'd been and how far she'd come and he watched for signs of backsliding. But yesterday when Claire had called with disturbing news he'd kept it from Brynn, unwilling to send her into another tailspin.

"You're worried." Brynn came up behind Simeon as he sat in the living room. Since yesterday he'd been quieter than usual and there was a dark shadow in his eyes. "Did something happen?"

Simeon looked up at her and realized that he had to tell her now. He took her hand and pulled her into his lap. She wrapped her arms around his neck and kissed him.

"Tell me what's bothering you."

"It's Merle. He's in the hospital." He felt her stiffen. "It doesn't look good."

She didn't move as his words penetrated. Thoughts whirled around in her head and all she could see was the first time she'd laid eyes on Merle when she was fifteen and a young dance student trying to learn her craft. He was the young dancer and choreographer who yearned for his own company. How the years passed so swiftly, she thought, suddenly seeing all the events in their shared lives. And it was all ending. "Why is this happening to me?"

"Brynn?" Simeon was startled by her remark and looked at her strangely.

"I want to go to him." She disentangled herself from his arms. "Now." Moving away almost dreamlike, she went into her bedroom and closed the door.

He had his eyes closed, and Brynn watched quietly from the doorway, unwilling to disturb him. Merle looked as if he were in a sound sleep but she was startled when his eyelids fluttered and his dull gray eyes found hers. He raised a finger, beckoning to her. She went to him and stood looking down at him too overcome to speak. Her chest rose and fell.

Merle held out his hand. "Star bud."

She smiled and took his hand, sitting in the chair beside the bed. He'd called her that all those years ago when they'd met and he'd first observed her in dance class. He'd said that she had the stuff that made stars. "Merle."

"I'm sorry, Brynn. Forgive me?"

Surprised, she said. "Forgive you?"

"I shouldn't have kept this to myself for so long," Merle said, blinking his eyes. "I should have told you sooner, honey." He looked disgusted. "It wasn't fair to you, and then to ask you to carry on . . . I'm not leaving you enough time to prepare, Brynn."

"Please, don't say that, Merle. Please." The lump in her throat made it hard to swallow.

"I thought that I would be one of those statistics that beat this thing. I really started treatment long before I told you." He grunted disgustedly. "Time was on my side, I thought, because I'm not finished with my

work." He shook his head. "So much to do yet. So
many ideas." He gave her a wan smile. "You have to
do it now, star bud. You understand. Always did know
what was in my head. You gave life to my work." He
gave her a piercing look. "Just like there are other star
buds coming along who will bring *your* creations to
life." He saw her lashes flicker and squeezed her hand.
"I know, honey. You'd rather be on the other end," he
said.

"You know I won't deny that," Brynn said quietly.
"But, I'm dealing with it." She paused. "Simeon is
there."

Merle studied her. "He is, isn't he?" When Brynn
nodded he said thoughtfully, "Have you two been working with his composition?"

"Yes." She thought about her frenzied visit with her
mother. "It's still incomplete." His eyes darkened.
"Why?"

In the old familiar gesture he pushed back his hair
that was no longer thick and wavy and made a small
sound of disappointment. "Years ago I heard what he
was writing. Even then I could see you with your own
fantastic style making glorious movement to his music.
That was a secret dream of mine." He moved his head
in time to the rhythm that was in his head, keeping
time with his hands. "Ah, what a vision." He caught
her look. "Now," he said, winking, "with things the way
they are, it would be a dance of love. The rhythms of
love would fill the theater to the rafters. It is like that,
isn't it?"

Warmed by the picture Merle painted, Brynn said,
"Yes."

He laughed. "So breathless, she is," he said to the
ceiling. "Come here." When she sat closer he hugged
her for a long moment and then kissed her cheek. "I

would have given you away, you know," he said in a tight voice.

Brynn nodded and sat down. She still held his hand. "There could have been no one else," she replied in a low voice.

"It's been one helluva ride, Brynn. Wish I could stay for all the encores to come, but . . ." His thin fingers moved helplessly. "You'll see to everything. I'm at peace knowing that."

Brynn's heart ached as she watched Merle drift. With one last squeeze to his hand, she leaned over and kissed him. His lids fluttered and a tiny smile lifted the corners of his mouth. "Sleep well, Merle," she murmured.

When Merle died three days later, Brynn was by his side. His fatigued parents, who had slept by his bedside for the last few days, had left the room to refresh themselves. He stirred once in his semisleepy state, opened his eyes, saw her, and closed them again. She heard him take his last breath but she sat there, stunned, refusing to believe that he was gone when the nurse who'd rushed into the room brushed her aside. Brynn left.

Simeon was scared. That cold feeling that had touched his soul once before was back and he wondered if history was repeating itself. Ever since that day when he'd told Brynn about Merle he couldn't get her response out of his head. "Why is this always happening to me?" Those words had made him shudder. Had he fallen in love with another beautiful, selfish, self-centered woman whose only aim in life was to feather her own bed? To the detriment of those around her?

The night that he had learned of Veronny's true nature had devastated him. He'd bought a ring and had planned an elaborate romantic evening starting with the proposal in Veronny's apartment. Minutes before he left his house to meet her, she called to say that she was still in the hair salon but for him to let himself into the apartment and she'd get there as soon as she could. Disappointed, yet anxious to get the evening started, Simeon waited. Her machine was on and two messages were left, each relating to possible theater work. The next call chilled him and in the same instant curdled his blood.

"It's Cal. Veronny, baby, where the hell are you? I thought you wanted to give me mine first, before you hurried on back to that man of yours. Damn. Guess all his money can't give you what you *really* want. The starring role in my new TV show. When you get this message, hightail it on over here. I'm more than ready, baby."

Simeon had cracked the bottle of champagne and waited. When Veronny had walked in he was feeling no pain, but he deliberately sat unmoving. He steeled himself when she sat beside him, kissing his lips, her soft fingers caressing his face. He cringed. She smelled of hair salon.

Deadly calm, he said, "You were at the beauty parlor."

Surprised, Veronny said, "Of course, darling. Didn't I say that's where I was going?"

"Was that before or after?"

"What are you talking about?" Veronny's eyes narrowed with curiosity.

"Before or after you gave Cal his?"

When she had tried to speak, Simeon put a finger to her lips. Just touching her revolted him. "Shh, no lies." He took the ring from his pocket and tossed it up and down in the palm of his hand. "As my wife I would have given you my love and whatever it was in my power to do for you. But that wasn't enough. You want the love of the world, and there I can't help you."

"H-how did you know?"

Simeon had walked slowly to the telephone and pushed the message button. When Cal's voice came on he shrugged into his jacket and walked to the door after dropping his key on the table. "See you in the movies." He closed the door softly behind him.

Simeon shook himself out of the past and into the present. He remembered that for weeks he was a numb man, acting by rote. Working, but listlessly. Art was there, and as with Simeon's mother and sister, not once had Art said, "I told you so." But Art was his cushion and had been there through the recovery. Not until Brynn Halsted wiggled her way into his heart had he ever equated the words *love* and *woman* in the same thought.

But Brynn's words still haunted him. Was he making the same mistake? But how could he be? He'd never felt for Veronny what he felt for Brynn, the woman who was his heartbeat. What, then, if history were repeating itself? He had no answers.

After Merle's death, it was no shock to Brynn that the Merle Christiansen Dance Company was still on its feet. News of his death had rocked the dance world and much speculation had been given to the company's early demise. But as saddened as the company was they were all professionals and life went on, especially the business of keeping Merle's dream alive.

Brynn still found it hard to enter the theater without attempting to seek out Merle for his opinion on something. A new dance step, a certain way to have a dancer move, whether she should have one or two dancers in a set area, or which side they should enter from. Things she'd hardly ever concerned herself with before now crowded her mind. Her day was filled with administrative duties, choreographing, working closely with the assistant artistic director, and now acting director, who relied on her heavily.

She knew that he was only following Merle's directive to lay it on her, preparing her for the future that would inevitably hold many surprises and setbacks, but in the end, always joy. At night, she went home happily tired, though pensive about her new roles.

She found that Saturday was the only day she devoted to working with Simeon. At times she wished that the score were completed because she wanted to be with him, not working, but doing things that didn't involve either of their professions. She loved that man and couldn't think back to the time that he hadn't been in her life. But tomorrow, Simeon had promised, they were taking a deserved day off. He was driving them to his place in the Pocono Mountains in Pennsylvania, not far from his brother Conrad's home. Maybe there, Brynn thought, she would get Simeon to tell her what was bothering him.

On Friday evening, looking forward to a restful weekend, Brynn was on her way out of the school when she passed by Claire's office and was surprised to see her still at her desk.

"I thought I was the last one in here," Brynn said. "What's up? Art out of town?" She knew that the lovebirds rarely spent time apart when he wasn't playing at the supper club. Claire often made it her business to be with him whenever she could. Taken aback by the look on her friend's face, she went inside. "What is it?" She sat down in the chair across from the desk.

"I miss him," Claire said. She fell back in her chair and looked around, lifting her shoulders in a helpless gesture. "I can't help it."

Brynn knew immediately that it wasn't Art she was talking about. Her eyes clouded. "I do too," she said simply. Almost as if their old friend, teacher, and mentor were in the room with them, Brynn cast a smile to the four corners. "He knows what we're feeling. Don't you think so, Merle?" she said softly.

"It all happened so fast," Claire said. She tapped the paperwork on her desk. "I was looking forward to doing this. Just relishing a new career. But, I just knew that he would be here to see me through the rough period. To hold my hand and guide me through my mistakes, like he always did when I was onstage." Her eyes glinted. "I know, out of all of us, you're hurting deep, Brynn," she said quietly.

"I'm okay," Brynn answered.

"On the surface, yes," Claire said, giving her a sharp look. "But you're torn up inside. I can see it if no one else can. You watch those dancers, put them through their paces, and I can see the yearning in every move you make. It's almost as if with just one wish, you would have things as they once were. One morning I saw you rush out of there on the pretense of going to get your notes. Only I knew where you went. You were praying for your old life back. As it was before your accident. You haven't fully accepted, Brynn. Have you?"

A chill passed through her almost as if Merle's ghost were hovering over her. *How would Claire know?* Brynn thought. The place she'd gone was the secret room she and Claire had found behind an old storage closet. Often the two would go there to rant and rave over what they thought was the too-harsh scolding they'd received from Merle or another hard-driving taskmaster.

"Of course I have," Brynn answered. "What are you talking about?"

Claire was smiling sadly. "It's me here, Brynn," she

said, and began to straighten her desk. "Don't go back inside yourself again, old friend. I'm here whenever you want to unload. I do it to you." She stood and her face had lost the shadow. "We set the date," she said softly, almost shyly.

"What? When?" Brynn said, recovering from the somber tone of their conversation.

"I decided not to have the whole big circus my parents were looking forward to," Claire said. "I told my dad that he can keep his money in his pockets. Just save the big bucks for his grandkid." She gave her friend a sly smile.

Brynn, who'd stood, dropped back in her chair. "You're kidding!"

"I kid you not, Auntie." Claire's laugh tinkled as she too sat back down, a wondrous look on her face.

"When?" Brynn was having a hard time finding which question she wanted to ask first.

"The wedding or the birth?" Claire said, then laughed. "Oh, I'm sorry for springing it on you like that. But there was never a right time." She splayed her hands. "Considering everything."

Brynn was out of her chair and hugging Claire around her neck, planting kisses on her cheek. "An aunt? At last! Oh my God." She plopped back down. "Are your parents going a little nuts over this?" she finally said.

"Some." Claire spoke in a matter-of-fact tone. "It just happened, and I wasn't going to get rid of it. Art and I made a baby and I wasn't going to kill it. Of course, my folks would have wished I'd put the horse before the cart, but . . ." Her eyes clouded. "I conceived the night we got back from Boston."

Merle had been buried in his hometown and Brynn remembered leaving Claire huddled in Art's arms after she and Simeon had exited the taxi they'd shared from LaGuardia Airport.

"I was out of it that night," Claire said. "I wanted Art near me, in me, I couldn't get enough of him. I didn't want to be alone."

Brynn remembered a similar scene after she and Simeon had reached her home. "I can understand," she murmured with empathy. After a moment she said, "So you're about four weeks?" Brynn calculated.

"And a half," Claire answered. "The baby is due in January."

"And the wedding?"

"Will you and Simeon be available two weekends from now?"

"You know we will be," Brynn said, feeling happy for her friend.

"I'm glad. I didn't want Art to say anything to Simeon until I told you." Claire smiled. "So tell your man to expect a call from him tonight. Art's like a kid trying not to spill the beans about what his parents secretly bought him for Christmas." She stood and turned off her desk lamp. "We're going to marry at St. Martin's and then have a small dinner party at my parents' home. That's where I'm headed. Mom still wants to do her thing, big to-do or not."

"You can't blame her, Claire. Only daughter and only child," Brynn said. Sadly she thought about her own nuptials and knew the pain her mother would feel with the absence of her husband at their daughter's wedding.

Almost guessing Brynn's thoughts, Claire said, "Has Simeon asked you yet?"

Brynn shook her head. She still wondered what was on Simeon's mind.

"He will," Claire said knowingly. "The man is crazy in love with you." She grinned. "But I guess I'm not telling you that the world isn't flat." Claire linked arms with Brynn as they left the building and walked to their cars in the small adjacent parking area. "Don't make him wait too long, sweetie. Life's way too short and we should all make our dreams happen while we're still able."

"Will you go away?" Brynn said as she unlocked her car door.

"Uh-uh. Art's working and we're so busy here at the school. Maybe around Labor Day we'll steal away for a few days." She opened the door of her black Volvo. "Call me Sunday night when you get back from Pennsylvania." Suddenly she clapped her forehead.

"What's up? Forget something?"

"And *what* I forgot to tell you!" Claire's eyes grew steely. "A little while ago Mom called me. She said that the crackerjack lawyer that Buddy hired was finally able to appeal the judge's no-bail ruling. He's free to walk around with decent folk again."

"What?" Brynn choked. "You can't be serious!"

"Sure as I'm standing here," Claire answered. "But we don't have to worry about a thing. The fool's got to be crazier than we know he is if he even thinks of coming near either of us. There's still a trial to be held." She blew Brynn a kiss. "Get that look off your face. He's probably on his way out of the country until the trial date. Don't forget to call me when you get back Sunday. But early. Before Art comes from the club." She winked.

After Claire pulled off, Brynn sat for a while waiting until the red haze of anger disappeared from her eyes. Where was the justice in this world for the victims? she wondered. Unconsciously, she wiggled her left foot, as if feeling a twinge of pain.

* * *

"Just a *little* something, you said?" Brynn stood in the middle of Simeon's "living space" as he called it. The big, two-level house was in a suburb of the town of Bartonsville, and was surrounded by woods. Only glimpses of neighboring houses could be seen through the trees, offering secluded privacy.

They were on the second level where Simeon was sitting on a kitchen bar stool watching Brynn walk around. He was amused because he'd noticed that whenever they entered a new place he could see her visualizing a dance space. Although they were supposed to be relaxing he knew that when she went downstairs, her feet would move and her body would sway in anticipation of dancing. The piano would do it for her. It had taken him weeks to convince her to come up here. He knew it was what she needed and was annoyed that it couldn't be for more than two days. Last night he'd sensed that the news about Buddy's release had disturbed her more than she was admitting.

He waited for her to come from the master bedroom and connecting bathroom where there was a huge Jacuzzi with a skylight overhead.

"I love it, Simeon." Gesturing toward the master bath she said, "There's room for a crowd in there."

"Just for two," he said softly, giving her an intense look. Her eyes crinkled at the corners in the way that he loved and as usual he felt the tickle that started in his belly and traveled downward to his groin. He slid off the stool and extended his hand. "Come. Let's go downstairs."

Brynn caught his hand, then slid her arms around his neck and kissed his lips. "Thanks," she murmured.

"For?" Simeon hugged her, inhaling the sweet-tart lemony scent of her hair. "Whatever it is, you're more than welcome," he said between kissing her ears, her neck, and capturing her lips.

"I needed this," Brynn said against his onslaught of affection. "My body is telling me exactly that." She leaned into him, stroking the hard muscles of his back.

"*Your* body?" Simeon was rising against her and he caught her hands as they moved tauntingly low. He was ready to love her where they stood but he wanted her relaxed. He wanted to knead the tension from her shoulders and lather her body with scented oils and then love her into a deep sleep. But she wasn't ready. "Sweetheart, I want to show you something," he murmured. He took her hand and preceded her down the stairs.

"Oh my," Brynn whispered, as she stood at the foot of the stairs, staring at the gleaming black baby grand piano in a far corner. She walked across the room that was bare except for a futon and a few straight-back chairs. The wood floor shone as if beckoning to dancing feet.

"Suitable?"

"Wrong word," Brynn breathed as she circled the room that ran the length of the house. Except for support beams the room was unencumbered, and one could move freely about. "It's similar to your home work space but this is so much more!" She turned to him. "It's fabulous and I love it."

"Thought you might. Sometimes I bring the guys and we cut up making crazy noises. Some dancers have used the space effectively."

"I bet they have," Brynn exclaimed, feeling a twinge of jealousy, and wondering if she knew any of them.

Exactly as he knew she would, Brynn stepped out of her sandals and ran her bare feet across the smooth wood. She wiggled her toes and flexed each foot.

"Uh-uh," Simeon said in her ear. He caught her waist from behind and held her against him. "No warming up. We're not here to work this weekend. Rest is the order."

Brynn squirmed around until she was plastered against his middle. She laughed. "You're kidding, right?"

"No, I'm not," Simeon said, trying to be firm, but caressed her breasts with his thumb tips. "Monday will be here soon enough," he rasped.

"Isn't that sad?" Brynn whispered in his ear. "I could stay here for the rest of the summer. You held out on me," she accused. "You knew I'd fall in love with it."

He let out a sigh of relief. "Then I'm glad you fell in love with me first or I would have my doubts." Then, quietly, he asked, "Do you really love me, Brynn?"

"What kind of question is that?" *So there is something on his mind,* she thought.

Simeon shrugged. "A silly one. Forget that." He pulled her to him. "Now where were we?" He nuzzled her neck.

"Right here," Brynn said, loving the way he was making her feel. But she sensed he was not telling her something. She was tugging his navy polo shirt from his khaki jeans, while planting little kisses on his mouth and playfully pulling on his chest hair.

"Ouch. I'm wounded." Simeon caught her teasing tongue and nibbled.

"Not as much as you're going to be," Brynn murmured. She had his belt buckle loose and was slowly pulling his pants zipper down.

"Brynn, sweetheart," Simeon said, husky-voiced, and melted at the look on her face. Her swollen lips trembled and she was silently asking to be loved. All his plans for loving her later, and slowly, flew to the four winds. "Lord, not here," he rasped as he hurried her up the stairs. In the bedroom he quickly lost his clothes. "Now, anything you want."

Brynn kept her eyes on his naked body as she let her skirt fall to the floor. She lifted her arms as Simeon pulled her blouse over her head. He unhooked her bra and she shivered as he slid her panties over her hips. He followed them down to the floor, raining kisses on her belly, and all the curves he could find, his tongue darting teasingly over the thin flesh of her inner thighs, and finally lingering maddeningly at her throbbing sex. He pulled her onto the bed, holding her against his stomach.

Closing her eyes and clutching his shoulders, she savored his tender touch on her searing skin. Her juices were beginning to flow and she wanted to be absorbed by him. When his hot tongue continued to taste her, suckling her nipples while his fingers probed her inner core, her body went limp. Bereft of his touch momentarily she knew he was searching in his jeans for his condoms and experienced delightful anticipation when he deftly reversed their positions, ready to love her.

Simeon stroked her sex and when she arced against his hand, whimpering and touching his erection, he moved rhythmically against her and was instantly sheathed in her moist heat. "You have me, love," he murmured, while thrusting deeply into her.

It was as if all furies were unleashed in their bodies as they sought and found the perfect tandem that they had come to know. But Brynn's body was electrified as it had never been before by him and she moved wildly, sounds of delight bursting from her throat. If she'd thought she'd been loved thoroughly by him she'd been mistaken. Never before had her roiling blood seared her flesh nor had his touch left burning sensations on her tender parts. His kisses were like nectar and she drank them as a thirsty woman while calling his name. Her response to him was frightening and she was bewildered by it. What happened that she wanted to lose herself in this man who loved her madly? It was almost as if they loved for the last time. Was what she'd been feeling this last week an omen? The thought sent her body in a writhing spiral as she clung to Simeon, wrapping her legs high up around his muscular thighs, straining to keep him inside her. A soft cry escaped as she sought to maintain the high but their bodies rose one last time and then shuddered as, spent, they fell, clinging limply to each other.

Simeon's body shook with the fiery tremors still coursing through his body. His heart was pounding in his chest and he gulped for air. The woman beneath him was as a stranger whose body he'd yet to explore. He thought he knew every erogenous zone and teased and pleased them to her ultimate satisfaction. But his every kiss, caress, and thrust had opened something new in her and her responses had driven him over the edge.

Nearly stunned at the ferociousness of their lovemaking, Simeon looked in wonder at the desire still in her eyes and in her touch as she caressed his back. Brynn clung to him and he saw the fleeting look of panic in her eyes before she closed them. He eased his weight from her.

"Brynn," he said softly, "what is it?" He kissed her eyelids and she looked at him.

"I love you so much, Simeon."

That wasn't what this was all about, he thought. "I know, sweetheart. I love you too." He studied her. "You're cold." He pulled the sheet over them and melded his body to hers. But when she closed her eyes, Brynn was still shivering.

Later Brynn stood on the upstairs deck after setting the table and bringing out the dishes of food. She smiled when she heard the soft curse in the kitchen where Simeon fought with a stubborn wine bottle cork.

It was after twelve o'clock, and she was amazed at the fleeting time. Tomorrow afternoon was fast approaching and would be all too soon to leave this lovely place, she thought. She gazed out over the natural wood railing where there was nothing but yards of full green trees. There were no houses on this side of the property and Brynn felt as if they were all alone on top of a mountain.

Though she should have felt at peace after such a sound sleep, Brynn could feel the frown on her face and the tensing of her body. Try as she would she couldn't shake the feeling of uneasiness that had captivated her during her torrid lovemaking with Simeon. She was certain that he'd felt it but after asking her that one question he didn't pursue it, and she hadn't answered because she didn't know herself.

The feeling that she was going to lose him terrified her. How could she explain something like that to him? She shuddered and leaned her head back. The strange feeling she had was unnerving. Since her accident and then her mother's and Merle's illnesses she hadn't felt like this. What else could happen? Seeking comfort, out of habit she touched her neck. Surprised to find it bare, she remembered that she'd left her necklace on the dresser. *Everything's fine,* she told herself. *We're in love and neither of us is going anywhere. At least not me,* she thought, vaguely thinking that with all their professions of love, neither had ever broached the subject of marriage. She couldn't imagine them going their separate ways.

Simeon watched Brynn with a thoughtful look as he poured the wine in tall crystal flutes. It was a long time since he'd seen her feel for her pendant. By now he knew that habit came after she'd had a troubling thought or she was thinking of her father. Wenona had just spoken to them yesterday and was feeling fine, so that couldn't be it, he thought. So why was Brynn bothered?

On a hunch, Simeon walked to the bedroom. He stared down at the sparkling emerald in its bed of gold. Feeling that he was intruding on something private between Brynn and her father, Simeon hesitated. But feeling so strongly that the woman he loved with every breath he took was distressed, he reached out and gently fingered the stone. He drew his hand back as if he'd touched a flame.

"Well, I'll be damned!"

Fourteen

Brynn stood up to help Simeon when she heard him at the screen door. She slid it open and he set the flutes on the table. As she uncovered a bowl, the smell of fresh dill and cucumbers wafted to her nose. "Mm, the salad smells delicious."

"You know we made too much. There are still three lamb chops left." Simeon joined her at the table.

"Then we'll just have them for dinner. You wouldn't mind, would you?" She tasted the broiled chop. "I know I wouldn't," she said, eating with relish, realizing that she was hungry.

Simeon was not quite recovered from feeling the emerald move under his finger and he tried to shake off the strange sensation that tickled his gut. He didn't believe in myths and omens or black magic, although he'd never sweated anyone else who did. Live and let live, he always thought. It hit him that Brynn believed that her premonitions were real. He knew that now and was curious at just how strong the bond had been between father and daughter. It was almost as if Joseph Halsted were communicating with her from the other side. Warning her. As far as Simeon knew, nothing else in that realm bothered Brynn. So was there something to this thing? Was she being warned of something! The chill inside him turned icy and he shuddered.

"Simeon?" Brynn was embarrassed. She'd been

making a pig of herself and just realized that Simeon hadn't spoken a word since he sat down. He'd never even answered her about dinner. Concerned about the shiver he made, she said, "Are you cold?" She looked at him and her eyes widened. "What's wrong?"

He was torn as he steepled his hands on the table. Should he mention it to her or let her find out for herself? Would she lose it and try to hurry home to see who was sick? Or call her mother in a panic?

"Brynn," he said quietly, "I need to know something."

She could only nod. He was scaring her.

"I know you still hurt inside." He steeled himself to continue. "Not as raw as you were months ago, but you have a lot of pain. Something has been weighing heavily on your mind. Merle's death knocked everyone for a loop. He laid a burden on you and you're doing your damnedest to measure up." He speared her with an intense look refusing to let her look away. "I know you still want to dance in the worst way. You haven't completely let go, have you?"

Claire's words, Brynn thought. "You know I haven't. But it's not because I'm not giving it my best shot." She tried to tease but instead lowered her head. "I'm trying, Simeon. I really am."

"I don't know," Simeon said. His voice was sharp.

"What do you mean?"

"There's more inside you to give, but you're holding back for whatever reason," he said, intensely. "You haven't made the separation yet."

"Separation?"

"Between dancer and teacher. You're still seeing how *you* would perform a movement. Or how Merle would tell you which way to move. Or in just what way he would handle a certain problem."

How could he know these things? she cried inside.

Simeon sat back and searched her face. "And besides that there's something gnawing at you that has nothing to do with the theater and I'm stumped as to what it is." He cocked his head. "I'm wondering if it could be me," he said in a low voice.

Brynn's head shot up. "H-how could you know that?"

His heart nearly stopped. So it *was* true! Remembering their lovemaking earlier he'd wondered if he had something to do with her angst. But he was surprised and not a little hurt that he was one of the reasons at the core of her pain. His finger tingled where he'd touched the loose jewel. Was she being warned against him? he thought.

"I felt it when we made love." Simeon's voice stiffened as if he couldn't believe what was happening. "Do you really love me? Do you want me?" Veronny flashed before his eyes.

"Oh no," Brynn said, shocked. She dropped her head in her hands. "It's true," she said woodenly. "It is us."

Simeon went cold. "What is us?" She shook her head in her hands. "Talk to me, Brynn," he said tersely.

She lifted her head and stared at him. "I just know there's something happening," she said. "I don't know why I keep feeling that it's between us. That w-we're not going to be together. Th-that we'll separate. Soon."

His eyes were hooded. "Is that your wish?" he said harshly.

Her eyes widened. "My wish? God no! How can you ask me that when I love you with all my being?" She looked bewildered. "It's as if you're there one second and the next you've disappeared. I seem to just want to hold on to you. Never to let you go. It's so fragile. The time, I mean. There just seems to be so little time before it h-happens. And I don't know what it means.

I—I haven't had those strange feelings, no, premonitions since, well, in a long time. I—I can see us being apart." Suddenly the air felt cloying and she pushed away from the table and went to the railing gulping huge breaths. Her heart was beating wildly. "What's wrong?" she whispered.

Simeon sat unmoving, still shaken by his own thoughts of losing her. And she was thinking the same of him. That she no longer wanted or loved him had left wounds so deep that he could put a fist through them. *Lord,* he asked silently, *what's going on?*

Brynn felt Simeon's arms go around her waist, hugging her close to his body. His chin was cradled in her hair, and she shuddered and leaned back into him. He rocked her back and forth and all she wanted was to stay like this forever. Not to think. Unconsciously, she touched her throat.

Her gesture brought a troubled frown to Simeon's brow. That was at the root of her anxiety. "Brynn, there's something you need to know."

On the sofa in the cool living room, Simeon waited until she tasted the red wine he'd poured for them. He took her hand. "The last time that you removed your pendant, was it okay?"

"Of course. It's on the dresser." Brynn gave him a curious look. "Why?"

"The emerald is loose," Simeon said. He watched her closely.

"What?" She stared at him and a scared look came into her eyes. "It can't be. It's never loose. I don't believe that part of the stone's prophecy!" Then as if realizing what it meant, she said in an awed voice, "Oh my God. Simeon, it's you! Are you . . . ?" She couldn't speak the words.

"No!" Simeon said sharply. "I'm not sick. So get that out of your head. You're not going to lose me too."

Brynn was silent. Her shoulders sagged against the sofa. "I could feel something," she finally said when she met his eyes. "How did you know?"

"I had a feeling," Simeon said. "Ever since this morning, even before then, I sensed something was wrong. I was drawn to it when I saw you touch your throat. I had to know." He left the room.

When he returned, Simeon held out his palm and Brynn took it from him. She touched it and the expected wobble didn't unnerve her as it could have. Simeon had prepared her. She set the pendant with the loose emerald on the table in front of the sofa and stared at it.

"Are you okay?" Simeon asked.

Brynn nodded. "I still think it has something to do with you and me."

"No," Simeon said firmly. "I'm in your life, sweetheart. You can believe that if you don't believe anything else. You're the woman I want and will always want. If marriage isn't in your plans now, then I can wait. For as long as it takes for you to decide that you'll wear my gold band on your finger."

Stunned, Brynn stared at him. "You just asked me to be your wife!"

"I did, didn't I?" He smiled. "Guess I've wanted to for a long time now but I had to make sure it was me you fell in love with and not some chivalrous knight to your rescue."

"You thought that?"

"You needed someone. I was there."

"You were hurt in the past," Brynn said softly.

"There was someone a long time ago." His eyes narrowed as he thought about that time when his world had come to a stop. He looked at Brynn, who was watching him with love in her eyes. "Her name was Veronny. She was beautiful, talented, and wanted a career as an actress. It was her passion." After a brief pause he told Brynn about the woman who'd soured his soul.

When he finished, Brynn took his hand. She understood. "I didn't fall in love with you because I was grateful, Simeon."

"I realize that now." Simeon ran his knuckles up and down her cheek. "I had to be sure because this is going to happen only once in my life, sweetheart."

She brought his hand to her lips and kissed the strong, slender fingers. "I know."

"Then is that a yes?" he breathed.

"Yes." Brynn brushed his lips.

Simeon didn't let her go but deepened the kiss hungrily, savoring her sweetness. He closed his eyes against the image of watching her walk out of his life. Separation? Never happen!

"Ooh," Brynn squealed at his bear hug.

"Sorry, sweetheart. I was just holding on."

"I'm here, Simeon. For always."

After a while, each stared at the emerald on the table and knew there was still an unresolved issue. Simeon broke the silence.

"What are you thinking about that?" he said softly, nodding at the stone. "Since I'm not letting you out of my sight, it can't be me, so get that out of your head."

Brynn stirred from the cocoon of his arms. "I only know that it's someone close to me," she said solemnly. "I know that now." She trembled. "I don't know what I'd do if anything happened to you. It would be more than I could bear." She shrugged helplessly. "So much tragedy in so short a time . . ." Her voice broke.

"Shh," he said. "I promise you I will be fine." He pulled her back into his arms. She was quiet for a long time when Simeon asked, "Would you like to go out for a while? Walk down by the lake? It's peaceful there."

"It's even more so here," Brynn said, loving the feel of his hard body. "I was just thinking about how odd life can be sometimes. So just one minute and unfair the next."

"Buddy?" Simeon asked quietly. He wanted her to talk about her feelings.

"Uh-huh. Claire and I talked about it last night. Uncanny," she said in disgust. "I bet there are hundreds of deserving men on Rikers Island that should be walking the streets now. Instead, the one slimy criminal in the barrel escapes his due."

"He'd better enjoy his freedom now because his days of walking free are very few." Simeon's eyes darkened.

Then with an ease that surprised her, Brynn put the evil man from her mind. By now, she knew that whatever the stone prophesied, she would know all too soon what the future held. When the time came for her to know she would face it. The love of her life was in her arms. And once she called the other two dearest people in her life, all she would have to do is wait. And pray that her loved ones would be safe from harm.

Brynn stood. "I'm going to call Ma and Claire," she said simply.

Later, at seven o'clock, the sound of music drew Simeon downstairs where he saw Brynn lying very still on the futon with her eyes closed. Her rapid eye movement told him that she wasn't asleep and the book lying on her belly was a definite giveaway. He knew that she was mentally marking her choreography. Last week they'd been overcome when they realized the score was finished. She'd immediately notated the final movements and was so eager to try them together it was all he could do to contain her. But this was to be a weekend of rest, not work. He sat on the floor beside the futon.

"Hey," he said when she opened her eyes. "No working, remember?"

"It's going to be so beautiful. I can see it."

A lump caught in his throat at the sadness in her voice. He knew what she was thinking. It was going to be one of the hardest things for her to do to select the dancer for her choreography. And it would take months for him to face the reality of a stranger performing at the premiere.

She swung her legs to the floor making room and he sat beside her. "It can be nothing else," he said, successfully masking his own feelings. "It's *your* vision."

"Merle would have loved to be sitting up there in the rafters, that stern look on his face. Of course I think we would have differed on a few things, but we'd have gotten through it." She brushed slender fingers over Simeon's brow. "I'm sorry. I know what it meant to you. All those years and now . . ."

He caught her hand. "Don't. You and I'll be sitting up in the rafters that first night. Merle will be there too." Weeks ago they'd decided that another pianist would play Simeon's score. He smoothed her curls. "Together we'll discover what needs fixing."

"They're going to be tough, Simeon." A new season always brought new fears, new stars, and old critics with new ways to harp and nitpick. Her new role would be sharply watched as well as her premiere ballet. Would she stand up to the pressure? Meet Merle's expectations?

"Then we'll be tougher."

A shudder went through her. "I'm so afraid that I won't be ready. The dancer won't feel it in time. She may not even get it! We've only a few months! Maybe

we should postpone until next year. I'll be better prepared what with all the other duties I now have . . ."

"No." Simeon sat up straight and caught her by the
shoulders. "That's not what you really want to do, is
it?" His voice was firm. "By next year Nick will be gone.
There will be no miraculous expanse of time to mount
a new ballet. Your season will be helter-skelter at best,
filled with revivals, ancient repertoires, and guest choreographers. Is that what you plan for Merle's legacy?"

Brynn quieted and her shoulders relaxed. In anything she ever did she had given her all to perfection.
Merle knew that and to do less with his company would
be to ruin his life's work. "No."

"All right then. A few months is not a lot of time so
you know what you have to do, and like yesterday, don't
you?"

"Fill the role," Brynn answered.

"Anyone in mind?" he asked, satisfied that she was
once more focused on her goals.

Her shoulders drooped and she shook her head.
"No one."

He knew what she was feeling. She'd seen only herself dancing the role she created. Simeon faced her
squarely. "Not really true, is it?"

Brynn looked at him curiously. "Why do you say
that?"

"Take yourself out of the picture, Brynn." He waited
a moment. "Now who do you see?"

Emotionally detached she answered readily, "Layle
Ambris, Paige Toure, Marvis Chambourd, and Virginia
Makei." Admiration sprang into his eyes and Brynn
knew Simeon respected her choices.

"See?" he said, a smile tugging at his mouth. "They
were in your mind's eye all along." He cocked his head.
"Bet that bourree movement was meant for Layle,
wasn't it?"

Without thinking, Brynn nodded. "It suits her and she could execute the transfer of weight from foot to foot so easily and without the least bit of difficulty." She wondered at his grin, and then realized what she was doing. "No wonder you're so successful at anything you attempt to do. You're in tune with the world, aren't you, Mr. Storey?"

"With you," Simeon said with a solemn look. "In all that you do."

"Truly amazing," she said, smoothing his cheek with a gentle caress.

Simeon caught her palm and kissed it. "Yes, you are." Then, with raised brow, he said, "One stage, one dancer. Have you narrowed it down?"

Acknowledging her dilemma, Brynn gave him a rueful look. "I think Paige and Layle. But I'd like all of them to audition."

"Good. I think before long you'll have your star. Merle knew how to fill his company," he said. "Future divas all." When she would have dropped her eyes he tilted her chin to hold her gaze. "And you will become the new star maker."

Suddenly Brynn was aching to get started. "Do you think Claire would beat up on me if I asked her to call them for a Monday meeting?"

"Whoa," Simeon said, laughing at her excitement. "I said yesterday, sweetheart, but give a guy a break. Art's only time with Claire this weekend is Sunday night and you want to call her to make a slew of phone calls. How about a call on Monday to meet on Tuesday? Soon enough?"

Brynn fretted. "But today's only Saturday," she persisted.

"And her and her mother's heads are filled with wedding stuff. Remember?"

"Darn!" But then she leaned back against his arm.

"I still can't believe it," she said, a smile brightening her face. "I know her parents are wild. A son-in-law and a baby practically in one breath. And me an aunt!"

Simeon was amused at her reaction to Claire's news. He'd never known how she felt about children until now. He'd supposed that the woman he chose for his wife would automatically want to become the mother of his children. But was Brynn's joy over becoming aunt to Claire's child satisfying enough for her to forgo having her own? As old as he was getting, once they were married he didn't want to wait forever before fathering a child. Would she be too wrapped up in the company even to think about getting pregnant? Unable or even unwilling to break her striding toward filling Merle's big shoes?

"What is it, love?" He had become so strangely silent.

"We never talked about children, Brynn. Would you want ours?"

How oddly he posed that. Brynn was thoughtful. This time last year, a man in her life, a husband-to-be at that, and a child growing in her womb were like booking a trip on a commercial flight to the moon. For some others, but definitely not on *her* goal list.

She was taking so long to answer that Simeon found himself holding his breath. Was he right?

"Years ago when I heard my mother crying late one night after my father got home from work I stopped asking for a brother or a sister." Brynn frowned at the memory. "I listened to them talk softly to each other, my father telling my mother that it wasn't God's will that they could have more babies but that they had a beautiful daughter that would fill their lives as if they'd had a houseful of kids. They were blessed, he said. My mother said it was their punishment for giving me up for the first five years of my life." She hesitated, sadness creeping into her voice. "I wondered what it would be like to hold a little baby brother or sister in my arms. I was sad that unlike some of my schoolmates I would never have that chance. But later when I was so into my own little world, being doted upon by all the adults in my life, I wondered whether I would have loved a tiny usurper. Was there enough love in my heart to give to that little person?"

Brynn smoothed the tightness from Simeon's mouth, and fingered the hard ridge of his jaw until it softened under her tender caress. "Don't be frightened, love," she murmured. "I've learned a lot about what I'm made of. There's infinite love in me for my man and his children. I'd thought that my career would sustain me until forever. Yes, Simeon, I want to have children with you. My own tiny babes, to love and to spoil." Her body warmed just thinking how the precious babies were made. She leaned into him teasingly, her hands sliding down to his chest, her fingers feathering the nipples through his shirt, and like the temptress she'd become, smiled wickedly when he got her message.

Remembering his earlier thoughts, Simeon pulled Brynn up and hurried upstairs. In the master bedroom he became a wizard shedding his clothes in the wink of an eye, and zipping into the bathroom. In seconds the giant whirlpool was beginning to fill.

Turning to Brynn, he began undressing her. The smoldering desire in her eyes and the gentle touch to his burgeoning sex nearly blew his skull off, and he worked feverishly with nimble fingers, as if tickling his eighty-eights. When she was naked against him, he devoured her mouth. "I'm not frightened, sweetheart."

"Bitch." Buddy watched Claire leave her mother's house, smiling and waving and skipping down the stairs as if she were tripping on clouds. She had that same big smile on her luscious lips as she'd had when she was thirteen years old. "Getting married, huh?" he sneered in the darkness of his car. Unnoticed, he started the engine of the borrowed Maxima and followed Claire as she pulled away from the curb.

Like a whirligig his mind worked overtime. For months the pent-up fury had been constantly fueled by images of Claire Jessup. His fantasies on how he would have her became nightmares, waking him up in cold sweats to the anger of his cellmate. During the day she was like a fever turning his blood hot and cold. But he knew once he had her she would be calling his name. Thinking about it made him hard and he gripped the wheel to maintain control.

"No, baby, not tonight," Claire said. "No more talk of wedding plans until tomorrow." Her voice was firm.

Art chuckled into his cell phone. "Now don't be so hard on your mother, baby. She's getting her kicks out of doing this thing, so cut her some slack."

"But Friday, all day Saturday, and now tonight? No way." Her voice softened. "What time should I expect you? Do you mind spending a quiet evening at home?"

"I'd like nothing better," Art said in a sexy voice.

Claire blushed. "Call me when you start looking for a parking space and I'll put the chops in the broiler."

Art chuckled. "Nah," he said. "I'm not going to be *that* hungry for chops. They can wait for a little later." He still had a smile in his voice when he said, "Baby, I left your apartment key on my dresser, so don't get scared when you hear the bell."

"Have no fear, honey. Just drive carefully. I'll be waiting."

Though tired from running with her mother, she

was happy that they'd accomplished so much. Unwilling to lay out ridiculous sums of money for a lavish affair in a hall on such short notice, Claire was firm on what she and Art wanted. The small guest list was finalized and the invitations addressed. Her mother would mail them tomorrow. Her aunt who worked for a caterer would provide the food, and she entrusted her aunt and her mother to select a delectable menu. Her father would take care of the liquor and other beverages. All she wanted to do was to have a party where all could come toast the couple's future and enjoy themselves.

Claire pulled the plug from the tub, reluctant to climb out of the warm water scented with her favorite vanilla fragrance. She toweled herself and bathed her skin in the same complementing lotion, then walked naked to her bedroom. As sleepy as each of them would be she knew that dreamland would remain a faraway place. At least until their love was satisfied, she thought wickedly. As Art had, she chuckled and said, "Yeah, later for the chops."

From her lingerie drawer she selected a man-killing royal blue teddy edged with ecru lace. The thigh-high-cut garment, naughty but nice, teasingly covered her feminine pleasures and the thin spaghetti straps were ineffective in keeping the wispy fabric from demurely showing her deep cleavage. Thoughts of her man made her nipples tauten as she stared at her body in the mirror. No matter how she twisted and turned she could see no evidence of the tender life that was growing inside her. She hoped it was a boy so at last her father could have a grandson.

Claire frowned at the soft sound she heard coming from the kitchen, then shook her head in annoyance. If those mice were back she'd pitch a boogie-woogie again, she thought. Once this year was one time too many! She'd have to speak to her landlady first thing in the morning and suggest she change her exterminating company.

"My, my, my, my, my! All for me, darling?" Buddy sniffed the air. "And as sweet-smelling as a vanilla ice cream cone on a Sunday afternoon in the springtime."

Claire whirled in horror, staring at the grinning man standing in her doorway. Her body froze. "H-how did you get in here?" she stammered as she looked about wildly. Her hands were wrapped around her middle as if to save the precious life. Because as sure as she breathed she knew that Buddy Randolph was going to rape her. But she had to fight him. She had to, she thought, as her glance searched the room. There was nothing within her reach to use as a weapon. In the quiet block and the equally quiet brownstone she knew there was no one around to help her. *Oh, God, please.*

Buddy laughed when he saw her panic. He stepped between her and the windows. "Now you wouldn't want to hurt yourself trying to jump to the ground, would you? Even second-floor falls can injure you for life. End your dancing career like your diva friend. Is that what you want?" Laughing nastily, he whipped off his jacket. "I'm getting naked as a jaybird for this one, darling. We have all the time in the world. I'm gonna make it real nice for you." His eyes raked over her like a greedy falcon about to swoop down on a cowering prey.

Claire screamed and swung, flailing and kicking, trying to aim for his groin.

Buddy eluded her wild swings and continued to undress. "Ain't nobody in this building but you 'cause I already checked. Lover boy is playing his jazz-loving heart out for some jerks, so it's just you and me. Make all the noise you want. Suits me fine 'cause that's what I like to hear." He grabbed for her but Claire swung her fist and caught him on the chin. His eyes glittered as he lunged toward her. "Yeah, baby, yeah."

Claire screamed as her lingerie was torn from her body and fell in a rag at her feet. "Art," she cried as Buddy flung her on the bed. She rolled toward the edge. When he pulled her back she kneed him and he yelled and slapped her sharply across the face.

With one hand she pulled his hair and with the other raked his cheek. She screamed and yelled, "Art!"

Buddy became enraged. "Not what I want to hear, darling," he said, and punched her twice on each cheek. "What's my name?"

Art had his hand poised to ring the bell when he heard Claire scream. "What the hell . . ." He kicked the locked outer door to the building. "Claire," he yelled. "What the hell's the matter?" He banged and kicked again. "Damn! Claire?" He was at the top of the stairs and he leaned over trying to peer into her living room window but couldn't see inside. Art heard a crashing sound in the rear of the house. He took the stairs two at a time and raced around the building toward the noise but all he saw was a man scrambling over a fence. He looked up to see Claire at the bedroom window. She was naked and crying.

"Claire, open the door," he barked and ran back to the front of the building and up the steps. His heart beat wildly as his imagination got the best of him.

"Art," Claire moaned.

"Damn," he croaked when he saw her face. "Sweet Lord."

Claire was still naked and she shivered in Art's arms as he led her back inside the apartment and to her bedroom. He saw her tattered lingerie and swore but found her robe and slipped it around her shoulders. "How did he hurt you?" he said through clenched teeth.

Her body vibrated with shock wave after shock wave and she couldn't catch her breath. The horror of what might have happened churned her emotions as if she were being whipped around in a giant bowl of batter. Her teeth chattered when she tried to speak and she bit her lip but winced from the pain where she'd been hit.

"Baby," Art said gently, "I have to know. You need attention right away, if—"

"Y—you stopped him," Claire stammered. "Buddy didn't have time to r—rape me."

Art closed his eyes and swore as he held her tenderly. "Buddy Randolph," he said softly. There was murder in his eyes.

Fifteen

At midnight, Brynn picked up the phone, always fearing that a late-hour call was bad news from her mother. With barely contained breath she said, "Hello."

"It's Art, Brynn."

"Art?"

Simeon sat up in bed when he heard, a tight knot forming in his chest. He waited.

"Claire was assaulted. Attempted rape. She's at North General Hospital. I'm staying with her through the night so I don't know whether you want to come . . ." Art stopped when he heard the cry.

Brynn dropped the phone and jumped out of bed, racing out of the room.

"What the . . . Art? What the hell's going on?" Simeon heard Brynn gagging in the bathroom and he stood ready to go to her. "What happened?"

Art repeated the grim news.

"My God." Simeon dropped back to the edge of the bed, staring at the phone as if it were something foreign, then listened in shock as Art told him that a search was already underway for Buddy. He hung up assuring Art that they'd be there.

Brynn was leaning over the bathroom sink, dousing her face in cold water. Her gown was soaked down the front and water was splashing everywhere. She couldn't seem to get enough of the cold and wished she were in the shower. Ice. She needed the numbing powers of ice. She turned wild eyes to Simeon when he walked into the bathroom.

Simeon turned off the water faucet. "Brynn, take this off. It's soaked." He lifted the gown over her head and tossed it in the bathtub. She was naked and he grabbed a towel and patted her dry. "You're like ice," he said, rubbing her skin briskly.

Weakened, Brynn sank to the edge of the tub and held her head in her hands, shaking it from side to side. She moaned. "I knew it. Oh God, oh God, this can't be happening. It can't! Why?"

He took her by the shoulders and pulled her up. "You have to get something on," he said firmly. "Claire is sedated but Art thinks she might need you when she wakes up. Her parents are basket cases and her mother had to be sent home. Come, I'll help you get ready."

In the bedroom, Brynn sat woodenly on the bed while Simeon searched her drawers for fresh lingerie. She watched with panic in her eyes. Mechanically, she stepped into panties and then hooked her bra. She put on the same slacks and blouse she'd worn earlier on the drive home from the mountains.

"Ready?" Simeon was dressed and waiting. He extended his hand and she took it. They walked to the door and when he opened it, he turned to her with a puzzled look. "Forget something?" he asked.

Brynn pulled back. "I can't," she whispered. "I can't."

"What are you talking about?" Exasperated, he said, "Claire needs you."

The look in her eyes turned dull as she stepped back in the foyer. "Why is this happening to me?" she whispered. "I don't understand. What have I done?"

Simeon looked at her strangely. Her same words

when Merle had died. "It's *Claire* who was assaulted, Brynn." She'd backed up inside the apartment. Time stopped as, disbelieving, he stared—and waited. "All right then," he said with tightened jaw. "Lock up behind me." He turned on his heel and sprinted down the steps, knowing instantly and with fear that the woman he'd just left was not the woman he was going to marry.

At noon, Brynn lay in a huddle in the bed. Earlier she'd stirred when the school called asking whether she was coming in. They'd heard the news about Claire. She'd said no and hung up. Ruth had come and quietly performed her duties, fixed a meal, and then left. Brynn had called her mother to tell her about Claire, and Wenona had been horrified. Still numbed by the vicious attack on her friend, Brynn went into herself, unable to shed the cold that traversed her body. It was a mild day yet she was chilled to the bone. There had been no call from Simeon, and Brynn wondered where he was. He must have left the hospital by now, she thought. Seeking solace from sleep, Brynn closed her eyes. There was no pain, no horror in sleep. She slept and awakened throughout the day. Monday evening, still unwilling to rouse herself, she slept.

Tuesday at seven in the morning she awoke. Brynn looked quietly at her familiar surroundings. She was in her own bed, not in that horrible place she'd been transported to, that she remembered so vividly. She felt as though she'd taken her own odyssey through a valley filled with demons attacking her from every angle. The cold, stark reality was that all the demons had her face! She was her own worst enemy! Only there had been one face that hadn't been hers. Simeon had looked at her with censure through amber eyes that burned like golden fire. She closed her eyes against the disappointment and sadness.

Brynn reflected on her torturous night. Her mind played back all her thoughts since that early morning call from Art. The strange look Simeon had given her when he left. The accusatory silence from her mother when Brynn told her she hadn't gone to see Claire yet.

It's Claire who was assaulted, Brynn. Simeon's words slapped her as if a brick had been slammed into her face. She remembered what she'd said to invoke such scorn in his voice. *"Why is this happening to me?"* she'd said. Her hands flew to her mouth to cover the hoarse cry. "To *me?"* Her body went limp. "Lord, what have I done?" she cried, then in horror remembered. She'd said those very same words when Merle was dying! Now she knew what she'd seen on Simeon's face, and her fears became a reality. He was leaving her!

Flinging her feet over the side of the bed, Brynn held her head in her hands, moaning shamelessly. *She* wasn't the one whose body was ravaged and ultimately claimed by death. *She* wasn't the one who'd lost a breast to an insidious disease. *She* wasn't the one who'd been beaten and subjected to a woman's deepest, secret fear.

There was nothing she could do for Merle or her mother except silently ask their forgiveness. But Claire was the one hurting now. Maybe her dearest friend *would* forgive her.

Within the hour Brynn was dressed and hurrying from the house. When she reached the hospital her heart was still fluttering. *Forgive me, Claire,* she prayed. Outside of the room, Brynn stopped. She couldn't face anyone now but Claire. The accusation in Simeon's and Art's eyes would be more than she could bear right now. Stepping inside the quiet room she breathed easily. Her prayers had been heard. In the shade-drawn light Claire lay with her eyes closed as Brynn stared in horror at the blue-black bruises on her face and arms. She was startled when Claire opened her eyes.

"Brynn." Claire held out her hand. "Are you all right?"

A stifled cry escaped and Brynn flew to the bed and caught her friend's hand. "Me? You ask about me and you're lying here—"

"Shh," Claire said, patting Brynn's shoulders. She waited until her friend quieted and moved to the chair. She stared at Brynn's drawn face and noticed that she had the same panicked look in her eyes as she did when she had been the one lying in a hospital bed. "I'm going to be okay," she said.

"I'm sorry I wasn't here for you," Brynn said. "Will you forgive me?"

"There's nothing to forgive," Claire said. "I understood what you were feeling." She looked thoughtful. "Now I know the hatred that was in your heart for Buddy for what he took from you. Sunday night I could have killed and not given a second thought to what I'd done. I was ready to spend the rest of my life in jail, gleeful that Buddy was rotting underground. I had murder on my mind. It was consuming me." She looked curiously at Brynn. "Is that how you felt?"

Remembering brought a throbbing ache to Brynn's head. "Yes." But the calm voice and the eyes without anger baffled her and she asked, "You don't feel the same, now?"

A shadow crossed Claire's face and it took a moment for her to answer. "I feared more for Art." She saw Brynn's confusion. "Art was going to do it for me. He was going looking for Buddy. If he'd found him, Buddy would be dead and Art would be in jail. *I* may as well be in jail if that happens. I wouldn't want to go on with my life knowing that he was dying a slow death because of me." She paused. "I asked him not to leave me. And he didn't."

Brynn couldn't understand why it had taken her months to rid herself of murderous thoughts and self-pity when her friend had done it overnight.

As she noticed Brynn's look, Claire's eyes darkened. "But I hate him, Brynn. God forgive me, I still hate him," she said woodenly. "It will be a long time before I get the foul smell of him from my nostrils and the feel of him off my skin. I want to scrub the grubbiness away until my skin is raw." She looked at Brynn with fearful eyes. "I'm so afraid that this hatred will stay in my heart until it drives me insane. If that happens, then what kind of life will Art and I have together? I'm trying hard to let it go. If I feel like this and I wasn't raped, how must all those women feel who didn't get away? Lord, Lord, I am so thankful! Now I know what my mother felt all those years ago."

"Oh, Claire," Brynn said with tears in her eyes.

"We prayed," Claire whispered. "Neither of us was so strong and forgiving. We had help. Reverend Johnson came and prayed with us. Art and I prayed together. All day and night."

"You let him go?" She wasn't so sure that Art wasn't combing the streets right now.

Claire smiled and then winced as her cracked lips stung. "Art is okay. I'm not worried about him now. He wouldn't do anything to jeopardize separating us. We need each other. Oh, Brynn, don't look like that. We're not so holier-than-thou and unfeeling. We're hurting inside. My body is sore. I was abused, shamed, and my spirit almost broken. I'm still angry but it's not overtaking my life as I was about to let it do. Buddy Randolph was an evil, spiteful boy and grew up to be an evil, unctuous, angry man. I'm not going to allow his black-heartedness to encircle me, robbing me of the life I planned with the man I love and who loves me. I'm going to be okay, Brynn. I have my life and to God I'm thankful." She blinked her eyes. "And I know He'll give me and Art other children to love and spoil. I believe that."

"You lost the baby?" Brynn was incredulous.

"There was nothing they could do," Claire said with a small helpless gesture. "They tried." She closed her eyes. "I just couldn't hold it."

The silence allowed Brynn to compose herself. All the suffering that Claire endured and she was still looking forward to the future with hope in her heart.

"Simeon's mad at you." Claire's eyes drooped, but she gave her friend a stern look.

"He has every right to be," Brynn answered. "He couldn't believe I wouldn't come."

"*I* understood," Claire said. She gave Brynn a warning look. "Don't let that go on. You don't want to lose him." Wearily, she closed her eyes.

Brynn leaned over and kissed her friend's cheek. "I won't," she whispered. But Claire had fallen asleep.

Sometime during the day she called her mother and they talked for a long time. She called Mr. and Mrs. Jessup, who were like her family. She even called Art to apologize but he wasn't in and she prayed that he'd forgiven her. Simeon was not at home when she called him but after the third time she didn't try again. She didn't wonder that he was probably home thinking long and hard about the kind of uncaring, vain, and selfish woman that he'd gotten involved with. She wasn't Veronny! Oh, what had she done?

In the evening after forcing some nourishment into her body she sat quietly in the living room. She'd had so much uninterrupted time to think. She had to laugh at herself once or twice. What had happened to that strong resolve after that period of enlightened self-discovery in Roensville? She had pitied Leria for the hate that had driven her all these years. Hate so strong that she glorified in reviling Brynn Halsted.

Brynn questioned her sincerity in accepting what was and what was to be. In the end of her stark self-examination, she realized that she had come to terms with reality. But she also understood that in the months to come she would feel a little sad about what had been lost. In time she knew that she would tingle with excitement each time one of her dances had its premiere. As Merle always had. She would worry that her dancers didn't show passion for their work. She would cry with the dancer who didn't get that coveted role. As once she had. That was going to be her life from now on!

She thought of Claire and Art and the strong love that knit them together in their time of stress and strife. Wenona and Joseph Halsted had had a love like that. And she hoped that Simeon still loved her because she was still in love with him. He would know that before too much longer but first there was something she had to do, something that had been nagging at her since she'd awakened from that dream this morning. With quiet determination she walked to the bedroom.

The emerald lay twinkling in the jewel case on her dresser. Brynn picked it up. Though still loose it hadn't popped out of its gold bed. As she stared at it she remembered something her father had once said to his wife after she'd laughed at one of his mythological stories. "Sometimes you have to believe the unbelievable, Wenona."

Whatever the prophecy of the stone she was not going to let this one incident dictate her behavior. There was nothing she could ever do about the feelings or the premonitions that she felt from time to time and that she could never begin to explain.

Somehow, she'd known that a loved one of hers was going to experience some kind of danger or illness. She was still stunned by Claire's beating and the loss of her baby. But from now on, Brynn thought, she would never be forewarned. At least, not by a beautiful stone that had helped turn her into a mindless, incoherent woman. Her father didn't intend his gift to cause her to walk in fear, to weaken her strength and character.

Years ago as the gift was intended, it had given her the courage and hope to pursue her creative potential. She'd achieved everything her heart had desired and more. It was time to let go of legends.

Carefully, Brynn placed the pendant in a small velvet-lined box and gently closed the lid. She carried it to the living room to an old chest that held many mementos of her accomplishments over her long career since she was seven years old. After placing it on the bottom beneath many yellowed programs and newspaper clippings, she was solemn when she walked back to the bedroom. She was wondering what would become of the stone and if the next wearer would see it for what it was. Only a beautiful jewel.

A short time later, Brynn was dressed and at the front door. It was dark and late, but she wasn't going to let another hour pass before talking to the man she loved. She locked the door and hurried down the stairs.

Simeon was tired and one glance in the car visor mirror at his two-days' growth of beard and his blood-shot eyes told him he was a proper candidate for vampire flick number twenty. He parked the car, mercifully not too far away, and started the walk down the street. His habit the last thirty-odd hours of eyeing every man that walked by or standing furtively in doorways was over.

Since leaving Art and Claire at the hospital in the wee hours of Monday morning, he'd had practically no sleep, catching winks wherever he happened to be watching from his car. There was no way that the busy police precinct could spare the bodies to do what needed to be done. Simeon felt as charged and restless as a wildebeest and was determined to make something happen.

The private investigator that he'd hired had a directive not to spare the cost or the manpower. Simeon knew that if Buddy hadn't run in that first hour it was his foolish mistake, because a network of men blanketed the city. Simeon was part of the mix, working right along with them hour after hour, watching the streets surrounding Brynn's home and combing every mode of transportation out of the city, including the airports. He even had men watching Newark Airport in New Jersey for Buddy Randolph, in case he'd gotten that far.

Simeon knew that Brynn was in danger. When Claire had described the way Buddy had taunted her and laughed at what he'd done to Brynn, cold fingers of dread had tickled his spine.

He didn't buy it that Buddy was on his way out of town, at least not immediately, because once he was caught he knew that he was going away for a long, long time. And Simeon knew that when Buddy was in jail it would be because he'd gotten his due. If not with Claire, then the other woman he hated would do. Buddy wanted Brynn Halsted too. Simeon had been around the man for too long not to pick up on his sick mentality. He knew that he would not stop or rest until Randolph was caught—and before he got to Brynn.

The intense surveillance had paid off. Not two hours ago, Buddy was spotted leaving an old girlfriend's house and furtively scurrying with bag in hand to a waiting taxi. Simeon and Art were at the precinct when Buddy was led away. Gone was the pretty-boy swagger. There was nothing but fear in his eyes as he was marched by Art, who held his hands in balled fists at his side. Buddy glanced away from Simeon altogether, seeming to be in a hurry to be taken away.

Simeon stopped when he saw a woman walking toward him. Brynn. Surprised to see her, he tried quickly to pull it together. He'd wondered what they would say to each other when this moment came. The last time he'd seen her she wasn't the woman he'd fallen in love with and he'd searched deeply into his heart for his true feelings. Now that she was out of danger he would be tested.

Nearly bumping into the stolid figure that hogged the sidewalk, Brynn looked up in annoyance as she broke stride to avoid the man. "Simeon."

"Why are you out here, alone?" he asked brusquely, trying to recover. The sight of her and his name on her lips gave him his answer. He knew that he would always love her but would it be against his better judgment?

Brynn peered closely at him. The reserved stance of his body. Had she lost him?

"I wanted to see you," she said in a soft voice.

They stared at each other.

"I was coming to see you," Simeon said, shifting his position for a passing couple.

Dared she hope? "Then would you like to come to the house?" He was looking at her so strangely, but the darkness didn't allow her to read his eyes.

"Buddy Randolph is in jail."

"Oh," Brynn said with a skipped breath. "Is that why you were coming to see me?"

"Yes."

A moment passed. "That's not why I wanted to see *you*," Brynn said quietly.

"No?"

"Will you come?"

In the apartment, Simeon excused himself and went straight to the bathroom where he splashed cold water on his face and he was instantly reminded of his last visit. When he joined her in the living room, Brynn had fixed him a scotch and soda. She was holding one too.

"I thought you might want that," Brynn said.

"Thanks." He drank heartily, then set the glass down. "Why did you leave here so late to come and see me? That was pretty dangerous considering you didn't know Buddy was arrested. And foolish." His eyes glinted.

"I wasn't thinking about myself," Brynn said.

Simeon questioned that with a steely gaze.

"I went to see Claire," she said, guessing what he was thinking.

"I'd heard."

"You're so cold toward me, and I'm not surprised." Brynn shut her eyes for a second. "I didn't like me either after I realized how I'd sounded to you. Selfish, cold, completely self-centered, all the things you thought about that woman who flew blindly past you in the theater, years ago."

He listened.

"I was so afraid of losing myself again. I also knew that this time it was left to me to pull myself back from that crazy state. And I did but only with help from unexpected sources."

Skeptical, Simeon said, "What sources?"

"Merle. Claire and Art. My mother. You. And my father."

Startled by her response, Simeon saw her fingers go to her throat in the old gesture. "And the emerald?"

His sarcasm didn't go unnoticed but Brynn only said, "In a way."

Simeon got up and fixed another drink. He swallowed, then turned to her in disgust. "Brynn . . . about us . . ."

"I saw you." Brynn was by his side. She took his hand and led him back to the sofa, but dropped it because he was so unyielding. "You came to me." She closed her eyes and began to speak softly about her dream.

She talked, and Simeon listened to her vivid description of how she had fought her way back from the frenzied world she was lost in. He listened to her revelation about her ill behavior and how she'd once again discovered who she really was. The quiet strength he saw and heard cast a new light in his eyes. He was doubtful. His whole life depended on what Brynn was saying.

As he listened, Simeon stood and walked to the mantel where there were framed pictures of the people in Brynn's life. Her parents. Merle. Claire. There was a photo of a costumed Brynn in her *Princessa* role. There was another picture of her where she was dressed in a pale blue dress and the camera had caught her looking serious yet with a mysterious half smile on her lips. That was one of his favorite photographs of her. It captured her beauty, her sensitivity, her caring, and her love of life. She was sincerity itself.

Brynn watched Simeon's struggle with himself, his fears, his values. She waited.

Simeon turned to her and jammed his hands in his pockets. "While you were fighting your demons, I was fighting mine, Brynn." He spoke softly. "When I left you Monday, I believed that I was walking out of your life because you'd become someone I didn't want to know."

"Veronny."

His lashes flickered. "Yes. As the hours passed while searching for Buddy, you were in my thoughts. I didn't want that man to hurt you ever again because if he did I wouldn't be responsible for my actions. Yet I knew that I couldn't spend my life with you in a constant state of wonder. In your new career there will be many inevitable and intense moments. I could never be certain just when that stranger would surface."

"She's gone, Simeon." Brynn caught and held his gaze.

He studied her. Simeon knew that he was looking at the woman he'd fallen in love with. And still loved. Whatever she'd gone through had returned her to him. He dropped his gaze to the chest beneath the window. There, she'd buried her fears. He stared at her. "There to stay?" he asked gently.

"Yes." Brynn went to him.

Simeon was overcome. He was so shaken with the possibility that their love had been lost that he reached for her hands and gripped them as though they were his lifeline. "Come here," he said gruffly, pulling her against his chest. "You're too far away."

"I'll never be again, love," Brynn murmured, as she drank in his kisses.

EPILOGUE

Five months later

In September, Simeon was as excited as the rest of the dance world with the advent of the opening season. Much talk had been bandied about in proper circles about the Merle Christiansen Dance Company and its new leadership, and the curious had made it possible for sold-out signs to be included in the advertisements for most of the performances. Diehard fans and naysayers alike looked forward to the new offerings of former star dancer Brynn Halsted.

Simeon was filled with pride for Brynn. She'd worked so hard with the school and with her choreography that he'd had to pull her back a few times to take some downtime. It was a feat to be able to steal her away for a few weekends in the country. Even there, he had to pull her from downstairs where she rehearsed, adding, deleting, and refining. Her determination and ideas vibrated off the walls of the theater and had the company on its toes. Although they all missed Merle, they felt his presence through her and joked about it. Brynn shrugged it off but was secretly pleased that she wasn't falling on her butt.

The theater was filling up fast and Simeon, who was backstage, said to Wenona, who was standing beside him, "Why such a crowd for a full dress rehearsal? I've never seen this much media attention before the premiere."

Wenona smiled. "You know how gossips are," she answered with a twinkle in her eyes. "They're waiting for my baby to fall flat on her behind. Ready to call her a washout."

"Yeah," Simeon growled, "you're probably right. But are they in for the surprise of their lives!" He looked at his watch. "Where's everybody?" he asked. Usually the dancers were huddled in their places or warming up or preparing themselves. At Brynn's request Simeon was playing for the dress rehearsal. The talented pianist that they had selected to play Simeon's composition appreciated the opportunity to see the concert in full.

Simeon was both ecstatic and sad. He would be playing his music but not for Brynn, who had ultimately chosen Paige Toure for the role. The lithe young woman was perfect and danced her heart out interpreting his score and Brynn's movements, giving the ballet her own style. Most important, she understood what Brynn and Simeon were saying in the ballet that Brynn called *Home*.

"Mm, I think you're right. Everyone will be floored tonight," Wenona said. She peered out at the audience. "I'd better take my seat. It's almost curtain time." She stood on tiptoes and kissed the cheek of her future son-in-law. "Don't be nervous. You're going to be fine." She left with a wink and a light step.

Simeon looked after her. All summer, she had been a frequent visitor to Harlem and her old home. He saw the sense of peace about her and he knew that she no longer worried about her daughter being left alone. She'd given her blessings to their upcoming marriage in January, at which his mother was ecstatic. He checked his watch again. "Where's Paige?" he muttered, then left to take his place at the piano.

Claire and Art, smiling to beat the band, kissed Brynn on the cheek.

Brynn hugged them. "Go on, you two," she said, "before Simeon guesses that something's up. He's already annoyed because no one is where they should be, including me and Paige." She waved them away. "Shoo. We'll meet backstage when it's all over." She eyed Claire. "You be careful on those steps," she admonished. Calling her a mother hen, they waved and then disappeared. After a two-month postponement, Claire and Art had been married. Now she was two months pregnant and Brynn thought she'd never seen two more awestruck people.

The theater was hushed in anticipation. Simeon was oblivious of all but the instrument before him as he riffed through the overture.

When he played the first chord of his score, a soulful A minor that would introduce the dancer, the curtain rose. Simeon's eyes glittered. *Brynn!* His fingers ran across the black and ivory keys not missing a beat as he played and Brynn dropped to the floor. As she moved slowly, dragging herself up, she met his eyes. A smile was not in keeping with the drama but he saw the twinkle in her eyes.

Simeon was overwhelmed. If he thought dreams did not come true he was wrong. The woman he loved was dancing for him. And he played for her. With misted eyes, Simeon played.

Brynn glanced at the audience as she took her bows to standing ovations and shouts of "Encore! Encore!" She knew there was much affection from devoted fans who never minded that she wasn't the Brynn of old, whose leaps weren't as high, and who had bobbled once or twice, but she was overjoyed. She'd danced a farewell performance onstage before an audience! And for the first and last time for her lover.

With tears rolling down her cheeks she smiled at her mother and the symbolic empty seat on the aisle. As Brynn had begun her professional career with her father's spirit, so it had ended. Beside her mother were her dearest friends, Claire and Art, who were stamping and applauding wildly. There should have been another empty seat. But Brynn looked up into the rafters and blew a kiss. Merle was there.

When the curtain dropped for the last time, she felt Simeon's hand slip into hers. She turned to him and saw that his cheeks were as wet as hers.

"Come here, you," Simeon said huskily, pulling her tightly against him. "Thank you, for my dream," he whispered in her ear. He clung to her, inhaling her musky sweetness, and kissing the salty sweat from her throat and lips. Her heaving breasts rubbed against him and he moaned from the erotic pleasure. "How did you pull this off? And able to keep it secret from me?" he murmured, staring into her beautiful eyes. He saw the desire and he shivered.

Brynn gasped as she felt her nipples ripen against the fine cloth of his tuxedo jacket. Unperturbed that all could see their passion for each other, she caught him around the waist and blushed at the fire in his amber eyes. "I have other secrets to share," she murmured. "But not here. They're for your ears only."

Simeon caught her hand and hustled her through the crowd of admirers. "We're on our way, sweetheart."

Dear Reader,

I hope you enjoyed Brynn and Simeon's story; hers of self-discovery, his of finding the courage to trust in love again.

Also, a heap of thanks to you all for the wonderful letters about MIDSUMMER MOON. To those who asked, at this time I have no plans to revisit beautiful Oyster Bay for Caleb Lancaster's story.

As always, I'm grateful for your support and hope you continue to write. For a reply, please include a self-addressed, stamped envelope.

Thanks for sharing,

Doris Johnson
P.O. Box 130370
Springfield Gardens, NY 11413
e-mail: Bessdj@aol.com

About the Author

Doris Johnson lives in Queens, New York, with her husband. She is a multiplublished author. During her travels, she's always looking for that one snippet of conversation, that interesting face, or that unusual occupation that will fire her imagination to eventually create a fascinating story. She enjoys antiquing and collecting gemstones.